TABLE O~

Titan's

Chapter 1 - - - - -
Chapter 2 - - - - -
Chapter 3 - - - - -
Chapter 4 - - - - - 25
Chapter 5 - - - - - 31
Chapter 6 - - - - - 36
Chapter 7 - - - - - 41
Chapter 8 - - - - - 47
Chapter 9 - - - - - 54
Chapter 10 - - - - - 59
Chapter 11 - - - - - 64
Chapter 12 - - - - - 67
Chapter 13 - - - - - 70
Chapter 14 - - - - - 74
Chapter 15 - - - - - 80
Chapter 16 - - - - - 82
Chapter 17 - - - - - 89
Chapter 18 - - - - - 100
Chapter 19 - - - - - 103
Chapter 20 - - - - - 107
Chapter 21 - - - - - 109

Tainted Mars

Chapter 22 - - - - - 112
Chapter 23 - - - - - 121
Chapter 24 - - - - - 133
Chapter 25 - - - - - 141
Chapter 26 - - - - - 147
Chapter 27 - - - - - 151
Chapter 28 - - - - - 159
Chapter 29 - - - - - 165
Chapter 30 - - - - - 177
Chapter 31 - - - - - 190
Chapter 32 - - - - - 194
Chapter 33 - - - - - 197
Chapter 34 - - - - - 211
Chapter 35 - - - - - 230
Chapter 36 - - - - - 235
Chapter 37 - - - - - 244
Chapter 38 - - - - - 252
Chapter 39 - - - - - 255
Chapter 40 - - - - - 268
Chapter 41 - - - - - 272
Chapter 42 - - - - - 276
Chapter 43 - - - - - 279

The Blood Covered Earth

Chapter 44 - - - - - 285
Chapter 45 - - - - - 289
Chapter 46 - - - - - 297
Chapter 47 - - - - - 304
Chapter 48 - - - - - 313
Chapter 49 - - - - - 320
Chapter 50 - - - - - 330
Chapter 51 - - - - - 338
Chapter 52 - - - - - 345
Chapter 53 - - - - - 354
Chapter 54 - - - - - 358
Chapter 55 - - - - - 361
Chapter 56 - - - - - 366
Chapter 57 - - - - - 372
Chapter 58 - - - - - 375
Chapter 59 - - - - - 384
Chapter 60 - - - - - 387
Chapter 61 - - - - - 390
Chapter 62 - - - - - 400
Chapter 63 - - - - - 402

Copyright © 2024 Jonathan Yarm

Issue Date : 08/08/24

All rights reserved.

No part of this book may be reproduced, or stored in a retrieval system, or transmitted in any form or by any means, electronic, mechanical, photocopying, recording, or otherwise, without express written permission of the publisher.

This is a work of fiction. Names, characters, business, events and incidents are the products of the author's imagination. Any resemblance to actual persons, living or dead, or actual events is purely coincidental.

Thank you to my wife for her patience and proof reading. Also thanks to Jay, Jim and Adam for giving feedback.

I dedicate this book to the memory of my sister-in-law Dorothy.

Titan's Deadly Tunnels
Inspector Danks mysteries
Book 1

Chapter 1

The spaceship had arrived at Titan on time. It was a small ship as few people wanted to come this far out into the solar system. Its maximum capacity was the crew plus twenty passengers and most of them were workers for the mining company that operated the base station on Titan.

Inspector Danks was in his early fifties and was wishing he was somewhere else. He'd just been sick and the spaceship hostesses were cleaning up the mess.

His claustrophobia and nausea had got the better of him. If only he'd gotten out of the pod faster he may have avoided the worst effects of his sickness.

The spaceship hostesses were very understanding. They didn't make him feel bad about his predicament.

The drones had tidied up the mess and afterwards the hostesses had instructed them back into their storage cubicles.

Danks was rather embarrassed about the whole incident and just wanted to get out of there. So, as soon as the drones were stowed away he took the opportunity to make his escape. He thanked the hostesses and glided off down the passageway.

Dodging the other passengers that were extracting themselves from their pods, he headed for the exit. He sped up past the occasional person that looked like they were about to vomit. It seemed that the longer the trip, the more likely passengers would be sick. It turned out he wasn't the only one to be afflicted as he dodged another individual who was retching near him.

Arriving at the spaceship exit he guided himself down the short connecting tube and came out into the main foyer of the spaceport that was orbiting Titan.

The foyer had conveniently positioned signs displayed in front of him. The luggage pickup was to his right, straight on was towards the shuttle bay for passengers descending to Titan's surface and to his left was the hotel attached to the spaceport.

He headed right to pick up his holdall.

Arriving at the luggage store, he scanned his ID chip that was embedded under the skin on his arm into a console in front of him. A few minutes later a drone appeared with his large black holdall. He slipped one arm through a handle of the bag swung it around onto his back and threaded his other arm into the remaining handle. It was a bit clumsy in these weightless conditions, but he wanted to get to his accommodation to tidy himself up.

Even though he'd been in stasis for eight months he still felt he needed to refresh himself and have a hot drink to warm his insides.

He had to grab some nearby rails to steady himself with his new load on his back.

Back on Earth he'd had to hurriedly pack in order to catch the next departure to Titan. They left once every eight months and he had only that day left to catch the next one.

Manoeuvring around with his holdall on his back, he managed to avoid everyone in the busy luggage pickup area with the exception of one collision. He apologised to the man and they both saw the funny side of it. Everyone knew how chaotic it was in the baggage area.

Once he'd gotten himself orientated in the right direction he had to negotiate his way back to the foyer. He was heading for the hotel reception.

He pulled himself through to the foyer. To get to the hotel he had to travel down a clear cylindrical tube. As he floated down the tube he could see Saturn looming majestically with its delicate rings in the distance. Below him shone the hazy orange crescent of Titan.

Entering the hotel reception he drifted over to a large screen which had an AI human face displayed on it. He spoke to the screen and the face responded.

"Please hold your ID chip over the pad below the screen" the slightly monotonic voice instructed.

He scanned his ID chip and a few seconds later the AI confirmed his reservation. "Your ID chip will operate the door to your room. Just place it on the pad next to your door". The lift door opened to the right of the screen. "We hope your stay is a pleasant one. The lift will take you down to your accommodation floor". Then the AI human went silent.

He entered the lift, strapped himself in and secured his bag next to him. Scanning his ID chip on a pad inside the lift, the door shut and he felt it manoeuvre around before it started its descent.

Danks knew that the lift had to start rotating at the same rate as the accommodation floors. It then had to align itself with one of four lift tubes which connected reception to the floors below.

The lift started its descent but it wasn't long before it came to a halt and the door opened. He unhooked himself and then his bag. The bag had some weight now and it fell to the floor of the lift with a bang.

He picked it up and slung it on his back as he stepped out into the corridor. The artificial gravity was about the same here as on Earth. It was a relief to be out of the weightlessness.

There were no windows in the accommodation as it was a 'no frills' hotel. It was primarily for the workers on Titan. Every two weeks out of eight they spent in the hotel so that they didn't lose too much bone or muscle mass. Also, passengers departing Titan had to spend a week here in order to acclimatize to the gravity back at their destination, which was usually either Mars or Earth.

Squeezing past people that were walking the other way and others that were standing in the corridor talking he eventually arrived at his room. He scanned his ID chip and the door slid back. It was a pokey room with only the bare essentials. He swung his bag off his shoulder and stood it up in the corner.

There was a narrow bed along the wall, barely the width of his shoulders. He lay down on it for a rest and to collect his thoughts.

Danks knew the name of the base station was Tartarus and he thought it was a most appropriate name. In ancient Greek mythology the Titans were banished to the underworld and were imprisoned in a place called Tartarus by the Olympians after a ten year war. Tartarus on Titan was deep underground. It was a cold and forbidding place.

This was a trip that he thought he'd never have to do. The sad news had arrived back at Earth that his older brother and his sister-in-law had died here on Titan.

The cause of death was thought to be asphyxiation. He had to discover how this could've happened. His brother was meticulous and cautious. It just didn't add up that they would die in that way.

Danks had sent a message to Titan before he left Earth. He wanted the bodies to be preserved until he'd had a chance to meet with the pathologist. It was imperative that he found out what the cause of death was, whether that was asphyxiation or something else.

Chapter 2

Inspector Danks lay on his bed composing himself. This trip out here was going to be a difficult one.

After a few minutes of rest he decided he needed to tidy up his appearance if he was going to have a video call. Rolling out of his bed he checked his face and hair in a mirror. He was ready for a shave as he hadn't had chance to have one on the day of departure from Earth. The trip out here was short notice. He couldn't have a video call if he looked like a yeti.

After he'd washed his hair and had a shave he felt he was ready to dial up the pathologist. He started the call on his watch and then with a flick of his finger across its face in the direction of a screen in his room, a phone symbol appeared on it. There were a few rings before the call was answered.

An image of a man in his mid forties with close cut mousey coloured hair appeared on the screen. His complexion was pale, probably because he'd been on Titan for quite a few years.

"Hello, Dr Shutt speaking. How may I help you?".

"Ah, hello doctor, I'm Inspector Danks. I'm calling about the autopsies you performed several months ago".

"I did many autopsies around then, could you be more specific?".

"It was a married couple that you reported as dying of asphyxiation. Their names were Ambrose and Mary Danks".

There were a few seconds of silence before Dr Shutt's response.

"Ah, I have my notes on my screen now. Yes, they seemed to have died of asphyxiation. The ventilation unit in their apartment seems to have malfunctioned. Instead of fresh air being pumped into their accommodation it was replaced with one hundred percent nitrogen".

"What exactly failed in the ventilation system?" probed Danks.

"Apparently, nitrogen is mixed with oxygen prior to being passed into their room. The oxygen was somehow cut off".

"How was the oxygen cut off?".

"I questioned the head engineer about this and he said - let me see, ah yes, here it is. He said that the oxygen valve had frozen shut. Sorry, I haven't seen these notes for some time".

"Can you send that document to me?".

"Of course. Although I don't believe you'll find anything about why the valve froze shut".

"That may be true doctor but it does have the name of the engineer you interviewed and his report on the valve. I'd like to talk to him at some point. By the way, did you store the bodies as I asked?".

There was a short period of silence as the doctor looked confused.

"I'm sorry but I was told to dispose of the

bodies in the usual way".

"And what is the usual way?". Danks was getting concerned that his request had been ignored.

"They are returned to the spaceport and from there they are sent on a trajectory to intercept Saturn. It's best to remove the corpses otherwise they'd start piling up on Titan's surface. Then they would freeze into solid rock at minus one hundred and eighty degrees Celsius".

"Didn't you get my instructions to keep the bodies until I arrived?".

"Yes, but I was told by the base subcommander to ignore that and proceed with the usual disposal method". The doctor sounded rather sheepish.

Danks was quite annoyed. His instructions had been blatantly disregarded.

"What is the name of the base subcommander?". Danks was going to pursue this when he got down to Tartarus.

"That would be Subcommander Paul Rees".

Danks made a mental note of the name. This person had deliberately ignored his instructions.

"Do you have the usual holographic scans of the bodies?" he said in a sterner voice.

"Yes I do. Do you want me to retrieve them?".

"Yes doctor. I'm only here in this hotel for one night. I'll be catching the shuttle down to Tartarus in the morning, so make sure you're free tomorrow. I'll be coming over to your labs shortly after I've checked into a hotel".

"My diary is pretty empty at the moment. So, see you tomorrow" said the doctor and with that Danks terminated the call.

How could this subcommander do that? He had destroyed some potential evidence. At least the holographic images should help as long as the doctor still had them.

That evening he prepared a simple meal and watched some local television channels for a few hours but most of it was boring. In the end he turned in for the night as he had an early start the following day.

Chapter 3

Inspector Danks had a restless night's sleep. From what he could remember he kept dreaming about his brother and sister-in-law. He kept seeing them clutching their throats trying to breathe. The nightmares were waking him up through the night in a cold sweat. He just wanted to get up out of bed and find that they were both still alive.

His watch woke him from his troubled sleep. He only had a short time to get ready. With his bag packed, clean clothes on and hair combed he left his room heading for the hotel reception where he paid his bill.

Floating back to the foyer he turned down the corridor that led to the shuttle bound for Titan.

Arriving at the shuttle entrance he registered his ID chip and a screen showed where his seat was located in the shuttle.

Leaving his bag with a drone to be stowed away, he floated into the connecting tube to find his allotted seat.

As Danks entered the shuttle a male attendant showed him to his seat. He sat in it, secured himself in and looked out of his side window. It was an amazing sight. The sun was a tiny disc in the distance and somewhere in that direction was the blue planet Earth. The only one in the solar system that could support life without the human engineered environments. Below was the forbidding hazy orange yellow glow of Titan with Saturn looming in the distance.

After ten minutes all the passengers were aboard and secured in their seats. The crew closed the hatches and at first there was silence. The AI attendant on the screen in front of the passengers announced what to do in the event of something going wrong. Danks thought that was more than likely pointless as they'd all be dead within seconds if anything were to go wrong. Out here, there was little or no room for error.

A jolt indicated that their trip to the surface had begun and Danks could see the spaceport drift off into the distance. Titan had started getting bigger.

The atmosphere of Titan extends out further than on Earth and soon they had begun their entry into it. At first it was gentle with light plasma streams streaking past the window. It gradually got rougher as they went lower. At about ten kilometres up the plasma streams died away and the shuttle entered a spiral descent to the surface.

Danks could see some faint lights ahead. They were the landing lights showing the way to the Titan shuttle port. Several minutes later, a couple of jolts indicated that they'd touched down and they taxied until they came to a halt on a rectangular platform.

After the shuttle had stopped, the platform started to descend below the Titan surface. A set of doors closed above them to seal off the outside extreme cold. They went through a couple more sets of doors on their downward journey. It was several minutes before their descent stopped. Once they came to a standstill Danks didn't have to wait long before the shuttle hatches opened.

He unclipped his seat belt and made a move towards the exit. It was quite tricky as the gravity here was slightly less than on the Earth's Moon so he had to be cautious.

Exiting the shuttle and moving down a connecting tube, he entered a low ceilinged hall. It was sub-zero outside the shuttle. Everyone had gloves, hats, thick coats and heavy lead soled boots on. The temperature was just below the freezing point of water. All the walls, ceilings and floors were frozen ice. It was a delicate balancing act to keep the temperature quite right. If they didn't warm it enough the temperature would plummet making it uninhabitable for humans and if they heated it too much the ice would melt.

Danks had dressed in suitable clothing when he left the shuttle. Ahead of him was a border control desk and a queue of passengers had formed in front of it. They were checking in with the Titan authorities. He joined the back of it.

After about ten minutes of watching his breath in the cold air it was his turn at the border control. He scanned his ID chip on a pad on the desk top.

"What is the reason for your visit to Titan, Inspector Danks?" came an abrupt voice from the border guard.

"I'm here because the Interplanetary Police Agency sent me to investigate some unexplained deaths" replied Danks.

That wasn't true. The IPA had given him compassionate leave to collect his brother's and sister-in-law's bodies. The plan was to bring their ashes back to Earth. But the local authorities didn't know that and, besides, he now knew there were no longer any bodies to cremate.

"I'll have to clear that with the base commander" came the reply.

A few minutes passed while the border guard was talking to the commander or one of his minions over his head phones.

"You've been given permission to enter Titan. But you need to check in with the commander within one orbit of Saturn".

Danks knew that Titan's orbit was roughly equivalent to fifteen Earth hours. He had plenty of time to check into his hotel and then head over to Dr Shutt's lab. After that he'd go and see the base commander.

He left border control and went to the baggage collection area. A drone carrying his bag dashed over to where he was standing. It had located him via his ID chip. He removed the bag from it and slung it over his shoulder.

Not far away from Danks was an escalator that descended deeper into Titan. He headed towards it and stepped onto it. It carried him downwards towards Tartarus.

At the bottom of the escalator he stepped out into a large public square. Across the other side of it were shops, restaurants, cafés and a gym but more importantly there was a small hotel.

Danks headed over to the hotel to check in and once inside he booked a room on the first floor. He didn't like being on the ground floor as it was too easy for criminals to observe his movements. It was much better to be on the first floor or above.

Danks was pleased that this Tartarus hotel was an improvement on the spaceport's equivalent. Although any hotel would have been better he thought. Firstly his room was much bigger and secondly it had a window overlooking the main plaza. He always enjoyed 'people watching'. The fun was guessing what they did and where they were going. Thirdly and probably most importantly was that the room was a pleasant eighteen degrees Celsius. It was a relief to get out of the cold.

He unpacked his bag and put the items into the cupboards in the room, but he was hoping to be here for no more than two weeks. After that he'd have a week back up at the orbiting spaceport before catching the shuttle back to Earth.

The returning shuttle was the very same one that Danks had arrived in. If he missed that he'd be stuck here for another eight months.

Once he'd settled in, it was time to find Dr Shutt's lab. He checked where it was in relation to his current position. It was only a couple of blocks away, he could walk that. He needed some exercise as he was getting out of shape with all the travelling he'd been doing prior to his eight months in stasis.

On leaving the hotel, he headed right to a lane that led off the main plaza. He turned down it and walked about half a kilometre then did a sharp left. After one and a half kilometres he took a sharp right.

As he was walking he'd noticed that he was being followed. A shadowy figure had been trailing him since he'd left the hotel.

Danks thought it was time to lose the person as he didn't want them to know where he was heading.

He looked at the map on his watch and could see several small lanes leading off the one he was currently on. He took the next left, then there was a cross roads, he turned right. Not far up that lane was a recessed door, he stepped into it and pressed his back hard against the door. He was in the shadow of the overhang and it would be difficult to see him in here even if someone walked straight past.

Danks covered his mouth with his gloved hands so as to reduce his breath. It could easily give away his position if the person shadowing him saw it.

He heard footsteps quickening then they seemed to stop then try another direction. He could hear an angry voice but he couldn't quite make out what was being said. The footsteps started again but this time they were getting quieter with every step.

After about five minutes, Danks decided the coast was clear and he resumed his previous course but not quite in the original direction. He would take a more tortuous route.

At last he was standing outside the building where Dr Shutt's lab was located. He touched the screen that was on the door and Dr Shutt's face appeared.

"Ah, you managed to get here inspector. Please come in".

The door slid open and Danks stepped inside. He did a quick check up and down the street and was confident that the shadowy figure hadn't managed to locate him.

He could see Dr Shutt standing outside his lab down the far end of the corridor waving at him. He made his way towards him.

"Welcome inspector". They shook hands and Dr Shutt showed him into the lab.

"I've managed to extract the holographic images of Ambrose and Mary Danks. You can view them on that table display over there". He pointed towards the corner of the lab where there was a rectangular flat surface that was the projection system specifically for analysing images of corpses.

Danks walked over and swept his hand over the table top. A menu popped up with lots of names. He quickly scrolled down to the surname Danks. There were only two entries. He selected Ambrose first.

A holographic image of a body appeared. This shocked Danks as it brought home the reality that his brother was dead. He took a few seconds to wipe some moisture that had suddenly accumulated in his eyes.

"Okay.." Danks's voice sounded croaky. He cleared his throat and composed himself. He started again, "Okay, what evidence do you have of the victim's asphyxiation?".

"If you see, there are no signs of a struggle. It's almost as though he has fallen asleep. The body is not aware of the lack of oxygen with nitrogen asphyxiation unlike carbon dioxide".

Danks zoomed in on the holographic image and panned around looking for something out of place. He moved up to the head and began searching for anything unusual.

"And where were the bodies found?" enquired Danks.

"They were found in their apartment as the report stated".

"Then there is something odd about this. Ambrose's eardrums have been blown inwards as though there was a rapid pressure increase". Danks pointed to the damage in that area.

Dr Shutt looked nervously at Danks.

"Did you know this already?". Danks could see he was holding something back.

"Regrettably I did".

"Then why didn't you put it in the report?".

"I was told I shouldn't include it otherwise..". The doctor hesitated.

"Go on doctor, I'm waiting for an explanation. I don't want to have to arrest you for falsifying a forensic report and hindering an IPA investigation".

Inspector Danks could see the doctor was struggling with his conscience.

He decided to try the good cop approach on the doctor.

"Look, I'll keep this between just the two of us. But I need to know all the facts you have on this case".

The doctor seemed to brace himself and pulled his shoulders back. "I did find that he'd been exposed to a sudden pressure increase and also extreme cold. It's as though he was suddenly exposed to the Titan atmosphere. Practically every cell in his body had ruptured which is consistent with a very cold temperature.

When I arrived at the apartment the temperature in there was very low. The strange thing was that his body was frozen solid. So I suspected he hadn't died in the apartment.

He died elsewhere and his body was returned to the apartment afterwards. It must have been shortly before I arrived".

Danks's gut feelings had proved right again. This was now a murder investigation.

"Did Mary die in the same way?".

"I'm afraid so. It looks like they died together as they have exactly the same injuries".

"Who was it that told you to falsify the forensic records?".

"It was the subcommander. He turned up here with two body guards. One of the guards whispered to me that my family would be in danger if I didn't comply. That's why I've made the decision that my family and I are moving back to Earth. Those men were very scary".

"I know the subcommander is Paul Rees, but what are the names of the two bully boys?".

"I don't know the names of the two guards but I think they are twins as they looked almost identical".

Danks shut down the hologram and transferred the image data of his brother and sister-in-law to his watch as evidence.

"Okay, tell no one that we've discussed this otherwise you'll be in danger" Danks advised Dr Shutt. He continued, "Is there another exit from this building?".

"Yes, it's down here. Why do you ask?".

"Oh, just the usual precautions". He didn't want

to alarm the doctor by saying he'd been followed.

The doctor hurried off down the corridor to an exit at the rear of his labs. It was quite a small door. "This is used for deliveries normally". The doctor pushed the catch and opened it onto the alleyway behind.

They shook hands. Danks checked the coast was clear and then slipped out into the alley.

Once back on the main street he resumed his course. He'd been longer than he anticipated at the doctor's lab, so he felt it was now a good time to check in with the base commander.

Chapter 4

The base commander could be found in the main government building which was several streets away.

After about five minutes of walking Danks arrived outside the grand building where the commander's office was located. He could see that vast amounts of money had been spent on this building. The whole of the front facade looked like white marble. Importing that from Earth would have been hugely expensive.

He climbed the stairs to the front archway and walked inside through a set of automatic doors. It was awe inspiring. It had vaulted ceilings with artwork reminiscent of ancient Roman temples.

There was a person sat at a desk in the middle of the hall. He beckoned Danks over. As he headed towards the man he could make out that he was a security guard.

"Can I help you sir?" the guard asked in a bored voice.

"I'm here to see the base commander. My name is Inspector Danks".

"Do you have an appointment?".

"No, but I'm sure he'll make room in his schedule to see me".

On hearing the reply the guard perked up. This is someone he could boot out of the building. He enjoyed booting people out of the building. It was one of the perks of the job.

"He's an extremely busy man. He won't be able to see you at such short notice". The man was sitting more upright now. He was getting ready to do some booting.

"Well, let's see what the commander says shall we?" replied Danks in a firm voice.

The guard seemed reluctant to call the commander but decided to give it a try just so he could tell this annoying guy to piss off.

"Sir, there's an uninvited 'gentleman' here requesting to see you".

There was a pause while the commander replied.

"His name is Inspector Danks. I was about to.." the guard stopped mid sentence. There was a surprised look on his face. The call terminated and the guard turned to face the inspector.

"It's your lucky day mister, you can go through to the commander's office. It's up the stairs, straight ahead and through the big doors". The guard looked annoyed that he couldn't do his usual job of repelling unwelcome plebs that wander in from off the street.

"You see, I'm a likeable bloke when you get to know me" Danks said with a sly smile as he walked past the guard.

The stairs were just ahead and he climbed up them. At the top was a grand arched doorway that looked like the entrance to a cathedral. He took a few steps towards it and as he did so the two doors in the doorway swung open automatically.

Stepping through the doors he entered a large room with a lofty ceiling. It was warmer in this office than the foyer he'd just come from.

There were rows of tables running the length of the room with a civil servant sat at each of them. At the end of the room was a grand desk with a large man behind it. He beckoned Danks forward as though he was a serf.

A chair was in front of the grand desk specifically for visitors to be seated. Danks sat down. The man's hands were oversized and the fingers curled as though he was holding an invisible cup. He had short black hair and he was clean shaven.

Danks guessed from the desk height that the man was a very tall individual. He estimated him to be over two meters tall.

Danks felt like a little boy sat in front of the teacher's desk about to be told off.

"Inspector, I'm Adrian Cross, the base commander".

A weasely looking man who had been scolding some of the civil servants broke off from what he was doing. He walked over and stood next to Adrian.

"This is Eric my brother. He's my deputy assistant".

Eric nodded at Danks.

"It was good of you to check in so promptly. I must say, we didn't know that Ambrose was related to such a pre-eminent inspector" said Eric.

Danks thought there was something familiar about these two. He couldn't quite put his finger on what it was.

"I thought it only polite to come over sooner rather than later so we don't get off on the wrong foot" replied Danks.

The commander added, "You presumably wanted to collect your brother's and sister-in-law's bodies. No doubt you've read the forensic report. They died due to an unfortunate malfunction in the ventilation system. Their bodies were then mistakenly disposed of in the usual way here on Titan".

"I sent explicit instructions to the forensic team to wait for my arrival before the bodies were 'disposed of' as you put it. Why were they ignored?".

"Sadly, there were some crossed wires and the subcommander ordered the funeral to proceed as usual" said the commander.

"Who ordered him to do that?". Danks was getting frustrated with them not explaining what the 'crossed wires' were.

"I think it was the subcommander himself. He's rather impetuous. By the time we realised what had happened to the bodies it was too late to stop it. The bodies had already been sent towards Saturn" replied Eric.

Danks thought he should try a different angle to try and put together a picture of what happened. "Who attended the funeral?".

"It was only the subcommander and near friends" said the commander.

"Did either of you attend the funeral?".

"No, we were rather busy that day" the commander added.

"Why not? You are the base commander and isn't it your duty to attend?".

"Look, I don't know where your questioning is

going, but it takes a lot of dedication to keep this base operational. We are needed one hundred percent of our time here" replied the commander sharply.

Danks had to suppress a scoff as that sounded ludicrous. He could see all these civil servants at their desks. Couldn't he delegate the work to one of them for the short time he would be at the funeral.

"I think it's important for me to speak to the engineer who's named in the forensic report, it's a Colin White. That will hopefully shed some light on what happened. Can you tell me where I can find him?".

"Ah yes. The subcommander sent him down to the lower levels. He's coordinating operations in the mine as some of the machinery has broken down". Adrian then leaned forward, put his elbows on the desk and placed his finger tips together, rather like a pyramid shape. Danks thought it looked rather menacing.

Adrian continued, "You'll have to go down there to interview him yourself as communications are poor down there". An evil smile seemed to cross his face after he said it.

"Before I do that I'd like to speak to the subcommander. Where can I find him?" asked Danks.

"He'll be in his office. You'll find his room back at the foyer two doors down on the right" replied the commander.

Danks stood up to leave.

"We hope your stay is short on Titan inspector. Tartarus is a busy and dangerous place. We don't need any distractions. The sooner this is put behind us the better" said Eric.

Danks got the impression he didn't like him being there on Titan.

As he headed for the door he was sure he heard Eric whisper something to Adrian and then they both sniggered.

Chapter 5

Once outside the commander's office he turned right and moved down the corridor. He found the second office on the right and pressed the intercom screen in the centre of the door. A video image popped up of the subcommander.

"Is that Inspector Danks?".

"Yes it is. I'm hoping you can help answer a few questions about my brother and his wife".

"Come on in inspector".

Danks had to wait a few seconds before the door slid open.

A tall man with blonde hair was waiting for him as he stepped in.

They shook hands and the man gestured for Danks to be seated. The man then returned to his seat on the other side of his desk.

"The commander warned me you were coming to my office".

"Did he warn you about anything else?" Danks jested.

The subcommander looked confused.

"I'm only joking. I've only come to ask you a few questions about Ambrose and Mary Danks".

"Fire away inspector".

"Did you attend their funerals?".

"Yes, along with a few of their friends. It seemed only right that they got a respectful send off".

"Do you know where and how they died?".

"I only know what was in the report".

"Why don't you remind me as to what it said?".

"Well I have a copy here somewhere".

"Let's dispense with that. Just tell me in your own words what you think happened". Danks was hoping the subcommander might slip up in what he believed to be the circumstances that surrounded their deaths.

"Well, I think they died of asphyxiation in their flat".

"They didn't die elsewhere then?".

The subcommander looked awkward again.

"Look, I know nothing of what happened other than what the pathologist said in his report".

Danks thought, "Either you, the commander or the pathologist is lying. Which of you is it or are all of you lying?".

Danks couldn't let on that he knew the pathology report had been falsified. That would put Dr Shutt in danger if he was an innocent party.

"Why did you send their bodies to be disposed of?".

"It's standard practice and I was told by the commander to dispose of them. Only later did he inform me that you'd asked for their disposal to be delayed until you arrived".

That didn't agree with what Eric had told him earlier.

"What was his reaction when you told him they'd been disposed of?".

"No reaction other than he shrugged his shoulders".

"I understand you sent the engineer who did the report on the ventilation system down to the mining operations. His name is Colin White. I want to speak to him".

"That's right, I sent Colin down there as we are having issues with the refrigeration units and one of the farming machines. There are serious issues that needed his immediate attention".

Danks didn't know what they were mining for here on Titan. All he knew was that his brother and sister-in-law were both experienced biologists. They were sent here by the mining company and their primary task was to look for life on the moon. Some exotic lower life forms had already been discovered on the moon Enceladus, so why not Titan.

"What exactly are you mining for?".

"About two hundred kilometres below the surface there's a salty ocean. Bore holes have been drilled down to it over many decades. Harvesting machines have then been released that swim about collecting nodules that are floating about in the briny solution. The nodules are exceedingly high in osmium and other rare elements. The harvesting machines return the collected material back to the main farming machines which are at the bottom of the bore holes. From there the nodules are liquidised and the resultant solution is transported back up to Tartarus where it gets processed. It makes this mining operation very lucrative".

"Do you get a large slice of the profits?".

"We usually get a nice bonus every month from the company".

"Why didn't the commander attend the

funeral?".

Paul looked uncomfortable with this question. He hesitated before replying.

"Well they are busy people".

Danks suspected that he wasn't being quite truthful.

"Really and that was enough for the commander to avoid the funeral. Wasn't it his responsibility to attend?".

"I'm just the subcommander. I'm not privy to their thoughts".

Danks decided he wouldn't push the questioning too much at this time as he needed to gather more information from other people. He'll ask more difficult questions at a later date.

"How do I get down to see Mr White on the lower levels?".

"I'll come with you if you like".

"No, that's okay. I just need to be shown the route". The last thing Danks wanted was a potential suspect looking over his shoulder at someone he was conducting an interview with.

"Well in that case, you'll need this pass to gain access and this is the route down there".

There was a map displayed on the subcommander's table screen. Danks touched his watch against a pad next to the map and the information was transferred.

"I'll be back to ask more questions after I've interviewed Mr White. I must say I'm interested in what he can add to why my brother died the way he did". Danks was hoping to sow some seeds of doubt in the mind of the subcommander to see what might develop.

Danks looked at the map on his watch as he stood. "Until the next time subcommander".

They shook hands and Danks left the office. His next destination was the mining lifts that were in a secure area about a kilometre away.

Chapter 6

Looming in front of Danks was a large industrial site with fencing all the way around. He could see guards patrolling the perimeter of the compound.

Inside the perimeter was the nuclear fusion reactor building that powered the whole of Tartarus and next to it was a second one as an emergency backup. Everyone's lives in Tartarus depended on the fusion reactors. If they failed they would all die not long afterwards.

He headed over to the main entrance that had a small building that straddled the fencing.

Behind a bullet proof window sat a guard. Danks pressed the intercom and spoke into it. "I'm here to conduct an interview with an employee".

The guard replied, "Name?".

Danks wasn't quite sure which name he wanted, so he decided to plump for the employee's name. "Mr Colin White".

There was a short delay while the guard looked at his list on the screen. He had only one person with that name and he knew he was down the mine. He replied, "No, your name!".

The inspector thought, "Damn, that was a fifty-fifty chance and it was wrong". So he tried his own name, "It's Danks, Inspector Danks".

The guard scanned down his list again. "There's

no one with that name on my list". The guard looked at Danks with narrowed eyes in a threatening manner. He lifted a gun up from behind his desk.

Danks then remembered the pass that the subcommander had given him. He pulled it out of the inside pocket of his jacket and placed it on a pad by the window.

Something changed on the guard's screen and the narrowed eyes changed back to being normal.

"It seems the subcommander has given you permission to enter the facility". The guard touched a pad on the screen and the door on the right of the window slid open.

Inspector Danks stepped though the door into a corridor with an arch of metal about a couple of meters down. This was the usual instrument for detecting any weapons or explosives.

The guard appeared on the other side of the arch.

"Step through the archway". The guard was brandishing his gun, just in case.

Danks walked through it. To his relief no alarms sounded.

The guard then frisked him to check for any other items that could be easily concealed. Danks was clean.

"Go across the courtyard to the building opposite. Inside there are ten lifts in a line. There should be at least one of them available at this level. You'll need the Mining floor. It's about two kilometres down. That's the lowest level. Ask the person at the desk there for Mr White. They should know where he is".

Before Danks could say 'thank you' the guard had disappeared back into his office and the door had started to close.

Danks shrugged his shoulders. "What an odd bloke" he thought.

Heading out of the guard's building he made his way over to the structure that housed the lifts.

Inside the lift building he could hear lots of strange squealing and grinding noises emanating from the shafts. An attendant handed him some crampons which he attached to the base of his boots.

Danks then walked over to a lift that was waiting. Stepping inside it an automated voice asked which floor he wanted. "Mining floor" he said.

"Please enure all loose items are secure. Then use the clamps on the floor to secure your feet" came the reply.

He zipped everything that was loose into his pockets, then he secured both feet. As soon as he'd done that the lift door slid shut and it started its descent.

The lift and he were in free fall. He looked at his watch to see how long this would last. After about forty five seconds he felt the lift start to decelerate. It felt comfortable as it was like being back on Earth.

The lift came to a stop and the door slid open. It was just above zero centigrade, the humidity was higher and the atmospheric pressure was slightly elevated. Water was dripping from the ceiling and there was a darkness that the lights struggled to penetrate.

Ahead of him there was an air conditioned office. He went over and stepped inside closing the door behind him.

It was pleasant to be in the warmth.

Someone spoke to him from the corner of the room, "Can I help you?".

A slim man in a green all in one jumpsuit was sitting on a tall stool. He swung around from the screen he'd just been studying.

"Ah, yes. I was told you could help me find a Mr White. He's the head engineer sent down here to fix some machinery".

"Yes, he's got a lot on his plate at the moment".

"Why is that?".

"Well he's got to fix the tunnel refrigeration units and then the farming machine down here. It's not normally above zero centigrade out there. That's why the tunnels are melting".

"Can I speak to him?" asked Danks.

The man swung back to his screen and entered Mr White into his keypad. A map popped up on the screen with a red flashing dot indicating where he was in the tunnel system. He transferred the information to one of several drones that were standing to attention along the wall. One of them stepped forward.

"This drone will take you to him. When you've finished talking to him just tell the drone to return and it will bring you back here".

It marched to the door and waited for Danks.

"Thanks for your help".

"That's okay. It's been a welcome break as I don't get to see many people down here".

The door slid back. Danks and his side kick

drone left the sanctuary of the air conditioned office. It was back to the cold and dank atmosphere in the tunnels again.

Chapter 7

It was eerie walking down the tunnels with two sets of footsteps and the dripping of the water in the background. Every so often a screeching or rumbling noise shattered the sounds that Danks had gotten used to.

He unzipped his pocket as he'd remembered he had brought a torch with him. Turning it on it illuminated the way ahead even more, with the drone's shadow elongated down the passage in front of him.

They passed a worker heading the other way with their drone guiding them along the tunnels.

Danks was thinking what if his drone ran out of energy it would mean he would be lost down here. He'd have to wait for someone to pass by.

After what seemed an age they entered a chamber. It was housing a large machine. The drone marched up to it and stopped.

Several people were working on the machine and one person seemed to be coordinating the operation. Danks went over to him.

"Are you Colin White?" asked Danks.

He was wearing a yellow boiler suit with oil stains on the sleeves. The light level was low but Danks could make out that he was dark haired and he was slightly taller than him.

The man wiped his sweaty forehead with a

greasy cloth. "Yes I am. Who's asking?".

"I'm Inspector Danks. Can we go somewhere a bit quieter?". Danks had to shout over the noise of the machinery.

The man pointed to a small box shaped building about ten meters away. "That's my temporary office down here. We can go there".

It was good to step back into a warm office again.

"So, inspector, I'm guessing you're here to ask me about Ambrose's ventilation system".

"Yes I am. How did you know?".

"Danks is a very rare surname so I assumed you are related to Ambrose".

There was a short pause before Colin continued.

"Also, he used to talk about you quite a bit. He was very proud of you".

"Yes, I am his brother and I was proud of him too. So, did you know him well?".

"Yes, Ambrose and Mary used to come down here quite a lot. They were conducting some research into potential life living in the ocean below. They would lower probes down into it and retrieve them a day or two later. The three of us would often meet in a bar and have a few beers when back up at Tartarus".

Danks was intrigued as to what they'd discovered down here. But for now, he needed to find out what the fault was in their apartment.

"I see from the forensic report that you stated that the oxygen valve had frozen shut on Ambrose and Mary's ventilation system".

Danks saw surprise on Colin's face.

"Is that what the report said?".

"Yes, didn't you read it?".

"No as I'm too busy fire fighting all the equipment failures down here".

"What do you mean by that?". Even though Danks thought he knew what he meant he wanted Mr White to elaborate.

"There isn't very much money to repair all the equipment around here. That's why the harvesting machine and the refrigeration units that cool these tunnels keep breaking down.

The tunnels are cut into frozen water and as you can see, the heat generated by the machines is causing the walls and ceilings to melt. If we don't get the refrigeration units operational soon some of the tunnels could collapse and we'll all end up trapped down here.

The guys out there are doing their best. I think, with a bit of luck, that the refrigeration units will be operational within the next few hours".

"How much do you get for the maintenance of the equipment?".

"I have a budget of only twelve million dollars per Earth calender year. It just isn't enough".

Danks couldn't understand why the budget was so low. This was a company that made over two trillion dollars profit a year and most of its wealth came from the rare elements extracted from Titan.

"You looked surprised when I mentioned what you'd been quoted as saying in the report. Why?".

"That's because the oxygen valve wasn't frozen. In fact, the oxygen and nitrogen are mixed where the nuclear reactors are.

Carbon dioxide is split back to oxygen and the nitrogen is recycled. This makes the equivalent of air. The resultant mixture is then piped to all the accommodations around the whole of Tartarus and down here. There is no oxygen valve that could freeze shut.

What I said was that someone or something had crushed the air supply line feeding their flat. I've never seen anything happen like that before.

I told Dr Shutt that and he seemed to take that on board. I assumed that was why you were here".

"That's useful information as that wasn't in the forensic report. I assume you attended their funeral?".

"Yes, there were several friends and the subcommander. I wasn't surprised that the commander and his brother didn't turn up".

"Oh, why was that?". Danks was interested to see if it agreed with their reason for not attending the funerals.

"Well, there had been a falling out between Mary and those two".

"That's news to me. Why did they fall out?". Danks thought that this was strange but added to the picture he was building.

"Ambrose confided in me one night at the usual bar. I think he'd had a few too many. It all happened when they had some disagreement with Mary over something. I don't know what as Ambrose refused to say any more about it and then fell asleep. I had to sling his arm over my shoulders and help him back to their apartment".

Danks could sense Colin's resentment of the commander and his brother.

Ambrose had never mentioned any of this to him although they hadn't spoken for quite a while.

It's pretty difficult having a meaningful conversation with someone when the signal takes between two to three hours round trip. They did at least send recorded videos every other month just to catch up on things.

"That's answered a few niggling questions I had. Thank you Mr White".

"Please call me Colin. Your brother did".

"Okay, Colin. How much longer do you think you'll be working down here?".

"Not sure. Once we've fixed the refrigeration units the farming machine needs repairing.

Something keeps clogging up the feed mechanism. The holes down in the ocean need constant clearing out otherwise they reseal. It's as though they're trying to heal themselves over. In fact Ambrose and Mary seemed very interested in that.

Anyway, I'd better get back and see how the guys are getting on with the repairs if that's okay?".

Danks had finished questioning Mr White for now.

"Yes that's fine. But let me know when you are back at Tartarus. I may have more questions to ask you. We could make it more pleasant over a few beers".

"That would be excellent" replied Colin.

They left the relative shelter of the temporary office and stepped outside. Danks was surprised to see his drone was standing next to the office door.

Danks and Mr White shook hands and Colin headed back to the refrigeration units shouting instructions as he went.

The drone stood silently waiting for its next command. "Drone, return" said Danks.

The lights on its head lit up and it sprang into life. It marched off in the direction of the tunnel they had come from. Danks followed not far behind.

Chapter 8

The drone entered the tunnel taking them back towards the lifts. Danks had to pull his attention away from looking around the vast chamber and had to hurry to catch up with it.

They marched past several side tunnels before it took a right turn down a darker tunnel. Danks didn't recognise this tunnel, but then he didn't recognise the previous ones.

After about thirty minutes he was beginning to think this wasn't the route back. He looked down at his watch to find the map of the tunnel system. At that very same moment the drone footsteps stopped so Danks instinctively halted too. The drone's lights had gone out and it was pitch black.

Danks heard a few faint crashes but they seemed quite far away. He unzipped his pocket and searched around inside it to find his torch. He was glad he'd brought it with him. Pulling it out he switched it on and scanned the light around. The drone was nowhere to be seen. He was in a high vaulted chamber. But as he lowered the beam to his horror he realised he was standing on the edge of a large black hole. It was three meters wide. He took a step backwards. Picking up a small block of ice that was near his foot, he stretched out his arm and carefully dropped it over the edge. It didn't make a sound and he didn't hear it hit the bottom.

Danks concluded that the drone had gone over the edge and on its way down it must have hit the sides of the bore hole. That would account for the crashes he'd heard.

Danks turned around as carefully as possible as it was quite slippery and he edged his way back down the tunnel. He wasn't sure how many turns they'd done so he looked at the floor. There were faint marks where his and the drone's feet had dug into the floor so he followed them. As he started walking back he could see gargoyle like faces carved into the walls. They were beginning to melt but still recognisable as faces. The old tunnel builders must have added them like an artist signs a painting.

He checked his watch for the tunnel map. It was no use as there was no signal down here.

A cool draught began wafting past him. Colin and his team must have managed to get the refrigeration units back on line. The draught soon turned into a cold chill as it drove the temperature of the tunnels down. It wouldn't be long before the surface water would start to refreeze. It was a good job he'd brought that thick coat with him. He slipped his gloves back on and zipped his coat right up.

It was awkward retracing his steps as the foot marks were difficult to see with all the surface water around. Danks had been walking back for roughly half an hour now and he just wasn't sure he was on the right track.

He came to a point where there were three tunnels. One went straight ahead, one went to his right, the other went to his left. He couldn't determine which was the correct route to take. Stopping at the junction he listened. He was sure he could make out faint voices coming from the one on his left. Deciding to take a gamble he turned down that one.

Arriving at a T junction he stopped. This could be the main tunnel that the drone had mistakenly turned off. He checked his watch again hoping it had reconnected. There was nothing. It just wasn't working this deep down.

Those faint voices could still be heard. Maybe he'd try waiting here to see if someone would come along the tunnel. So he crouched down and tucked his gloved hands under his armpits to keep them warm. His breath was visible as the temperature had dropped to below freezing.

Time seemed to pass slowly. He'd been waiting twenty minutes now, he was getting cold and concerned that no one was going to come by.

Then there was the sound of footsteps coming from his left. To his delight a drone appeared followed by Colin himself.

"Inspector, what are you doing here and where's your drone?".

Danks stood up and dug his hands into his pockets. "I'm not quite sure what happened with my drone. It took me quite some distance down this route". He pointed to the tunnel he'd come back through.

Mr White looked shocked. "That sounds like a malfunction. There are lots of abandoned mine shafts down there. Mainly because the ice was too unstable at the deeper levels. Some of the shafts go down ninety kilometres or more".

"Tell me about it. I nearly fell into one. The drone leading me disappeared down that shaft. I was stupidly looking at my watch while following it. It was only because the drone's footsteps went silent and its lights disappeared that I stopped".

"You were fortunate to have found your way back to this tunnel as it's like a rabbit warren around here. There are uncharted tunnels all around that area.

We'd better head back to the lifts to get warm and ask the drone operator to explain what happened.

You'll probably have to fill out a drone report as you were lucky to survive by the sounds of it.

In all the time I've worked down here that has never happened before".

"That's reassuring, but why my drone and why now?" said Danks suspiciously.

"No idea" replied Mr White.

Colin's drone started off again and they both followed it.

As they followed the drone Danks asked, "When you last saw my brother what did he say?".

"That was quite a while ago, but I can remember it quite vividly. He seemed excited about something. He said it'd make him and Mary famous".

"Did he say what that was?".

"No, but he bought an extra round of drinks to celebrate which must have meant it was pretty momentous". Colin laughed as Ambrose was usually slow at buying a round.

"Ah, yes. My brother kept his wallet firmly closed. The last time I saw him open it some rare and exotic moths flew out of it". They both laughed.

Danks continued, "On a more serious note, if you do remember anything else don't hesitate to contact me no matter how trivial. It all comes in useful when building a picture of the events leading to why they died".

They arrived outside the lift office and went inside. It was a complete contrast to earlier. It was very cold and dry outside. Inside it was warm and cosy.

The man in the green jumpsuit swung around again. "Hello gents. You're back!". He looked puzzled as only one drone moved over to the row of others and plugged itself into the power supply to recharge.

"What happened to the other drone? Did it break down?".

Danks replied, "You could say that. It led me off the main route and almost killed me by walking into a mine shaft. I nearly followed it over the edge. What I want to know is why you programmed it to take that path back?". Danks was seeing what the man's reaction would be to being accused of trying to kill him.

The man looked shocked. "I can assure you that I had absolutely nothing to do with that. I programmed it up in the usual way giving it the route to take there and back".

Colin added, "Actually, it did seem odd that it was waiting by the office door when we left my temporary office. They usually wait where they left you which was over by the machine. You know, where you started talking to me".

"Do these drones have the ability to hear sounds?".

"Yes, as you can issue verbal commands to them" replied the man.

"So, do you think it might have been listening in to our conversation in your office Colin?".

"I would think it could detect what we were saying. But why would anyone want to do that?".

"Precisely, if it had heard us could it relay it out of the tunnels?".

"There is a drone intercommunications that is linked to Tartarus. I suppose someone could listen in to the conversation" replied Colin.

"Are these things listening to us at the moment?". Danks was concerned that even now they were being monitored.

"No, once they plug in to recharge they enter a dormant state. All external stimuli are ignored" the man replied in a confident tone.

"Okay, that's good. I'm heading back to Tartarus now Colin. Are you coming up too?".

"Sorry inspector. I have a few more days down here. Now the refrigeration unit is back online I have to fix one of the farming machines. It's become jammed with debris. It takes a while to lower the probes down to the ocean below, figure out what has actually wedged in it then perform a suitable repair".

Danks shook Colin's and the green jumpsuit man's hands and left the warm sanctuary of the office.

He stepped out into the cold and walked to the nearest empty lift. He stepped inside, zipped up his pockets, secured his feet to the floor with the foot clamps and spoke to the lift. "Tartarus".

The lift door closed and it started its ascent.

He was hoping nothing would go wrong on the journey up. Although he thought that there were eight motors, one for each corner of the lift, so everything should be fine.

It reached maximum acceleration which was about the same as gravity on Earth. It then eased off and it returned to the Titan gravity. Then the decelerating kicked in and he felt he was hanging upside down before it came to a stop.

The lift door slid back silently and Danks stepped out. He handed the crampons back to the attendant and headed out of the building.

After exiting the mining compound he made for the nearest bar for a drink and something to eat.

After his meal he left the bar just as the lights of Tartarus were being dimmed. This was to keep everyone's internal body clocks in sync with the twenty four hours rhythm back on Earth.

He headed back to his hotel for some sorely needed sleep.

Chapter 9

Danks had had a good night's sleep. The day light hours were artificially created on Tartarus to help the citizens' circadian rhythms. Rolling out of his bed, he got up and prepared for the day ahead.

His first task was to send a message to the corporation operating Tartarus. He was interested in why a multi trillion company would only invest twelve million dollars into the maintenance of the site equipment per calender year.

He recorded the message and sent it to their headquarters back on Earth. It would be quite a few hours before he would receive a reply.

In the meantime he needed to have some breakfast. He'd seen a small café not far from the hotel which looked rather inviting.

Leaving the hotel he wandered over to the café. There were a couple of people inside who were already having their breakfast. He opened the door and went inside.

There were rows of private booths along the walls like the diners back in the USA. The seats were covered in that red easily cleaned tough material, typical in those types of diner. He took his coat and gloves off and slid himself onto one of the seats. Scanning the menu displayed on the table top he selected something that looked tasty.

A waiter arrived and took Danks's order. It was

a substitute scrambled eggs on toast with a hot coffee. He was hoping it would be palatable.

While he was waiting he caught sight of two people who were looking furtive outside. As soon as he'd spied them they came into the café and sat down at a table not far away. They were the same blokes he'd spotted earlier when he left the hotel. At the time he thought it was a bit suspicious but now this confirmed what he was thinking.

The waiter went over and took their orders and when he returned with their drinks they paid immediately. Danks knew this old trick. If they had to leave quickly they could do so without the waiter chasing after them. It was clear that these guys were following him, although not very well he thought.

His drink and meal arrived and he tucked in. He was pleasantly surprised as it was passable as almost real egg and the toast, being kosher, helped with the enjoyment.

He was quite amused by the two men who'd obviously been tasked with following him. They were sipping their drinks quite slowly as they didn't want to be sitting at a table with empty cups waiting for him to finish his meal. So, just to annoy them he ate his meal more slowly than usual.

Danks finished his drink and paid the waiter. He could see the two men in the café discussing something and looking restless. They must have been thinking he was about to leave. He didn't want to disappoint them so he slid along his seat and stood up. Putting his coat and gloves back on, he headed for the exit.

Leaving the café his next destination was the Tartarus Police HQ. He should at least make them aware that he was here on Titan.

Looking on his map he saw it wasn't too far away. Fortunately, Tartarus was a small and compact community.

Danks knew the advantages of a small outpost like this. The main one was that there wasn't much crime in places like this. Tartarus had only about two thousand people working here, so he guessed that the police HQ wouldn't be a big unit.

From the café he turned right heading towards the police station. As he moved down the street he heard the café door open and shut behind him. "Ah, here come the shadows" he thought to himself.

Danks didn't see any reason to shake them off like last time as he was only going to check in with the local police. So whoever had told them to follow him wouldn't get much information from this trip. He'd shake them off at a suitable time.

Crossing the street and turning down Cassini Street he could see the two men trying to keep their distance.

About half way down the street was the Tartarus Police HQ with a sign just above the main entrance and he went inside.

A police officer at a single desk in the small room was concentrating on the screen in front of her.

He approached the officer. "Can I see the police commander?".

"Take a seat please sir".

Danks sat down opposite the police officer.

"She's quite busy you know sir?".

"I'm sure she is".

"Can I take your name?".

"Yes, it's Danks". He paused a short time then added, "Inspector Danks".

The officer looked up, squinted at Danks then stood bolt upright and saluted. "Sorry sir. I'm Officer Helen Turner sir".

He surmised that the whole police force at this base consisted of a single officer. This really was a low crime rate area. But just to check he asked the question anyway. "Are you the whole department here at Tartarus?".

"Yes sir. It's only me sir".

"You can sit down Officer Turner".

"Thank you sir". She lowered herself back into her seat.

He looked around for any facilities at the police station. "Do you have a prison cell?".

"No sir, but we do have that chair over there". She pointed at a lone chair in the corner of the room. "It does come with hand and ankle restraints" she said with some sarcasm.

Danks couldn't believe what he was hearing. "And have you had to use it at all?".

"No, but then I've only been here a month. I was drafted here at short notice from the asteroid belt to cover for the officer who was here".

"Where is the previous officer?".

"That's just it sir. He's vanished along with all his belongings from his flat. I conducted some investigations and there is no record of him leaving Titan. In his flat there were only his finger prints. The case is still open. I've been conducting investigations but nothing has turned up.

Other than that, everything is very quiet around here".

Danks thought he should inform the officer as to why he was here on Titan. "I'm investigating a couple of deaths here at Tartarus. I'll need some assistance while I'm here. I assume you're not too busy to help me are you?".

"That sounds great. So where do we start sir?".

Danks told her the complete story so far. She listened attentively to everything he told her. "So now you're up to speed. I'm waiting for a reply from the headquarters of the company running the operation here on Titan. It should be coming in any time soon. In the meantime I want to check my brother's and his partner's belongings. I'm guessing they are over at the pathology lab".

Officer Turner scanned through some menus selecting the occasional item on her screen and then looked back at Danks. "The report says that they are at Dr Shutt's lab".

Danks stood and headed for the door to leave. "Well are you coming?" he said.

Officer Turner looked excited. She grabbed her cap, joined Danks and she locked the door behind her as they left the station.

Chapter 10

Once outside the police HQ they started walking along the street heading for the pathology lab.

"By the way sir, did you know we're being followed?" said the sergeant quietly.

Danks was impressed that Officer Turner had spotted the two shadows following them so quickly. "Yes I am aware. They've been tracking me since I left my hotel. I'm tolerating them at the moment. That's why I asked if you'd got a prison cell as we'll pull them in for questioning at some point.

You'll have to requisition another chair or we lock them both to the same chair" Danks said with a smile.

Officer Turner grinned.

They arrived at the pathology lab. Danks touched the screen on the door and Dr Shutt's face appeared. "Ah, inspector, you're back again. Come on in".

The door slid to the side and they went in.

Danks looked back and could see one of the two shadows was reporting back to his boss.

Once inside, he heard the door slide shut behind them and Dr Shutt appeared at the corridor end. "Come on through" he shouted.

They moved down the corridor and into the lab.

"How can I help you this time?" Dr Shutt

enquired.

"We'd like to see my brother's and his partner's belongings. The report says that you have them stored here" replied Danks.

"Ah, yes I do. Wait here". Dr Shutt then disappeared into an adjacent room.

Danks could hear him scrabbling about in the room. After a few minutes he appeared at the door pulling a trolley with two large sealed boxes on it.

"These are your brother's and his partner's items. I tried to separate them into his and hers when I collected everything from the flat".

Danks pulled the box that had Ambrose written on the top towards him . He pressed a button on the side and the lid opened. He found it difficult to search his brother's belongings. If only he'd kept in contact with him more, maybe he would have seen the warning signs and could've saved them.

Inside the box were Ambrose's coats, clothes, several pairs of boots, goggles and at the bottom was a tablet. This was his work tablet but the screen was broken.

Danks lifted the tablet out to check the extent of the damage. "Do you know how this happened?" he asked Dr Shutt.

"It was like that in the flat. It looks as though it has been stamped on with the heel of a foot".

Danks turned it on and it tried to flicker into life but then shut down. Not only was the screen cracked but also the batteries were damaged. "Did anyone try to recover the data from it?".

"No. The subcommander wanted it incinerating. He said there was probably confidential information on it".

"Why didn't you incinerate it?".

"Because I'd received your message that you were on your way so I thought you'd want to see it first".

Danks opened Mary's box next. There were similar items but no tablet.

"Did you find Mary's tablet?".

"I incinerated hers and an old tablet I had lying around. I then took the remaining bits to the subcommander to show him I'd done it. It convinced him and the commander that both had been destroyed. I kept your brother's safe as I thought that one could be useful" Dr Shutt replied confidently.

"Okay doctor, although you should have kept hers too. I'll take this tablet with me anyway. I may be able to recover the data".

Danks rummaged around in the box that contained his brother's belongings and pulled out a canvas bag with a strap. It was the case for the tablet. He tucked the tablet into it and slung it over his shoulder before addressing the doctor. "Put all this back in the storage cupboard".

The doctor replied with an affirmative answer.

"We'll be in contact if we need to look at them again" said the inspector.

Danks and Office Turner headed out of the lab. This time they left via the front door. The two shadows were still lurking just up the street behind a statue of Christiaan Huygens.

Heading back towards the police HQ they passed a shop that sold electrical items and spare parts for computers. Danks went inside. There were several people in there all stood at screens.

He went over to a screen and scanned through the available parts selecting items that he believed he could use to effect a repair to the tablet. He placed the order and paid by scanning his watch at the terminal.

It took a few minutes before a message appeared on his watch indicating the items were ready. They came racing down a chute into a sealed box and he scanned his watch on the box to open it. Removing the components he placed them in the canvas bag with the laptop.

They left the shop and continued on their journey until they arrived at the police HQ. They both went inside.

"Now Officer Turner, let's take a look at the two shadows following us with your security camera".

Officer Turner sat down at her desk and routed the video feed to her screen. She located the two men stood leaning against the building opposite trying to look nonchalant.

Zooming in she was able to get a closer image of each of them. Passing them through the image recognition system it popped out with two names, Ron and Reg Edwards. She pulled up their details.

"They are twin brothers. The previous officer had documented that these two characters were invariably in trouble. He arrested them a few times but had to release them as the subcommander vouched for their whereabouts at the time of the crimes".

"The subcommander keeps cropping up whenever something happens". Danks was now thinking that this guy had become the number one suspect.

It was time he headed back to his accommodation to try and recover the data from his brother's tablet. He said goodbye to Officer Turner and left the station.

As he headed back to the hotel he noticed that the twins had disappeared.

Chapter 11

Inspector Danks closed the door of his room and took out the damaged tablet putting it on the table along with the parts he'd bought. He was hoping that he could do some sort of repair, even if it worked for only a day or two. On previous cases he'd managed to recover data from damaged tablets in a similar manner.

He plugged in the hot air gun he'd bought and started heating up the edges of the screen. After a few minutes he pushed a plastic spatula into the edge between the screen and the back of the tablet. Luck was on his side as the back started lifting up. Running the heat gun along the edge he worked his way around the perimeter.

Eventually the back peeled away exposing the main board inside. He gently removed the damaged battery and put it to one side. Taking the new one out of its wrapper, he carefully inserted it into the main board where it made a satisfying click noise as it engaged. He plugged in a recharging pad and left the tablet on it. It would take a while to fully recharge, assuming that those parts of the board weren't damaged too. At least the charging symbol appeared on the screen.

In the meantime, there was a video message waiting for him from the HQ of the company back on Earth. He flicked it from his watch towards the

TV in his room and the video appeared.

"Play" said Danks.

"Hello inspector, I am Keith Stein Chief Financial Officer of Titan Mineral Corporation.

You asked why there was only twelve million dollars allocated for the repair of all the equipment on Titan per calendar year. I can assure you that your figure is incorrect. As you can see from the financial report here..". He pointed to a table of figures that were next to him. ".. the figure is actually one hundred million per calendar year".

Danks zoomed in on the table of figures displayed on the screen.

"We are unsure as to where your figures have come from. Maybe you should consult with the base commander. All funds are routed via him. He then distributes it among the various departments. I hope I've answered your question inspector. If you have any further questions don't hesitate to contact me". The video message ended and the screen went blank.

Danks turned the TV off.

"There's a huge discrepancy between what the company thinks is being spent on maintenance and what Mr White says the budget is. Maybe the commander can enlighten me on how the funds are distributed" thought Danks.

He called Officer Turner. "I'm heading over to see the base commander. I think you should accompany me as backup".

"Okay sir. I'll be there in about ten minutes", replied Officer Turner.

The video call ended.

Danks checked the tablet. It had built up enough

power now.

He touched the tablet face and a rectangle appeared where a fingerprint had to be scanned to unlock the device. That obviously wasn't possible. The screen was cracked in several places and his brother wasn't here any more to scan his finger. He selected the alternative option to enter a password.

Racking his brains he was trying to work out what his brother would choose. He knew it would be some complex biological word. His brother enjoyed using tongue twisting words, usually the Latin names. He would need some time to think about what that might be.

At that very moment there was a knock on his door. The hotel rooms on Titan were very basic. None of the modern conveniences that the inner planets enjoyed. Not even the video doorbells.

He went over and answered the door. It was Officer Turner. He put the tablet into the safe in his room and locked it with his thumb print. They left his room heading for the main government building where they were going to ask the commander some taxing questions.

Chapter 12

Danks and Officer Turner arrived at the building where the commander's office was. They entered the main hall and approached the main desk. Danks recognised the man behind it. It was the same guard that he'd encountered before.

"You're back again I see. Have you an appointment this time?". The guard looked slightly annoyed.

"Yes I'm back again and no I haven't an appointment".

"Then you can't see the commander, so fuck off". The guard grinned after he said it. It was his favourite part of the day when he got a chance to express his feelings.

Danks turned away from the desk and spoke into his watch. "Dial the Tartarus commander". It started ringing. Someone answered. It was one of the civil servants. Danks said he wanted to see the commander but the person said he was too busy.

"Can you tell him that I've been in contact with the company HQ back on Earth and they want me to report back to them ASAP". That wasn't true but he knew it would galvanise them into action.

He could hear a discussion going on in the background and then the person came back.

"The commander has a free slot right now if you'd like to come through". The person then hung up.

Danks and Turner returned to the guard's desk. The guard looked at them as though he was even more annoyed than before. He was about to tell them to sling their hook in not so nice a terms when his headphone rang. He answered it. A look of disbelief seemed to cross his face.

"I don't know how you're doing this but the commander says you can go straight through". The guard seemed to say that through gritted teeth. Danks quite enjoyed seeing the guard having to bite his own tongue.

This was the first time Officer Turner had been in this building and she couldn't believe it. There she was in a tiny police station without a prison cell. The only thing she had was a chair to restrain a criminal and here they seemed to be oozing opulence.

They strolled up to the base commander's desk. Danks sat down while Officer Turner remained standing. She was checking out all the people in the room. One of the main requirements of a good police officer was being observant.

"Well inspector, you said you'd been in contact with the company HQ. Was that completely necessary as I'm sure we could have helped you if you'd asked?" said the commander.

Danks could see Eric was standing a few desks away talking to one of the civil servants, but he kept staring in their direction. Officer Turner noticed it too and seemed to find it disconcerting. Normally if you meet someone's eyes they look away, Eric didn't. He just kept staring.

"Well commander, I'm interested in Tartarus's

accounts for the last two years. Is it possible to have a copy of them?". This wasn't really a request thought Danks, it was more like a command. If the commander refused he'd make it more official.

"Of course, I'll get it transferred to you straight away". The commander beckoned Eric over.

"Eric, can you get George to send Inspector Danks our accounts for the last two years?".

"Why?" said Eric in an annoyed tone.

"Just do it Eric" the commander said in a stern voice.

After a few awkward minutes of silence, George came over with his tablet. "Here is the information you requested inspector". He swept his finger across the screen towards Inspector Danks. His watch indicated that he'd received the complete report.

"Thank you commander we'll be in touch if we find anything we don't understand" Danks replied.

"I'm sure you won't. We have a very professional accounting department here at Tartarus" said the commander.

They said the usual goodbyes and Danks and Officer Turner left.

"I can check through that financial report for you sir. I was an accountant before I joined the police force".

"That would be really helpful. It'll give me time to see if I can access my brother's tablet".

Danks transferred the data to Officer Turner's watch and they parted company. She headed back to the police HQ while he returned to his hotel room.

Chapter 13

Danks arrived back at his accommodation to find that his door had been wrenched open and the inside had been turned over. He went straight to the safe. There were marks on the safe door as though it had been hit several times with a heavy object. Fortunately, whoever had done this was unable to gain access to it.

He contacted the hotel reception and they came up straight away.

A tall thin man with black hair and wearing black trousers, black jacket and red shirt appeared at the door. "I'm so sorry sir. I have no idea how this could have happened. I'll check the security cameras for this corridor. In the meantime I'll move you to an alternative room".

"That would be ideal and send me the video clips when you find them".

"I will sir".

Danks gathered all his belongings and stuffed them into his holdall. Opening the safe he took out the tablet and placed it in its bag.

The tall man showed the inspector down the corridor to his new accommodation.

Once Danks had closed his door and locked it, he unpacked the tablet. Placing it on the table, he sat down and started thinking about a suitable password.

Danks thought it could be from Ambrose's childhood. He tried several names of plants or flowers Ambrose liked but they were all rejected.

Just then the video footage of the corridor came in on his watch. He reviewed the footage on his TV.

It was obvious by their build and how they walked that the two intruders were men. They were both wearing balaclavas so as not to be recognised. Walking down the corridor they stopped. They then forced the door open that was in front of them. It was his old room. They entered and several minutes later they reappeared. Thankfully he knew they hadn't found anything significant.

Danks spotted something and froze the video. He zoomed in on several different frames where the men's hands were clearly visible. He could see from the high resolution images the marks on the back of their hands. They were age spots on the skin. "These are just like fingerprints. Everyone has them in varying degrees but they are all different" he thought.

Danks stored the hand images and labelled them accordingly. One hand was particularly identifiable where the age spots had merged into a larger recognizable shape. It looked a bit like a flower. Something like a rose or dianthus.

That thought triggered a memory. Danks suddenly remembered that his brother had selected a particularly beautiful flower for his lapel at his wedding. It was a Dianthus Caryophyllus. He tried Caryophyllus. His luck was in, the tablet sprang into life and up popped the home screen. He knew his brother well. When they were kids, they often challenged each other to guess what they were thinking. Danks always won that game.

Firstly, he scanned through the list of video files and found the most recent one. Playing it he sat back and watched his brother. He was looking worried.

"I think something dreadful has happened to Officer Smith. I talked to him two days ago about what Mary and I have found. He said he'd go and talk to the subcommander about it. I haven't seen or heard from him since. I went to the station and it was all locked up. I tried calling him and it returns the message that he's out of the area. I'll have to go and see the subcommander myself. Oh wait, someone is at the door. I'll continue afterwards". Then the video ended. There were no later recordings, this was the last one he'd done.

Danks played the next most recent video. This time his brother was more upbeat. "I've just spoken to Officer Smith and he's as excited about what we've discovered as we are. It's remarkable. Mary and I believe this will change everything here on Titan. Officer Smith has gone to tell the subcommander. I'm going to draft a video for the company HQ back on Earth. Mining will have to be suspended until we have further information". He saw his brother reach forward and the video terminated.

Inspector Danks could think of only one reason for stopping the mining. If his brother was this excited it means Ambrose and Mary must have discovered life here on Titan. He played the third video in the list.

"Mary and I have discovered that the nodules floating around in Titan's ocean are actually an amoeba like creature. They clump together for warmth and it seems they move from one vent hole to another to collect the nutrients that they need. After ingesting them they secrete the rare elements out as a protective layer around themselves which they shed every so often. The company will have to suspend mining while we evaluate an alternative method of collecting these elements. With the current method of mining we are killing these new life forms".

"So, that's possibly why Officer Smith disappeared and why my brother and his wife were killed" thought Danks. The subcommander must have had them eliminated so the mining wouldn't stop.

This whole case had suddenly become a lot more deadly. If he made a wrong move he too would go missing. He would have to tread carefully.

He would send a message to the company HQ to warn them and then it was time to throw a few testing questions at the subcommander without giving away what he now knew.

Chapter 14

Inspector Danks arrived at the government building and walked up to the check in desk. The guard had an exasperated look on his face.

"Name?" said the guard.

"You know my name" replied Danks with a smile on his face.

"It's protocol" replied the annoyed guard.

"Inspector Danks". He was getting fed up with this weird protocol.

"Who do you want to see this time?".

"I have some questions for the subcommander".

A sort of relieved look came over the guard's face. It was obviously easier to get a meeting with him than the base commander.

The guard called the subcommander and it wasn't long before he turned to Danks. "You're in luck buddy! You can go through to his office now".

Danks got the impression that the guard still had the urge to throw him out.

The subcommander's room wasn't far down the corridor. He entered the room and saw him dictating to his screen in his desk. Stood right behind him were two men who looked a lot like bouncers. He recognised them from the video that Officer Turner had captured of them. They were the shadows following him before.

The subcommander waved his hand over the screen to pause his dictation. "Hello inspector. Please take a seat".

Danks sat down and looked at the two men. They didn't look very happy. "I would like to talk to you in private". He was a bit wary of these two guys. Presumably they were the guys who'd threatened Dr Shutt.

The subcommander asked them to leave. They looked very reluctant to depart. One of the two men put his hand on the subcommander's desk while his other hand was on the back of his chair. He then leaned down menacingly close to the subcommander and whispered something in his ear.

Danks glanced at that man's hands and noticed the same age spot pattern he'd seen on one of the two intruders that had broken into his hotel room. These must have been the two guys who'd turned over his place. He kept a close eye on them as they left.

"What do those guys do here?" asked Danks.

"Oh, that's Ron and Reg. They're the commander's body guards".

"So they're nothing to do with you then".

"Certainly not, I wouldn't have them working for me. They're too uncontrollable and threatening. The commander insists that they accompany me occasionally".

"That's interesting" thought Danks. "What did that guy whisper to you?" he asked.

"That was Ron. He was warning me about you. I try not to take any notice of those guys but it's difficult when they are so hostile. Anyway, I'm sure you're not here to enquire about those two happy bunnies" said the subcommander with a touch of sarcastic emphasis on the 'happy'.

"I was just wondering what happened to Officer Smith. I've found some evidence that he came to see you just before he disappeared. Have you any idea where he went?".

The subcommander looked confused. "He never came to see me. I was down at the mining facility for several days at that time. I used to maintain the machinery before I became subcommander. When I was promoted Colin White took over my old job. I knew he was getting overwhelmed with the work so I went down to help".

"So if Officer Smith didn't see you who would he have seen?".

"It would have probably been the base commander. If he'd managed to get past the grizzly guard out there if you know what I mean". The subcommander half laughed as he said it.

Danks replied, "I certainly do. He seems to have a chip on his shoulder with anyone who doesn't have an appointment". They both laughed.

"On a more serious note. Did my brother come to see you?".

"I'm sorry about your brother and his wife. I liked them. They were most enthusiastic about their work here. I only found out that they'd died when I returned back to Tartarus. I went to their funerals as I like to think they were my friends".

Danks detected that the subcommander was being genuine. Either that or he was a really good actor.

"You vouched for the two twins a few times

when Officer Smith arrested them, why?".

"Ah, yes, Eric told me they were with him or the base commander each of those times. He told me to tell Officer Smith that they were accounted for when the offences took place. I wasn't sure I should intervene but he threatened to sack me if I didn't follow orders".

"You ordered the incineration of their laptops. For what reason?". Danks had an inkling of what the answer might be.

"For the simple reason I was ordered to by the base commander as he said there was secret company information on them. To make sure I told Dr Shutt he insisted that Ron and Reg accompany me to his lab".

"And falsifying the forensic report and disposing of the bodies?".

"All ordered by Eric".

Danks felt he was now getting somewhere with this case and his initial suspicions about the subcommander may have been misplaced.

Danks continued, "Why were the commander and his deputy unable to attend the funerals?".

The subcommander moved awkwardly in his seat. It was clear something was eating into him.

"Look, it's imperative that what I tell you doesn't get back to the commander or his deputy".

Danks leaned forward and the subcommander lowered his voice.

"I'm appalled at them for not attending".

"Oh, and why is that?".

"Well, I would have thought you'd know why".

"Really?".

"The commander and his deputy are the brothers

of Mary".

"What?". Danks almost shouted that out. He was stunned. He hadn't seen either of them at his brother's wedding otherwise he would've recognised them if they'd been there.

All of a sudden he realised why they looked familiar. It was their family resemblance to one another. Mary was a normal looking woman whereas Adrian and Eric looked more like caged rabid bulldogs in comparison.

Danks could only think what sort of despicable people wouldn't go to their own sister's wedding and funeral. He could only think they were complete arseholes. Thinking back now, he remembered that Mary's maiden name was Cross but he hadn't realised that there was a connection.

Danks's voice returned to normal volume as he sat back in his chair. "Do you know why the budget is so low for maintaining the equipment down in the mines?".

The subcommander leaned forward with clenched fists and thumped one down on his desk. "I've been trying to get them to increase the budget. One of the reasons I accepted the promotion was that I naively thought I could influence it. I even asked for a proper communication system to be installed down the mines for the workers but they refused".

Inspector Danks could see that the subcommander was quite emotional about the whole subject.

Danks stood to leave. "Okay subcommander. Thanks for your help. I'll be in touch if I need anything more".

The subcommander showed Danks to the door. Ron and Reg were standing outside.

Danks was wondering if they'd been listening to their conversation. "Have you two been over to my hotel today?" he asked.

"We've been here all day haven't we Reg?" grunted Ron.

"Yeah, what would we want to break into your room for?" added Reg and they both sniggered.

"These two are buffoons" thought Danks. They've just indirectly admitted it was them as he hadn't mentioned that his room had been broken into. However, he wouldn't do anything about it at the moment.

Danks headed off but could feel their eyes tracking him as he walked down the corridor.

As he entered the main hall, his watch rang and he answered it. "Hello inspector, it's Officer Turner. I've discovered something about the accounts. I think you should come over to the police HQ so I can show you".

"Okay Helen, I'll be there ASAP". Danks ended the call.

He looked up to see Ron and Reg were now standing next to the guard at the check in desk. They must have followed him down the corridor.

"Did they overhear that call too?" thought Danks.

He warily left the government building heading for the police station.

Chapter 15

"What have you got Helen?" asked Danks as he stepped into the police HQ shutting the door behind him.

Officer Turner looked up from her screen. "Well sir. I looked at the main accounts. There are several direct debits that transfer money to different departments. This all seems above board. However, not all the allocated money goes to each of the departments.

Take the maintenance budget. The direct debit transfers twelve million as we know. The remainder gets transferred to a company referred to as Titan Maintenance Corporation. If you look this company up they are supposed to pay out additional funds in the event of major equipment failure. But that is clearly way too late as it can take up to eight months to get any replacement parts if they're not in stock".

Danks jumped in, "But this company is clearly not paying out any additional funds as Colin doesn't see it".

"That's just it sir. This Titan Maintenance Corporation is listed on a local stock exchange here on Titan. I've looked up the owners of the company and they are none other than Adrian and Eric Cross".

Inspector Danks was beginning to see where this was leading. "If the company is receiving eighty eight million dollars a year and they're not paying anything out, where's that money going?".

"Precisely sir. It appears the company pays out large dividends to their share holders and guess who they are?".

"Hmmm, let me see, Adrian and Eric Cross?".

"Almost spot on sir. The lion's share goes to those two but about ten percent is going to Ron and Reg Edwards".

Danks now knew who Ron and Reg were reporting back to. It was either Adrian or Eric or both.

Suddenly the police HQ door burst open and Ron and Reg stormed in pointing guns at them.

Danks and Officer Turner stopped what they were doing and held up their hands.

The twins each had an aerosol cannister aimed at Danks and Turner.

Danks started to speak but was sprayed in his face. He started coughing and the room started spinning.

One of the twins was nearby. Danks threw a punch at him but missed. He stumbled forwards and fell to the floor. He tried to get up but he was feeling weak and nauseous. He could see that Officer Turner had slumped forward onto her desk. She was already out cold. He tried to resist the effects of the spray but it was no use and he passed out.

Chapter 16

"Oh, my head" said Danks in a croaky voice.
He felt a hand slap his face.
"Wake up" someone growled.
He opened his eyes to bright lights and focused on the person who'd slapped him. It was Eric.

Danks looked around and could see that he was inside a large glass dome that appeared to be on the surface of Titan. Outside was the orange haze of the atmosphere and he could see the methane clouds drifting across the sky above him. Rain was falling onto the dome and running down its surface to the ground outside. This wasn't precipitation as he knew it on Earth. It was methane rain.

Next to him was Officer Turner. She was strapped to a seat like him but she was still unconscious.

"I guess you've brought us here because you were getting nervous about us digging into your little scam". Danks was trying to goad Eric into telling him more if not everything.

"You think you're so smart don't you. Well out of the two of us, who's tied up?" snarled Eric.

About a couple of meters away from Danks, the floor slid back and Adrian Cross came up through the opening on a lift floor. It stopped when it was level with the main floor.

"Well inspector, what do you think of this

marvellous dome I had constructed? The floor is a meter thick white plastic that insulates us from the solid ice below. The dome is also a meter thick clear glass and plastic keeping us nice and cosy in here" Adrian gloated.

"I'm guessing you used the funds you were siphoning off the maintenance money to finance this little project". Danks knew that was what was happening but he wanted to hear it from the horse's mouth.

"Yes, and not just that. We're siphoning off from all departments. There's no way we could do something like this on the measly salary they pay us. It's nice to have a little luxury in one's life don't you think?".

While Adrian was talking Danks was trying to work out how he was going to get out of this sticky situation.

Danks heard Office Turner groan as she regained consciousness. He continued probing. "Ambrose and Mary discovered that the nodules you were harvesting for the rare elements contained living creatures. If that had got back to HQ on Earth the whole operation would've been shut down. That would then have put a spanner in your plans. The company would've sent a team out here and no doubt they'd have uncovered your little accounting scam".

The commander walked around Danks almost like a lion stalking its prey. "Yes, he made it very inconvenient for us. He sent Officer Smith over to demand that we stop mining. I suggested he, I and Eric both went down to see what all the fuss was about. It was quite tragic really. He slipped and fell into one of the mine shafts". Adrian smiled as though that was funny.

"Yes, he unfortunately lost his footing when I accidentally pushed him in the back" sniggered Eric. He obviously got some perverted kick out of murdering Officer Smith.

"I'm guessing that it was you who rerouted my drone when I was down the mine in an attempt to eliminate me". Danks's hunches were usually right.

"Yes, I was listening in on your conversation with that idiot White. Pity it didn't succeed as it would've solved all our problems. We could've said your drone had led you into an unsafe area" responded Eric.

"We deliberately limit the communication down in the mines so we can monitor what the workers are saying via the drones" declared Adrian.

Danks got the impression he was quite proud of that little scheme he'd put in place. "The subcommander said he wanted proper communications installing in the mines".

"Yes, but we didn't want it and he has to do whatever we command him to do otherwise we'd get rid of him" snarled Eric.

Danks knew what he meant when he said 'get rid of him'.

At that moment the two twins, Ron and Reg, came up on the lift carrying a couple of handguns. They obviously weren't that bright as Adrian looked angrily at them. "I've told you two before not to bring those pistols into this dome. If you fire them up here and it hits the dome it could damage it" growled Adrian.

The two goons seemed to cower when he rebuked them. They flicked on the safety catches just before they holstered the pistols.

"You brought Ambrose and Mary up here didn't you?". Danks had a feeling that they both died up here at the hands of these four.

As he asked the question he was trying to wriggle one of his hands out of the restraints.

"Very good inspector. Ambrose was about to tell the company HQ that he'd found a new life form in the ocean below. We couldn't have that. As you said, it would've affected our operations here. I sent Bill and Ben here to collect Ambrose and Mary". Adrian was of course referring to the twins.

The twins both looked behind them when Adrian pointed in their direction. Ron scratched his head and looked at his brother. "Who's Bill and Ben?" said Ron. Reg shrugged his shoulders in a 'Beats me' sort of way.

Adrian continued, "We then brought them up here. But they didn't seem to appreciate the views".

"Yeah, so I pushed them into that airlock and opened the outer door. It was such fun" laughed Eric.

Anger surged through Danks. His worst fears had been realised. His brother and sister-in-law had been exposed to the extreme cold and atmospheric pressure from the Titan surface. It was an horrific death.

"You complete and utter fucking bastard. I'll enjoy sending you to prison for the rest of your life. They were good people" spat Danks.

"Eric, restrain yourself" Adrian said sternly.

"Sorry brother. It's just that I feel we should get rid of these two quickly" replied Eric sheepishly.

"Presumably you returned my brother's and Mary's bodies to their flat shortly after you'd killed them".

"Yes. I got Ron here to crush the air supply to the flat to make it look like they died from asphyxiation. Then we called in Dr Shutt to do the forensic analysis. Of course he annoyingly worked out that they didn't die of asphyxiation so we had to gently persuade him to modify the report slightly" replied Adrian.

"Yeah, we said we'd relocate his family, if you know what I mean" sniggered Ron.

Danks knew exactly what these disgusting people meant. He also realised that Dr Shutt had deliberately said in the report that an oxygen valve had frozen knowing full well that there wasn't one. Was it his way of defying Adrian and Eric?

Adrian signalled to the two goons to untie Danks and Officer Turner.

Danks had just managed to wriggle a hand free as Ron bent down to untie his hands. Danks swung around and hit Ron with an uppercut to his chin. Ron staggered backwards. But Reg reacted quickly thumping Danks on the back of his head with the butt of his gun and he collapsed to the ground, stunned.

Reg secured the hand restraint on Danks again ensuring it was extra tight.

"Pick him up and take them to the airlock" commanded Adrian.

Ron and Reg grabbed Danks while Eric held

Officer Turner. They dragged them both over to the airlock and threw them in. Eric closed the door with a smirk on his face.

Danks was racking his brains as to what he could do to stop them opening the outer door. Otherwise, he and Helen would meet the same fate as his brother and sister-in-law.

It was very cold in this airlock. He needed to think of something quickly or they would die in here very soon.

"You do realise that if we mysteriously die due to asphyxiation or disappear like Officer Smith that the IPA will come swarming all over Tartarus". Danks was hoping this might stop them in their tracks. He also knew the IPA may not investigate it as he was supposed to be picking up his brother's and sister-in-law's ashes.

Danks could see Adrian mulling it over in his head.

"Wait" Adrian shouted to Eric as his hand moved towards the button to open the outer doors.

Adrian was rubbing his chin and looked at Eric. "Danks might have a point. If he and Turner both die the same way as his brother and sister-in-law that would look suspicious. If they were to disappear like Officer Smith that would also attract attention. Either way it would alert the IPA that something odd was happening out here".

Adrian paced up and down the floor trying to think of a solution. He suddenly stopped and looked at Eric. "On the other hand, if they were to die in a tunnel collapse while they were visiting the mines then we could pass that off as a mishap. We could add that they wandered into an unsafe area of the workings against our advice. It would look like we tried to protect them".

"Yeah, that sounds plausible and I could practise pushing them into one of the unstable tunnels" grinned Eric.

Adrian signalled for the inner door of the airlock to be opened. Danks and Officer Turner felt a blast of relief as they were released from the potential coffin. It was only a temporary stay of execution but at least he had more time to think of an escape.

Reg and Ron stepped forward. They each grabbed an arm of Danks and Turner respectively. Pulling them out of the airlock they frogmarched them to the lift floor. All six of them then descended down towards Tartarus.

Chapter 17

The lift came to a halt. Danks and Officer Turner were pushed out into a small room with an office desk and a few chairs placed in front of the desk.

Danks's head was throbbing from being hit. He could feel a trickle of blood running down the back of his neck.

"This is my private office. I have all my confidential discussions in here. It's where Officer Smith came just before we took him down to examine the mines" said Adrian with some amusement.

They walked through a side door and down a corridor towards a set of old fashioned scissor gate doors. Ron opened them. Danks and Officer Turner were unceremoniously pushed inside the cabin and the other four followed.

There were crampons hung on the lift walls. They each put a pair on. Ron and Reg kept their guns trained on Danks and Officer Turner while they donned theirs.

"We discovered this old lift and the corridor leading to it when we expanded my private office. It was hidden behind a partition wall. It must have been here from the very early days when they first started mining in this region. It's proved quite convenient recently" said Adrian.

They descended for ten minutes at a slow pace until it reached the bottom of the lift shaft. Ron and Reg prodded Danks and Turner in the back with their guns to move them out of the lift.

Ahead was a dimly lit tunnel that had a slight downwards incline. They descended down it.

They arrived at a T junction where they were instructed by Adrian to turn right. He wanted them to go to an area he knew was unsafe.

They pushed on into the warren of tunnels. They came to a domed chamber that had a shaft in the middle of its floor that descended down into the depths of Titan. Danks estimated the chamber width at about seven meters and the path running around the shaft at two meters. Safe enough for one person to walk around.

There was a tunnel branching away from the chamber ahead. Ron pushed Danks down it.

They walked for a short distance down the tunnel until Adrian ordered them to stop. "This is a suitable point" he said.

Strewn around the floor were shards of ice that had fallen from the roof. It was clear that this section was where he thought they could bury Danks and Officer Turner.

"Take their hand restraints off. They can't have them on when they're found" Eric added with a sound of excitement in his voice.

Ron stepped forward and took Officer Turner's handcuffs off first. He then shoved Danks face first against the wall. It stung where he hit the wall. He felt his hand restraints come off and Ron turned him around.

Danks reacted quickly. He brought his knee up

between Ron's legs with force. Danks could see the look of pain spread across Ron's face. He bent over in agony.

Danks shouted to Officer Turner to run.

They both started dashing down the tunnel away from Ron and Reg. They could hear shouting behind them. It was getting difficult to see in the tunnels as some of the overhead lighting had failed. Danks and Officer Turner both used their watches to light their way ahead.

Danks heard a shot ring out and he felt pain in his left arm. He was hit. They came to a intersection of three other tunnels. One tunnel went to the left, one straight on and the other to the right. Danks took the left one and Officer Turner the right.

As he ran, Danks recognised the tunnel he was in. It had those odd gargoyle carvings in the walls. He realised he was near the shaft that he'd nearly fallen into. He stopped running. "I need to move carefully here" he thought to himself.

Danks came out into the domed chamber that had the shaft in the centre where he'd nearly lost his life. There were no lights in this chamber. It was completely dark. Using his watch to illuminate his way, he moved away from the tunnel opening along the path that went around the central shaft.

Danks could hear someone running up the tunnel. He pressed himself against the wall hoping they wouldn't see him in the darkness. He moved sideways towards an opening that was another tunnel branching off from the chamber. He stopped and turned the light off on his watch.

The running was getting louder and Danks saw someone run out of the tunnel into the chamber. It was too late when Ron realised what was ahead. He tried to stop but his forward momentum carried him out into the blackness of the shaft. He tried to grab at something as he hit the wall of the shaft on the far side. Danks heard him shout "What the fuck" and started screaming when he realised what was happening. It went on for some way down getting fainter and fainter until he must have hit his head on the shaft wall. There was silence after that.

Danks edged his way around the path to the tunnel he'd seen just before Ron appeared.

In the light of his watch he could see that he was dripping blood. He tore the bloody sleeve off his shirt and he tied it around his wound the best he could with one hand.

There were no lights down this tunnel as the electricity to this area had been cut off a long time ago.

Danks could hear voices echoing around the chamber. Then from his dark vantage point Danks saw Reg appear first carrying a torch followed by Eric and Adrian. Adrian had a firm grip of Officer Turner's arm. She was handcuffed again.

They shone their torches around the chamber.

Danks heard Reg shouting for Ron. There was no reply.

Adrian shone his torch on the path and noticed drops of blood leading to a tunnel a little further around from where they were. They started moving around it towards the tunnel Danks was hiding in. He was thinking that he'd be really lucky to get out of this alive.

"Come out, come out, wherever you are inspector. There's no escape. We have your little helper here. You'd better come out or I'll push her into the shaft" snarled Eric.

"And what have you done with Ron?" shouted Reg angrily.

Danks thought that if Adrian was to complete his plan they couldn't push Turner into the shaft. They had to make it look like they'd been killed by a cave-in.

Danks moved further back into the darkness. He had only one chance. If he caught them unawares by attacking them as they turned into this tunnel he could possibly take one of them out of the equation.

He edged forward as the light from their torches became stronger in the tunnel. It would have to be an all or nothing attack. If he missed he'd end up plummeting to his death down the shaft.

Reg appeared first. This was Danks's opportunity. He leaped forward out of the darkness illuminated only at the last second by Reg's torch light. It was a flying kick and he made contact with him in the middle of his chest. Reg fired a shot as he flew backwards. He made a grab for anything to help him. Catching hold of an arm, he thought it would stop his backward motion, but it didn't. The arm belonged to Eric and all that happened was he started dragging him backwards towards the shaft edge with him.

"Let me go you idiot" Eric shouted at him. He turned to kick Reg with his boot but this was his undoing. His footing slipped and they both tumbled over the edge into the abyss screaming as they fell.

"Eric!" Adrian shrieked as he saw him disappear down into the blackness.

There was a rage in Adrian now. He dragged Officer Turner to the edge of the shaft.

"If you don't come out now I'll push her over the edge and damn the consequences".

Danks came out with his hands held aloft.

"How are you going to explain how your brother and the two goons have gone missing?". Danks's mind was racing. He was trying to think how he and Turner could escape. It wasn't looking good at the moment.

"I'll turn them into heroes by saying they went looking for you. In their attempts to rescue you both they fell down this shaft.

You see inspector, you are under the illusion that I cared about my brother. What I care about is money and you are getting in the way of that. In fact you've inadvertently done me a favour. You've single handedly increased my share by disposing of those three". Adrian seemed to visibly perk up at the thought.

Danks moved slowly towards Adrian and Helen. "But if we were to disappear it would create some doubts about you and what's happening here on Titan". Danks was trying to stall while he tried to think of a plan.

"I think you need to move down that tunnel" said Adrian. He gestured with his gun towards the tunnel they'd come through. It was particularly unstable and he was forcing Danks down it.

Adrian was gripping hold of Officer Turner as

Danks moved towards the tunnel.

"You could give yourself up. I'm sure the courts would be lenient with you if you voluntarily surrender yourself". Danks didn't think the courts would, but sowing that seed of doubt could swing it in their favour.

There was a moment when Danks thought Adrian was mulling it over but he suddenly snapped out of it. "Nice try inspector, but the good cop tactic doesn't work on me". Adrian took the handcuffs off Officer Turner and shoved her towards Danks.

"Now move down that tunnel" he said in a threatening voice, waving his gun in the direction that he wanted them to move.

Danks was hoping that an opportunity would present itself. He and Officer Turner moved towards the tunnel with their hands in the air.

Adrian was standing by the tunnel entrance as they turned into it. At that moment a piece of ice fell from the chamber ceiling with a crash.

Adrian was momentarily distracted as he glanced in that direction. Danks brought his right hand down in a chopping action onto Adrian's arm holding the gun. It flew from his grasp to the ground. Officer Turner dashed down the tunnel and Danks turned to follow.

Danks's coat was grabbed from behind by a big fist and he was pulled backwards. Before he knew it he was pinned against the cold hard wall of ice.

A big hand encircled his neck and he was lifted up the wall. Adrian's eyes seemed to be on fire. "I think it's time for you to die" Adrian growled menacingly.

Danks was being throttled. The huge hand was cutting off his windpipe. He had to do something, anything. He did a wild kick which made full contact with Adrian's knee. It must have pushed his leg backwards as he heard a load crack.

Adrian howled in pain and dropped Danks to the floor.

Danks turned towards the tunnel and dived down it following Officer Turner. They were in darkness. He could hear Adrian swearing fiercely.

Moments later Adrian came to the tunnel entrance pointing a torch and firing his gun wildly at any shadowy movements. Load echoes bounced around the domed chamber and cracking noises could be heard from all around.

Adrian concentrated his torch down the tunnel. The beam fell onto Danks. He had nowhere to hide. Adrian pointed his gun at him and began to squeeze the trigger.

At that moment a section of the tunnel ceiling collapsed in front of Adrian. The debris had such a force that it knocked the gun from his hand and he stumbled backwards. He managed to stop himself but his feet were now teetering on the edge of the shaft.

Danks moved quickly and climbed over the collapsed shards of ice towards Adrian. He was still flailing with his arms in an attempt to stabilise his position. But then the edge of the shaft that his feet were on gave way. He dropped down with his chest crashing hard on the ice of the footpath and with his legs dangling into the abyss.

Danks advanced cautiously as he wasn't sure how stable the rest of the path was. He stretched out an arm towards Adrian.

"Grab my arm" said Danks.

Adrian's large hand seized hold of Danks's hand.

"I'll see you in hell first Danks you bastard" he said as he started pulling him towards the edge.

Danks was slipping towards the shaft. He couldn't hold on much longer. The ice was breaking around the teeth of the crampons on his boots.

Officer Turner stepped up next to Danks and stamped hard on Adrian's arm. The teeth of her crampon drove through the sleeve and dug deep into the flesh beneath. A scream of agony came from Adrian and he released his grip.

Danks scrambled backwards pulling Officer Turner with him.

They watched as Adrian's face showed fear for the first time as he slipped slowly backwards. Danks saw him scrabbling with his arms to catch hold of anything but it was no use. In the end he seemed to resign himself to his fate and stopped fighting.

Danks watched as Adrian slipped over the edge. He was quickly engulfed by the blackness. It was utter terror. There was no sound from him as he fell into the abyss.

Officer Turner looked away as she couldn't watch.

"I didn't want to do that, but I couldn't see any other way of saving you" she whispered in tears.

"He gave you no choice. We gave him every chance but he turned them down. We did our best to save him" said Danks.

Danks and Turner were safe at last, but now they were lost. He'd managed to escape from this tunnel system before but he was lucky that time.

They both followed his blood trail away from the shaft back to the intersection. Now they had a choice of tunnels to go down. But which is the correct one?

"Hello" came a voice that echoed around them. Danks thought it had come from the tunnel on his left. He turned just as a drone appeared with Colin following close behind.

"Are we glad to see you!" said Officer Turner.

Colin was surprised to see them. "I heard voices and what sounded like gun shots so I thought I'd better come and find out what was happening. This area is very unstable and noises like that could trigger a collapse".

"Yes we found that out" replied Danks.

"Is there anyone else down here? I'm sure I heard other voices". Colin looked questioningly at them.

"No, there's only us two now" responded Danks.

The drone then led them back through the maze of tunnels, eventually arriving at the lifts.

The man in the green all in one jumpsuit was surprised to see them. They hadn't checked in with him to pick up a drone.

"You can't wander around in these tunnels without one you know!" he said sternly.

They told him they'd come down via a different route. But all would be revealed after they'd filed their reports. They left him with his line of charging drones.

A lift was waiting and all three of them stepped into it. At last they were heading back to Tartarus.

Chapter 18

As the lift headed up towards Tartarus Colin asked Danks and Turner, "How did you guys end up down there?".

"It's a long story, but there'll be some changes coming along quite soon" Danks informed him.

"How come?".

"Let's just say you'll be doing some interesting work quite soon".

"I don't think Commander Adrian and Eric will listen to anything you say. They were very clear that they don't like me as I keep complaining about the problems we are having down the mines".

"The management will be changing as they are no longer in charge" said Danks.

"Oh, are they leaving?" asked Colin.

"No. Unfortunately they fell into that abandoned mine shaft near where you found us" replied Danks.

"Oh no, that's dreadful". Colin was so shocked at the news he nearly went the colour of his surname.

"We found out that they were fiddling the books. So they tried to eliminate us by inducing a cave-in making it look like an accident. That's why you found us in that tunnel. Also, your maintenance budget was a fraction of what it should have been because they were siphoning off large quantities of it".

The lift stopped at Tartarus and all three passengers stepped out of the lift.

"At some point you'll have to set up a recovery operation at that abandoned shaft. I suspect there'll be at least four maybe five bodies to recover if there's anything left of them. Then you should seal it off so no one can ever go in there again" said Danks.

"I'll put a team together straight away to start the recovery". Colin shook both their hands and headed off to organise the operation.

After he'd left Danks turned to Officer Turner. "I'm going to see the subcommander to inform him of the situation. I think you should come along, but first I think I should see a doctor".

They left the lift building and walked over to the main gate. The security guard looked confused as he'd not let these two through that day.

"Where have you two come from and what happened to your arm?" came the response from the guard.

"We were here on police business and Inspector Danks received this injury in the line of duty stopping a criminal gang" replied Officer Turner.

"Criminals but how..where..when?" the guard was finding it difficult to comprehend. In all the time he'd worked there, it had been quite mundane and he'd not detected any unlawful activity.

"Look, I need to get the inspector to a doctor right now. He needs treatment for his wound". Officer Turner had become convincingly serious so the guard let them through with no further hesitation.

"You know you are wasted here on Titan Helen" whispered Danks as she hailed a taxi. He was in excruciating pain now that the adrenaline had subsided and he was beginning to feel faint from the blood loss.

"Thank you sir, I'm learning a lot from one of the best". She smiled as she pushed Danks into the taxi and climbed in after him.

The taxi sped off in the direction of the Accident and Emergency at the Tartarus hospital.

Chapter 19

Four days later, Danks was given the okay by the doctors and was discharged from the hospital. His arm had healed nicely and it was safe to enter stasis. That was a relief as the flight to Earth was due to leave in just over a week's time.

He'd returned to the hotel and he'd managed to pack his holdall. It was lying on his bed.

His wrist watch rang and he flicked the call to the TV. The new temporary base commander's face popped up.

"Hello Paul, how are you coping with your new job?" asked Danks. He took a sip of his drink that he was holding with his good arm.

"It's going slowly. We are gradually unravelling the complex web that the ex-commander and his deputy had set up to filter off large amounts of funds.

It seems much of it was being sent back to Earth into multiple accounts, some of which were owned by a mafia like syndicate. The authorities back on Earth acted quickly to freeze the money in them. The Titan Mineral Corporation are extremely happy you were able to break the hold of that gang. Also, Colin and his team are making headway in sealing off all the old unused shafts. There'll be no more people wandering into any of Titan's deadly tunnels".

Commander Paul talked to someone off screen for a second before continuing. He looked back at he screen and asked Danks, "How did you know I wasn't involved with that gang inspector?".

"At first you were my prime suspect. But when you said Adrian and Eric were Mary's siblings that made me realise those two were not quite what they seemed.

I knew Mary very well and she wouldn't hurt a fly. When you informed me that they'd fallen out with her, that just didn't add up. It could only mean that there was something odd about them. So the spotlight switched to them". Danks could see he'd stirred Paul's interest. "Besides, I checked out your statement that they were siblings and it was true. I was one of the guests at my brother's wedding and neither Adrian nor Eric was there. I would have recognised them otherwise.

What sort of individuals would murder their own sister. They couldn't even be arsed to pay their respects at her funeral". Danks's blood was boiling. He calmed himself down knowing that some sort of justice had been served on the two detestable siblings.

"Well I'm thankful you eliminated me from the list of suspects. I was constantly being threatened by Ron and Reg who reported back to Adrian and Eric" said Paul with some relief.

"I did get the feeling you didn't like them. I looked into their criminal records and they were involved with lots of illegal activity when they were back on Earth. It was only on Adrian's recommendation that they joined the corporation here on Titan. It appears he'd known them before.

So that reinforced the idea that you weren't involved".

Danks took a sip of his drink then continued, "Besides, I also checked your criminal record and you were clean". He smiled as he said it.

"You might be interested to hear that Colin and his team have set up a retrieval system in that old shaft and they've sent a remote camera down it.

It appears that the shaft was abandoned decades ago because the sides were unstable. They gave up drilling after only two kilometres. From the camera images they were able to identify Officer Smith's body. It seems his hands were handcuffed behind his back. What a horrific death.

There is a plan to erect a statue in his memory and the company is paying for it.

They are also offering financial assistance to his family".

"That's good to know" replied Danks.

"The dome has been opened to the public and the Tartarus school has started using it to teach the pupils about the Titan weather.

I'm not sure you're aware inspector, but there's a proposal to name the new life forms after Ambrose and Mary".

A tear welled up in the inspector's eye. He wiped it away with the back of his hand. He was sad that they weren't here to appreciate it for themselves. "They would have been honoured".

"Colin has come up with a few ideas on ways to extract the rare elements without harming the new life forms. But he's going to conduct some trials first".

"Sounds like the mining on Titan is in good

hands". Danks was pleased that improvements were being made.

"Do you think you'll ever return to Titan?" asked Paul.

Danks thought for a few seconds. "I don't think so, unless you are desperate for me to solve another mystery here.

My wife back on Earth thinks that these trips take a lot of time out of our relationship". He was keen to get back home as he would've been away for nearly a year and a half by the time he returned.

"Thank you for your help inspector. Have a safe trip and goodbye".

"Goodbye and good luck Paul". Danks signed off and the screen went blank.

Chapter 20

The buzzer for his door alerted Danks that there was someone outside his room. He went over and pressed the open button. It slid back and Officer Turner was standing in the corridor.

"Hello sir. I understand you need someone to carry your bag to the shuttle port". Officer Turner grinned as she strode in. She slung Danks's holdall over her shoulder.

Danks appreciated the help as his arm was still a bit sore and he could do with the company.

They left the hotel and headed across the square to the escalator that took them back to the shuttle port.

As they stepped onto the escalator Danks turned to Officer Turner, "So Helen, what are you going to do now that things have returned to being mundane here at Tartarus?".

"This was a temporary assignment and it's way too quiet for me. I like the excitement of pursuing the quarry". She obviously wasn't planning on staying on Titan and Danks liked her attitude.

"Well, I have a position available back on Earth. You would fit the bill perfectly but it'll mean a promotion to sergeant. Would you be interested?".

"Would I be interested! Of course I would sir". She was thrilled at the opportunity to work with him.

"So that's decided then. I'll look forward to seeing you back on Earth in about sixteen months time".

"Well actually sir, I'm booked on the same return flight to Earth as you. My posting here is finishing and my replacement arrives on the next shuttle. The new base commander was happy with me leaving early. Apparently the guard on the mining compound gate is going to cover as a community police officer until the replacement arrives".

They both laughed at the thought.

"The new base commander seems to have got everything under control. It'll be good having you there in the spaceport hotel as I could do with the company".

It was customary for passengers to spend a week in the spaceport hotel before their flight. It helped them get used to Earth-like gravity before their journey back.

Chapter 21

A week later Danks and Officer Turner gathered their belongings together and headed to the spaceport hotel reception.

They checked out of the hotel and floated off in the direction of the shuttle baggage check-in.

Once there, they scanned their ID chips which doubled as their boarding passes. A drone scuttled up and collected their luggage and whisked it off to be packed neatly in the hold.

Danks and Officer Turner floated into the shuttle and drifted down the corridor until they found their respective stasis pods. They swung their legs around and entered feet first.

Just as they were about to disappear inside their respective pods Danks stopped. "Well Helen, or should I say sergeant, see you at the spaceport back at Earth".

"Yes sir" she said proudly.

They both disappeared into their pods and the doors shut behind them and the suspended animation sequence began.

Helen felt a tingle of excitement at the thought of being a sergeant. She couldn't wait to be back to Earth.

Danks made himself comfortable. He wanted to get back to Earth too. He and Officer Turner had been very lucky to have survived their ordeal here on Titan.

Just as the suspended animation started he thought he'd have to make it up to his wife as they'd been apart for too long. Maybe treat her to some romantic evenings out.

The End

Tainted Mars
Inspector Danks mysteries
Book 2

Chapter 22

Inspector Danks never liked travelling on interplanetary ships as he wasn't sure if he was going to be sick when he awakened from stasis. It had taken six weeks to travel from Earth to Mars but to him it felt like only seconds.

Danks was an athletic man with wide shoulders so he always found the stasis tubes a tight fit. He was in his mid fifties and worked hard to keep his body trim. With his line of work he needed to keep himself in tip-top condition.

When he awoke it was a struggle to prise himself out of the tube before his claustrophobia and nausea started to well up inside him.

On his last trip to Titan he was sick before he managed to wriggle out of the tube. It resulted in rather a mess but fortunately the space stewardesses were accustomed to dealing with such situations.

The ship had arrived on time at Mars and was anchored to the space docking port some seven hundred kilometres above Mars's surface. He only had five minutes to rub his limbs to get the circulation going before he disembarked.

As he floated down the corridor, other passengers were beginning to exit their stasis tubes so he pushed on quickly to avoid the crush.

It wasn't long before he arrived at the only exit door on the ship. There were already several other passengers waiting at the door along with a steward and stewardess who were both smartly dressed.

After waiting several minutes listening to muffled banging and scuffing noises there was a loud hiss from the exit door. A cloud of condensing moisture swirled from around the edges as it opened. The pressure equalised between the ship and the space docking port interiors.

The people closest to the exit were briefly engulfed with a thin fog as the door rolled back revealing a long corridor stretching out in front of them.

A couple of space engineers, who had coordinated the docking procedure, drifted over into an adjacent cabin to avoid the exodus of the passengers.

To reduce the chances of a crush the space crew woke the passengers in a fixed order with the occupants of pods nearest the exit being awakened first.

Danks started to involuntarily drift down the corridor as a soft breeze pushed him and the other passengers along. He could see at the end of the corridor a large rectangular opening that was the entrance to the space-lift. The passengers entered the lift and were guided to their seats by attendants. Once all the passengers were securely fastened in, the doors were closed and the descent down to the surface would begin. The journey down would normally take a couple of hours to the main arrivals terminal. However, a storm was brewing on the surface and there would be delays to their departures.

As Danks drifted towards the space-lift he recalled that he was here at Mars on a special mission requested by the Central Mars Police Council or CMPC. At that moment his right arm was grabbed by a tall spindly figure.

Danks span around in the zero-g until he was facing the man. He grabbed a handy rail to stop himself from spinning any further.

The man, who'd caught his arm, was secured to the side of the corridor by long silvery tendrils that were coming out of the wall. They were attached to the back of his suit anchoring him in place. He was wearing a snugly fitting deep red suit. On his left sleeve was a badge showing the two moons Phobos and Deimos with the planet Mars in the background. It was the typical Mars Police uniform.

Danks estimated he was over two meters in

height. His skin was very pale and almost paper-like in appearance. He was a typical specimen of a healthy male Martian and someone who had spent their whole life on the planet.

It was over one hundred years since humans had first settled on Mars. Since then there had been at least a couple of generations that had spent their entire lives on Mars.

With the reduced gravity, native Martians grew much taller than adults from Earth. They had never developed a natural suntan because they lived predominantly underground and when outside wore pressure suits.

With the lack of sunlight they had to supplement their diets with vitamin D tablets. But an advantage of that was that skin melanomas were almost completely unheard of on Mars.

Danks reflected that even today, the majority of people on this space journey were emigrating from the over crowded Earth.

Politicians were too weak and were too late in declaring a limit on the number of offspring people could have. The starvation of the world's population in the years 2185 through to 2194 was a consequence of crop failures resulting from over stressing the land. Wars had broken out as aggressive countries tried to grab productive land and the food stores of those they had invaded. Global warming had triggered widespread fires and floods. Man's inability to recognise when nature was close to its breaking point was all too evident and man's inhumanity to man reached new heights.

By the year 2200 the world population had fallen back to thirty billion but it was still overcrowded. Earth relied heavily on the crops imported from orbiting space-farms and from the Moon colony's surplus crops.

The tall man pulled Danks to one side, out of the stream of passengers floating down the corridor towards the lift. The man had to shout to make himself heard above the chatter from the other travellers.

"Inspector Danks, my name is Sergeant Francis, I was sent by the CMPC to escort you down to the surface. We won't be using the space-lift. There is a police space patrol shuttle waiting for you down here sir". Sergeant Francis pointed to an almost invisible door in the main corridor wall nearby.

Danks noticed that Sergeant Francis had a large scar on his temple, dark hair, blue eyes and he reminded him of the matchstick men in the paintings of the twentieth century artist L.S.Lowry.

"I'll have to arrange for my luggage to be forwarded" responded Danks.

Sergeant Francis reassured him, "You needn't worry sir, there's an officer picking your luggage up for you down at the main terminal. They'll ensure that it'll be in your hotel room when you arrive at your accommodation. If you would follow me we can make a start on the trip down".

It was customary for the luggage of the passengers to travel separately via pods. These pods had been packed securely back on Earth. They were then transported up to the space docking port that was permanently in orbit. Once there, they were loaded into the side of the spaceship ready for the onward journey.

On arrival at the destination, the pods simply disengaged from the spaceship and were flown down to the main spaceport on the surface by autopilot where the luggage would be unloaded.

The passengers, on the other hand, travelled by space-lift. This was a much less bumpy route back to the surface and was, in most people's opinion, a much more civilised way to travel. Even though the journey took longer to descend to the surface than a shuttle, most people didn't mind.

Danks noticed that Sergeant Francis looked as though he was concentrating on something. A moment later the silvery tendrils withdrew from his suit and disappeared back into the wall.

Danks had witnessed for the first time a fully Integrated Headset Unit, known as an IHU. The headsets are implanted inside a person's visual cortex when they are between three and four years old. This allows it time to be incorporated into the brain of the child as they grow. This time is needed as the implant is partially biological and the body grows connections into the IHU.

Once fully established, the IHU directly projects images into the user's mind and is completely under their control. Wi-Fi links from the IHU connect each user to the Martian Global Internet, locally referred to as the m-net.

The sergeant had connected his IHU to the corridor's computer system and requested the tendrils securing him to the wall to be withdrawn. At regular intervals there were patches on the wall that incorporated these tendril units. The staff could then use them to anchor themselves securely before offering assistance to customers.

Danks didn't have anything like this as the technology had been banned back on Earth some fifty years before. In the early days, there had been too many fatalities. The scientist involved had moved to Mars where the technology was permitted to continue under strict control.

Danks thought that Sergeant Francis would come in handy when retrieving police criminal records as it would be considerably quicker than his wrist smart watch.

The door that Sergeant Francis had pointed to slid back quietly and a faint draught seemed to pull them towards the new corridor. Shortly after entering it, the door slid back with a faint hiss as it resealed behind them.

As they drifted down the corridor, there were viewing windows at regular intervals that gave Danks stunning vistas of the red planet below and the space docking port with the space-lifts anchored to it.

In the weightless conditions, Danks turned his head towards the sergeant and asked, "The commissioner at my headquarters ordered me out here to Mars at short notice. I didn't have much time to get any details from him as I had to hastily pack to catch the next available flight out here. Can you tell me why there was such an urgency?".

"I'm afraid I can't sir as I don't have high enough security clearance". Danks could sense a tone of annoyance in the sergeant's voice.

By now they were passing through the space patrol shuttle entrance. The shuttle had three rows of two seats with a narrow corridor between them running the length of the shuttle.

They both grabbed a front seat as they floated towards them. Gracefully swinging around, they manoeuvred themselves into their respective seats.

Automatic straps quickly wrapped around them securing them in position for the flight down to the surface.

Once they were secured, the shuttle door slid silently shut and, a few seconds later, there was a jolt as the shuttle disengaged from its moorings to the spaceport.

In front of Danks was a wide window that gave him panoramic views ahead. To his left there was a small side window and he looked out of it. He watched with fascination as the space docking port gradually drifted off into the distance.

The Artificial Intelligence pilot announced that they were beginning their descent. A few moments later there was a short burst of noise that thrust Danks into the back of his seat. The AI pilot had applied the thrusters for a brief period to start their journey down to the planet's surface.

Chapter 23

Danks was glad he was securely held in his seat as he could feel brief bursts of acceleration. The fine adjustments were being performed by the AI pilot to align the shuttle's trajectory with the best re-entry path.

"We should be back at the CMPC headquarters in under an hour sir" said the sergeant. "We may experience more turbulence than usual when we enter the atmosphere due to the storm front that's approaching but we'll be under cover by the time the main part of the storm arrives. It's not expected to last very long, maybe a day or two".

After half an hour Danks could see flashes of red light flickering past the windows as the shuttle started to enter the upper atmosphere. Sharp jolts shook the shuttle as it sped down through the thickening air. It was a strange experience to be weightless one second then thrust hard into the seat the next as the shuttle negotiated its way down.

"I much prefer the space-lift.." exclaimed Danks, "..it may be a longer trip but it's never as rough a ride as these re-entry shuttles".

Gradually the bumpiness subsided and the plasma streams died away as the shuttle slowed. At one point, as it banked on its approach to the landing site, Danks could make out the distant lights of the region's capital city, New Cambridge.

It wasn't long before the runway was visible ahead with pulsating lights that ran along its length. Danks looked out of his side window and he could see three small box shaped vehicles speeding down the runway. They were racing to catch up with the shuttle. Soon they were matching its speed and position. They disappeared under it and a few seconds later he heard some clunks followed almost instantly by a rapid deceleration.

Sergeant Francis leaned over and said, "The ground drones are the landing gear. They magnetically clamp to the underside of the shuttle and quickly decelerate it".

Once their speed had dropped right down, the shuttle was then guided by the ground drones to the CMPC hangar. It was highlighted by the pulsating lights that surrounded the entrance.

As the shuttle entered the hangar, the first set of doors closed behind them. The interior of the entrance chamber was quickly pressurised to what was nearly the same as on Earth. The inner doors of the chamber opened and the space shuttle taxied into the hangar. It swung around into a free docking bay and came to a halt.

The shuttle door opened with a slight hiss and a set of stairs was positioned in front of the open door so the passengers could now disembark.

Danks was acutely aware that here on Mars the gravity was less than half that on Earth. He had to be careful not to get out of his seat too quickly or walk as briskly as he usually did otherwise he'd end up launching himself into the air. That would give the Martians something to laugh about with his uncontrolled antics. A subtle and more sedate walking style was required. Danks carefully descended the steps to a waiting police officer.

Everyone on Mars wore heavy boots to make it easier to walk normally. Danks hadn't yet got his boots.

"Welcome to Mars sir, I'm Officer Robertson I will be escorting you to the CMPC headquarters. However, I just need to confirm your identity".

Officer Robertson moved forward in that strange Martian gait and raised a scanner to Danks's arm and read the information chip that was embedded under his skin.

Everyone had identification chips. These ID chips carry details on the individual, everything from full DNA mapping to complete 3D body images which are updated every year from birth to death.

There was no need for passports when an individual had their ID chip. It also recorded blood pressure, heart rate, oxygen levels and many more useful details.

The officer quickly checked the details against the information in the police central computer.

"Everything checks out sir, if you could put these boots on and then follow me".

Danks slipped his feet into the weighted boots. They were a perfect fit as they already knew his shoe size.

Once Danks was ready, Officer Robertson turned and proceeded towards a silver door positioned in the corner of the hangar. Danks could hear the buffeting of the building due to the storm as they headed for the door.

Officer Robertson continued, "You arrived here just in time sir as it sounds like the storm is getting worse. The good news is that it's not expected to last long and the space-lift will be operational again once it's passed".

The officer placed his hand on a metallic panel with a pulsating blue light next to the door. The blue light stopped flashing and it formed a thin solid line that quickly travelled down his hand. When it reached the bottom of his palm, the doors slid apart and a lift was revealed.

The three of them entered and Officer Robertson said in a clear voice, "One hundredth floor". The doors closed then a firm and authoritative voice echoed inside the lift, "For safety reasons passengers must ensure all loose items are secure and then place their feet on the outlines marked on the floor".

Danks had to quickly shove some loose items into his jacket pockets and zip them up. Then, as each of them positioned their feet on the markers, clamps wrapped around their ankles.

Once they were all secure the lift began its descent slowly at first but it then rapidly accelerated. As the lift descended, Danks had a feeling of complete weightlessness at first and then a feeling that he was hanging upside down. At this moment he noticed that the hair of his two companions was standing on end. He looked around and caught a glimpse of a reflection of himself in a shiny metal panel on the lift wall. He was grateful for having short hair!

Just as Danks was finding hanging upside down uncomfortable the lift started its rapid deceleration and he felt more like being back on Earth. To him it was pleasant, but it was obvious that his two companions were finding this part of the trip very uncomfortable.

Eventually the lift came to a halt and the ankle clamps were retracted. The doors slid open with what, Danks thought, sounded like a sigh or maybe it was his two colleagues sighing.

The three of them exited the lift and walked down a brightly lit corridor towards what Danks believed was a dead end. However, as they approached the end a line appeared in the wall and from nowhere a pair of doors slid back.

They entered a large room with white walls, grey floor and a blue ceiling. Opposite was an individual who was sitting at a long white table with a large screen behind him. Officer Robertson and Sergeant Frances separated and sat at opposite ends of the table.

The person who was sitting in the middle of the table gestured Danks to sit on the lone chair in front of him.

"Inspector, I'm glad you could make the journey to Mars at such short notice. We are sorry you've had to postpone your vacation. However, the circumstances meant that we needed you here as soon as possible. We have a problem on our hands and we believe that you are the only person with the abilities to bring this to a quick resolution. I can't emphasise enough how it's imperative that this is kept top secret. If the general public were to find out it could cause pandemonium" said the man.

Danks was no more than three feet from him. He noted that he had shortish black hair that was combed to the man's right hand side and he was slightly balding. There were beads of sweat on his forehead as he spoke. It was clear that he was worried by what had happened and was finding it difficult to articulate on the subject.

"I'm Commissioner Gilbert and I'll update you with the information we have so far". At that point the screen behind him jumped into life and pictures of seven people appeared spaced across the screen.

"I'm giving Sergeant Francis and Officer Robertson clearance on this as they will assist you in your investigations. These images show five people who have died in suspicious circumstances and two who have simply vanished. Three of the five were top people in the Martian corporation Cerebralnet".

The commissioner moved his hand over a screen set in the table and one of the images was highlighted.

"The first death was a Charles Lowe. He was the head of Research and Development at Cerebralnet. He was involved in a hover bike accident. He drove head long into a wall and yet he was one of the most experienced hover bikers on Mars".

The commissioner moved his hand again and the next person was highlighted.

"The second death was a Matt Hitchen who was the senior sales executive at Cerebralnet. He was involved in an accident where his vintage electric vehicle veered off the road and plunged into the Coprates Chasma canyon. There wasn't much left of him or the vehicle when the rescue teams arrived at the crash site.

The vehicle had recently been restored with the latest AI assistance, electric-inductive motors and braking systems. The recording unit was retrieved but we were unable to find any functional problems that could have caused the accident as the unit was severely damaged.

We interviewed all the engineers involved in the updates and they are some of the best in their field. They have done countless conversions. All of them thought the vehicle was working perfectly when it left the warehouse. They couldn't imagine what could have gone wrong".

Commissioner Gilbert paused to study his notes on the screen embedded in the table in front of him and then highlighted the next person.

"The third death was a Harry Ramsdale. He was the CEO of Cerebralnet. He was an accomplished pilot and was flying to the south pole where he has a residence. Apparently there was no distress message received before he crashed into the ice fields. We have a team on site at the moment. They haven't yet recovered the aircraft as it has fallen to the bottom of an ice fissure".

The commissioner highlighted two images next.

"The next two individuals were .." at this point the commissioner had to refer to his notes.

".. a Ms Anderton and a Mr Burgess. They were travelling in the same direction on the highway when their vehicles collided. This at first may not seem unusual, but such an event hasn't happened here on Mars for the last twenty years. Our safety records are second to none. We can't determine their connection to the other people. Mr Burgess was an AI software engineer and Ms Anderton was a reporter at the local internet news station".

The commissioner leaned forward and lifted a vessel of water. It looked like a child's beaker as it had a lid. These types of vessels were commonly used on Mars as it prevented the liquid inside from spilling in the low gravity. He took a sip of water from a valve that was on the top of the beaker.

The final two people's images were highlighted.

"These two people were Officers Jameson and Adamson. They worked here at the CMPC and I'd instructed them to find out what'd caused Charles Lowe's accident. However, only a week into the investigation their IHU's were detected entering a cave system near Olympus Mons.

Unfortunately, the loss of IHU communication in the caves is expected as no signals can penetrate that far into them. However, the two officers never came out and they haven't been seen since.

Their patrol vehicle was where they'd left it outside the cave system but they were nowhere to be found.

As a result of that I felt this case needed a specialist and that's why I called you in inspector.

Something bad must have happened to the two officers". The commissioner looked as though he felt responsible for their disappearance.

"Did anyone go into the caves looking for the missing officers?" asked Danks.

"That's what's so strange. Some officers went in with short range handheld IHU detectors but there was no sign of them" replied the commissioner.

Danks observed the recordings being played of each of the accident sites. He noticed something that wasn't quite right at the accident site of Matt Hitchen's road vehicle. "I would have expected to see skid marks from the tyres when Mr Hitchen realised something was going wrong. Had he lost consciousness?".

The commissioner looked at the screen. "We have no idea why he wouldn't have taken some evasive actions. There is also one other thing we are aware of, none of the vehicles involved show any sign of slowing. Normally vehicles are driven by the AI but for some reason the AI had been disabled. They were manually driving as though nothing was wrong right up to the point of impact. Also, they didn't send any distress messages via their IHU".

"Do we have any records of what they were viewing and who they last communicated with?" asked Danks.

The commissioner stood to his feet, "Strangely,

there are no recordings or communications which is rather odd. However, more information may have been uncovered by our investigators.

I would suggest that you meet with our chief scientist Doctor Mason. He can update you with the latest information that's been recovered from the individuals. Sergeant Francis will take you to see him".

"I would like a copy of all the recordings of the scenes of the accidents so I can study them in more detail". Danks placed his wrist watch on a pad on his chair and Commissioner Gilbert transferred the files to the watch.

The commissioner approached Danks and said in a quiet voice, "Inspector, you have the complete backing of the council but please keep this as secret as possible. The general public are already a bit jittery from the small amount of information that has leaked out. You, of all people, know what the press are like! They take a small amount of truth in a story, add a lot of false information and before you know it they've turned it into a catastrophe. The last thing we need is mass panic".

The commissioner turned and headed back to his seat.

Sergeant Francis stood up and gestured towards a corner of the room. Danks nodded in acknowledgement towards the commissioner and followed the sergeant. As the sergeant and Danks approached the wall another dark seam appeared, allowing them into an adjacent corridor.

Sergeant Francis said that they'd have to go down ten floors to where Doctor Mason's lab was located.

Chapter 24

As Danks and Sergeant Francis walked down the corridor, he quizzed the sergeant. "Do you have any ideas as to what might have caused these accidents? Commissioner Gilbert seems to think they are a cause for extreme concern"

Sergeant Francis looked at Danks, "This is the first time I've heard about the specific individuals involved. On the m-net news there were only sketchy details. But they did hint at there being rumours of a strange virus that's been disturbed as a result of some mining operations in the south pole. I guess that's why Commissioner Gilbert is concerned with the population finding out about it. If it's a virus and it's contagious it might cause a mass exodus of the planet. The virus would then end up being transferred to other colonies and even back to Earth".

"It seems to be a bit of a coincidence that three people out of five work for the same company. They would've had to have been close to the source. As far as I can see there are no indications that it's contagious otherwise more cases would have broken out since".

"The problem sir, is that Mr Ramsdale has a residence in the South Pole and had visited the mining site frequently" replied the sergeant.

"Have there been any reported cases among the workers in the mine?".

"Now I have clearance I can do a check for you sir". The sergeant seemed to go silent while he used his IHU to check with the CMPC central computer.

He continued, "There is a viral infection going around the workers in the mines at the moment, but no unusual symptoms have been reported. There are lots of viruses that regularly arrive here from Earth via the shuttle passengers. It's quite difficult to detect anyone who has an infection in the early stages. The only way we could stop them would be to put everyone into quarantine and not many people would agree to that".

"Well, maybe we need to visit Cerebralnet to find out more information on the employees who died. If it's a virus were there any early viral symptoms? What viral research projects are being carried out by the company and why was Mr Ramsdale involved with the mining at the South Pole?" replied Danks.

"I can tell you what Cerebralnet do sir. According to their m-site, they're the manufacturers of the chips that are implanted into people to give them their IHU's. They spend a great deal of money on new chip designs and software research to improve the user's experience. As a user, I regularly receive software updates into my IHU which fix software bugs or add new features. They don't say if they are doing viral research. However, the South Pole operations are mining for desperately needed minerals. There's no mention of any viral research being conducted on their site".

"Who is their chief scientist? I think we should talk to them about their ex-work colleagues and what research they're doing" replied Danks.

"According to police records the chief scientist is a Doctor Taylor. She has been with the company for the last ten years since she arrived here on Mars. She graduated from a University in England as a software engineer. She was promoted to CEO shortly after Mr Ramsdale's death".

"Can you set up a meeting with Doctor Taylor? In the meantime let's see what Doctor Mason has to report on uncovering any further information".

After descending the ten floors in the turbo lift, they were soon stepping into a tidy lab that had medical tools all neatly mounted on the walls behind transparent glass doors.

Bottles were neatly arranged with their labels facing outwards so that they could be easily identified. There was a strong smell of disinfectant that hung in the air and a humming noise coming from refrigeration units. These units stored the bodies and were along one side of the room.

There was a small office across the other side of the lab and they could see that someone was moving around behind the frosted glass windows.

As they approached the office, Danks thought he could make out someone whistling to 'The Dark side of Phobos' by Pink Sunset, a famous Martian band that is very popular back on Earth.

As they entered the office, there was a tall slim man with long hair that was tied back in a pony tail to keep it out of his way. His brown hair had grey streaks running through it. He wore a long white lab coat that reached down to his knees and a pair of white boots that he'd tucked his trouser legs into. They looked like the type of boots that had steel toe caps to protect the toes in case a heavy object was accidentally dropped onto the foot.

The man had his back towards them and was leaning over a holographic image of a body. He was passing his hand over the image and wherever he pointed his finger that section of the hologram would brighten and expand to show finer detail. The music was quite loud inside the small room and so the man didn't notice them enter.

Sergeant Francis moved over to a panel at the end of a desk and waved his hand in a downward motion. The volume dropped down at which point the tall man quickly stood upright and turned to see what had happened.

He was probably the same height as Sergeant Francis and a similar build. This made Danks feel a bit like a hobbit with these two tall Martians either side of him.

"I was wondering when you would put in an appearance Stuart. I have some more information about the clients" the tall man said to the sergeant. It was a strange terminology, but that's how he referred to the corpses.

"This is Inspector Danks. He's been brought in from Earth to investigate these cases" replied Sergeant Francis.

"I've heard quite a lot about you already inspector. I was particularly interested in your case on Titan. It sounded extremely dangerous and the new life form discovered there is fascinating".

"Actually, I was lucky to survive the ordeal but I had a lot of help in that investigation from my work colleague, Sergeant Turner, without whom I wouldn't be here now. Titan's a forbidding place and I don't know how people put up with living there for long periods of time. I couldn't do it.

Anyway, that was a couple of years ago and we are here to see what new information you've uncovered".

"What I've discovered is that they all appear to have been quite unaware of their situation at the point of impact. There are no signs of bracing before the accidents such as broken ankles and wrists. It's almost as though they were asleep.

Looking at the recovered recorded information from the vehicles they were clearly unaware of the danger. So I thought I'd do a check for any foreign bodies such as bacteria or viruses that may have impaired them. All I found were the usual ones that everyone carries with them through their whole lives.

There were no detectable unusual pathogens present. Their biometric chips indicated that their heart rate, blood pressure, temperature, insulin levels were all within their normal parameters.

However, that doesn't mean that a pathogen wasn't there, they could be well hidden. So, I ran a DNA comparison between a sample of their DNA and their stored DNA signatures on their biometric chips. They were all perfect matches.

So that left me with examining their IHU's. Unfortunately, the central IHU chips were all damaged and so there is no data accessible which is extremely odd.

The exception was Mr Burgess, he did seem to react as he shows signs that he braced himself. He appears to have been in the wrong place at the wrong time and he was the only one whose IHU was not erased. His IHU only shows him crashing into the tunnel wall". Dr Mason paused as he got distracted examining the holographic image.

"That seems to explain a lot in that four of the five were totally unaware of the dangers they were in. So the question is, how did they enter that state? Were they asleep, unconscious or were they already dead?" responded Danks.

Danks thought back to what he'd read about historical diseases such as the pneumonic plague of the latter part of the Roman empire. Some of the victims would feel unwell one minute and the next they would keel over dead.

Dr Mason pulled his attention away from the hologram and replied, "I've discovered nothing that could explain any of this but there are a few avenues I can pursue with the IHU's".

"Well doctor, keep us informed if you uncover anything new. In the meantime the sergeant and I are going to try and discover more about Ms Anderton".

"Why are we investigating Ms Anderton first?" whispered the sergeant.

"Why? Because it's a gut feeling. She was a journalist, so I'm interested in what she was last investigating. It might give us a clue about why she lost her life on the highway that day".

Danks and the sergeant signalled to Dr Mason that they were leaving and headed for the lift to return to the surface. As they left, they heard the volume of the music increase and Dr Mason started whistling again.

Once they arrived at ground level, the sergeant took Danks to one of the police vehicle bays where they climbed on board and strapped themselves in.

The sergeant entered the location of Ms Anderton's last known place of employment. The vehicle taxied out of the bay and entered a chamber. A door shut behind them sealing them off from the vehicle parking area and the chamber then depressurised to the same as on the Martian surface. The outer door of the chamber then slid to one side and the vehicle accelerated out. It glided up a slipway and onto the Martian highway. It was heading for Ms Anderton's old work place.

Chapter 25

Sergeant Francis and Inspector Danks pulled into the Daily Phobos news headquarters and a walkway tube extended out. It attached itself to their vehicle. They then had to wait for the external and internal pressure to match before the door opened.

Leaving the vehicle, Danks and the sergeant walked along the walkway. At the end of the tube they stepped out into the foyer and approached the reception desk. Behind it was a man who looked rather scrawny. He had a bald head that moved in strange up and down movements as he scanned one of the screens in front of him.

Danks was convinced that the man was listening to music, that's why he was moving in an odd way. Danks knocked on the reception desk surface and the man's attention was drawn away from the screen towards them.

"Oh, hello, welcome to the Daily Phobos. How may I help you?"

Before Sergeant Francis spoke, he showed his holographic CMPC badge. "We want to speak to the editor about a Maria Anderton. According to our records, she was an employee here".

The man at reception seemed to be disturbed by the request.

"Did you know Maria Anderton well?" asked Danks.

"She was one of the few people who would take time to chat. Most tend not to talk to me other than to say they have an appointment to see someone here. Everyone liked her and we were all shocked when we heard about the accident as we'd all seen her that day".

"Did she seem okay on the day of the accident?" asked Danks.

"She seemed her usual self so there didn't appear to be anything wrong. In fact she was happier than usual" the man replied.

"Do you know why that was?" probed Danks.

"She told me that she'd received some new information on a story she was working on".

"Did she say what it was?" asked Danks.

"No, she normally kept her work secret until the article was complete".

"Are there any colleagues she may have confided in?".

"Not that I'm aware of. You could ask the editor".

"Okay, thanks for your help".

The man glanced for a second at one of his screens in front of him and looked back at them.

"The editor is ready to see you. Take the lift to the top floor. His office is at the end of the corridor".

The sergeant and inspector thanked him and strode over to the lifts. They went up in silence.

Arriving at the designated floor, the doors opened and they walked down the corridor towards the editor's office. At the end there was a glass door. It slid to one side revealing a large office. It had long windows on three sides with panoramic views of the Martian landscape. Clouds of Martian dust swirled and dashed across the terrain in the distance.

The editor sat facing away from them taking in the views as they entered the room. "We might have to close the shutters if the storm gets any stronger" he said as he swung around on his chair to face them. "It's unusual for the CMPC to want to see me. So what can I help you with gentlemen?".

Danks settled in a chair opposite the editor. He couldn't help but notice that the chair he was in was lower than the editor's. Recognising that this was a typical psychological tactic to create a feeling of inferiority, he decided to stand up so as to reverse the roles. "We are following some lines of enquiry on Ms Anderton to help us understand the circumstances that led to her accident. Can you tell us what she was working on at the Daily Phobos before the accident?".

The editor leaned forward from his chair. "She came to see me some three months ago about a potential big story. She'd received an anonymous tip off saying there was something suspicious about the deaths of Charles Lowe and Matt Hitchen at Cerebralnet.

She was really excited that this was going to be the story that would make her famous.

At the time I didn't think there was anything unusual about the accidents other than they were the first couple for many years.

It was widely known that Mr Lowe was an adrenalin junkie and had a habit of driving his hover bike manually and doing some crazy stunts".

Sergeant Francis added, "That's correct sir. According to the CMPC records, Mr Lowe had received several points on his licence. They were for performing dangerous manoeuvres after overriding the AI driver on his hover bike that nearly resulted in a serious accident.

He argued that it wasn't a problem as he had it fully under control. But any more points and he'd have had his licence revoked. He'd then have to reapply for it".

"Do people receive points for overriding the AI driver here on Mars?".

"No, but it is recommended that the AI driver should always remain in control. Even when the AI is overridden it can still take control if it believes there is a life threatening event about to happen. It's the AI that reported Mr Lowe's incident that resulted in him receiving points on his licence. Completely disabling the AI is an offence".

"Why can the vehicle AI be disabled if it's an offence?" queried Danks.

"Well sir, it's like on Earth, you have speed limits on your roads but some people ignore them" responded the sergeant.

Danks pointed out that the speed limits had been made obligatory on Earth and that the AI could not be turned off. If anyone attempted to override the AI it would report them and their location to the police. The offender would end up with a long jail sentence.

Danks moved his attention back to the editor. "So, did Ms Anderton take your advice and leave the case alone?".

The editor gave out a quiet laugh, "You didn't know Ms Anderton did you inspector. If you did then you'd have known that she was a determined woman and like a true investigator she pursued what she thought was a story. Possibly a bit like you".

"How so?".

"She wouldn't take 'no' for an answer and she wouldn't give up. I assume you would doggedly pursue a case until you'd solved it?".

"Yes, that's very true". Danks had a wry smile as he continued. "How much did she tell you about the investigation before she died?".

"Nothing I'm afraid. She kept whatever information she uncovered a secret. She always double checked all her findings before showing me the draft article".

"Did anyone else work closely with her?".

"She always worked alone. As far as I'm aware she didn't reveal anything to anyone else. However, she did mention one thing inspector. She was heading to meet someone at an old bar called The Free Press down town. That was the last time I saw her. If only I'd known I could've stopped her". The editor put his head in his hands to cover his eyes. Discussing her death was proving difficult for him.

After a few moments he lifted his head from his hands, wiped the tears from his eyes, "Anyway, that's all I know inspector".

"Thank you for your help Mr?".

"Oh, it's Upton, Tom Upton"

"Remember Mr Upton, you can contact us via Sergeant Francis if you think there is anything new to add". Danks then turned and left the office with Sergeant Francis striding along behind him.

Chapter 26

Danks and the sergeant walked across the foyer of the Daily Phobos heading towards the walkway tube. They signalled thank you to the concierge behind reception and then entered the tube. As they approached the police vehicle the door opened. Sergeant Francis stepped into it, seated himself down in front of the main console and Danks climbed into the adjacent seat.

"So, Ms Anderton was investigating the accidents of both Mr Lowe and Mr Hitchen from Cerebralnet. She was also meeting some, as yet, unknown person at The Free Press. So our next step is to find out who that was as they may hold the key to this case" said Danks as the door closed behind him.

The sergeant replied, "The bar is in an expensive area of New Cambridge city that's frequented by many of the locals, particularly journalists. She must have been on her way to meet the person when the accident happened".

"How did it get its name? Is it because a lot of their customers are journalists?" enquired Danks.

"According to the m-net sir, the bar's name

came from an old pub back on Earth".

"Ah, I've been to that pub if you mean the one in Cambridge. One of my favourites" reminisced Danks. "Do we have any information on who sent the message to Ms Anderton setting up the meeting?".

"No, there's no indication as to who sent it".

"Was the name of the other person involved in the collision Jim Burgess?".

"Yes it was sir. He was a software engineer working on AI".

"What do the CMPC records have on him?".

Sergeant Francis thought for a moment while his IHU retrieved the information from CMPC central computer. "He was outstanding in his field, quite a dedicated worker according to his fellow colleagues and enjoyed solving complex puzzles in his spare time".

"So why was he on the highway at the same time as Maria Anderton?".

"The accident occurred at lunchtime and Mr Burgess's vehicle also had The Free Press entered as its destination.

The accident dossier says that Ms Anderton's vehicle veered out of its lane and collided with Mr Burgess's vehicle just as they were both about to enter a tunnel.

The AI driver on Ms Anderton's vehicle had been disabled only seconds before it lost control.

The resulting accident happened too close to the tunnel wall and the AI of Mr Burgess's vehicle wasn't able to avoid the collision.

The report says that Ms Anderton's vehicle rammed into the back of Mr Burgess's pushing it straight into the tunnel wall".

"I think we should visit The Free Press to question the proprietor. I can also have some food and a beer. I've not had a proper drink since I arrived and I'm parched".

"Sorry sir, what does 'parched' mean?".

"Yes, 'parched', an old Earth expression referring to the male condition of requiring a beer". Danks laughed but the sergeant looked a bit puzzled.

Eventually the sergeant replied, "Ah, I see. I've looked it up on line. I'll remember that one sir" he said with a smile.

The police vehicle, at that point, detached from the walkway tube and backed a short distance away. Once clear of the tube it turned and accelerated up a side road heading for the highway.

The storm that Danks had seen on entering the atmosphere was creating huge swirling columns of red dust whirlwinds that sped across the landscape.

Even though the police vehicle was being buffeted, it managed to seamlessly slide into the stream of other vehicles that were cruising along the highway that passed the Daily Phobos. Their destination? The Free Press.

Chapter 27

The sergeant steered them off the highway and negotiated several back streets before they arrived at The Free Press. They swung into the entrance and descended down a ramp through two pressurising doors that took them under the building where the bar could be found.

The vehicle travelled around until it found a free parking bay where it pulled in and stopped. The door hissed as it opened. Danks and the sergeant climbed out.

A large illuminated 3D sign was on the wall about ten vehicles away and it was flashing showing the direction to the establishment.

The Free Press occupied most of the space of one of the earliest buildings constructed on Mars. It was built underground to utilize the many natural tunnels found on Mars. It was perfect for sheltering from the Martian storms that hit the area from time to time and it was easier to insulate against the extreme Martian cold.

People could seek refuge down in the bar, have a few drinks and even stay the night if the storm was too intense.

Danks and the sergeant entered the building from the vehicle park through a set of glass sliding doors. As they stepped into the main room, their ears were exposed to a cacophony of music and chattering. The room was busy with several groups of people.

Danks and the sergeant had to squeeze past them before they arrived at the bar.

There was a couple of vacant stools so they each sat on one and swung around to face the bar. Danks started looking for a menu and beer list but couldn't see one. He started trying to gain the attention of the person behind the bar.

The sergeant could see Danks looking and guessed he was unfamiliar with the way things operated in Martian bars.

"I've got the menu here sir". He pointed to a screen behind the bar and as Danks turned to look, it appeared on it.

"Normally people get the menu via their IHU, but seeing as you don't have one sir I thought I'd display it on that screen for you".

"That's very kind sergeant, what would I do without you".

"Probably starve sir!" the sergeant said with a laugh.

After scanning the menu up and down a few times, Danks had come to a decision as to what he wanted to eat and drink. He conveyed his choices to the sergeant.

"Now, how do we place our orders around here?".

"I hope you don't mind sir, but I've already sent them through".

"Ah, I just can't get used to that. On Earth we speak to our wrist watches and then swipe it in the direction of the bar".

After about ten minutes the food and drink arrived via a tall waitress. As she placed the tray in front of them Danks asked, "Excuse me, can you tell me where the proprietor is?".

"Why do you want to know?" she asked in a somewhat defensive tone.

"We just want to ask him a few questions" said Danks.

"And you are?" she replied.

Sergeant Francis produced his CMPC badge. "I'm Sergeant Francis and this is Inspector Danks, we just want to ask him a few questions about some customers that were supposed to come here a couple of months ago".

She pointed across the room towards a man in a black double breasted suit with a yellow shirt and red tie. His black hair was short but the front was combed backwards over his head revealing his forehead. The hair had a sheen to it as though he'd used a complete pot of hair gel to hold it tightly in place. "He's over there talking to that group of people. I'll go and tell him".

The waitress collected a tray of drinks, carefully balancing it on one arm and then she moved off towards the group he was chatting to.

She talked to the proprietor for a few seconds and then pointed in Danks's direction. After that she moved off to deliver some much needed drinks to a group that were signalling for her attention.

The proprietor said something to the group he was with and they all laughed. He then waved goodbye to them and walked over to where Danks and the sergeant were sitting.

"Lizzy said the CMPC wanted to ask me some questions. I'm fairly certain we are a legal establishment and we haven't had any fights break out here for a few weeks now. So what do you guys want to chat to me about?".

"I'm Inspector Danks and this is Sergeant Francis. We aren't here to question you about any recent disturbances you may have had. We want to ask you about a Mr Jim Burgess. He had a reservation here some two months ago".

"Oh, okay. Let me just check". There was a short pause while the proprietor entered that usual trance mode while he retrieved the relevant information.

"Ah, yes, I've found the booking. He'd reserved a table for two people at 12:30pm which is quite unusual as he usually comes here with a large group of people.

Unfortunately, he didn't arrive and it wasn't until the following day that we found out he'd been involved in a fatal accident. It was quite shocking. He was such a likeable guy and a regular customer who tipped very generously".

"Do you know who the other person was?" asked Danks.

"No, I'm afraid not. However, he did request a private cubicle where people can talk without the noise from the other punters in the bar area".

"So, presumably you have no further information on the booking?".

"There isn't anything else I'm afraid. He placed a reservation but never turned up".

Danks pushed on with his questions. "Did you have another booking at about the same time for a Ms Maria Anderton".

Again, the proprietor went into a short trance and then replied, "There are no records of a Ms Anderton booking anything with us on that day. Should I know her?".

"No, we are just trying to build a picture of the events leading up to the accident. Okay, I think that's all Mr?".

"Oh, Gert Van der Waals".

"Thank you Mr Van der Waals. We'll be in contact if we think there's anything else you can help us with. Please give Sergeant Francis your contact details" said Danks.

The sergeant and Mr Van der Waals tapped each other's wrists together to exchange the relevant details.

"So, if that's all gentlemen I have a group of guests over there that are requesting my presence". He pointed in the direction of a rather noisy crowd of people. "I suspect they need to be encouraged to buy some more drinks or something like that". Then with a flourish he straightened his tie and strutted off in their direction.

Danks turned back to his meal as he was feeling hungry with the smell from his food. He started eating with a look of pleasure on his face as he hadn't eaten for ages, occasionally stopping to savour his glass of Martian beer. Although, he thought, drinking his beer through a valve on the top of the glass was a bit odd.

Sergeant Francis ate his meal in silence.

Danks took the last sip of his glass and placed the empty vessel back on the bar. "That was an enjoyable meal and the beer was excellent. Aeries ale must be one of the best I've had for ages. Maybe we can come back again if we get time".

"Yes sir, a really nice atmosphere here. It makes a change from the establishments that I normally have to visit. Most of them don't like me being there as I'm usually on CMPC business".

"Ah, is that where you got that scar on your

head?" Danks enquired. As soon as he'd said it he realised it was possibly a question he shouldn't have asked.

"Well yes it was. There was a disturbance at the Spirit and Opportunity bar in the rougher district. We arrived and there was a fight going on. Officer Robertson grabbed one guy while I grabbed the other. However, the thug I was trying to restrain broke free, turned and clunked me on the head with the bar stool he was using in the fight. I was knocked out cold and ended up in hospital for a few days under observation. The annoying thing was that he got away that night".

"Did you catch him in the end?".

"Yes, he went to prison for two years. Unfortunately, he's back out on the streets again".

"What was his name?".

"He's a well known criminal among the police community here on Mars. His name is Alex Lynch and should be locked up permanently in my opinion".

"Well, if we come across him again we can give him a hard time". Danks smiled at the sergeant.

They both swivelled around on their bar seats, stood up, brushed themselves down and headed for the exit.

On returning to their vehicle they climbed in and were soon back on the highway. The sun had already set and it was dark. They drove through the blackness with the headlights illuminating the road ahead with Martian dust blowing through the beams. Danks's hotel was the destination.

As they drove through the thin atmosphere of Mars Danks turned to the sergeant, "I think we need to visit Mr Burgess's residence to find out why he booked a table at The Free Press. Also, if he left a record of who he was planning to meet there and what he was working on at the time. But that'll have to wait until tomorrow morning. I'm looking forward to a shower, unpacking my bags and getting some shut-eye".

Chapter 28

Sergeant Francis pulled their vehicle up inside the pressurised dropping off point attached to Danks's hotel and he stepped out.

"See you at 8:30am tomorrow sergeant".

Danks stretched his back as it felt stiff after the journey. He thought he'd better go and check in so he walked up the steps into the foyer of the hotel.

Inside the reception area Danks saw the sergeant leave the dropping off point and watched as he accelerated off into the darkness, heading in the direction of the highway. He eventually lost sight of the sergeant as his vehicle blended in among the stream of white and red lights of the other traffic that was travelling along the same road.

Danks stepped up to reception and looked at the person that was standing behind it. She was a tall slim woman with blonde hair pulled back from her face with a blue ribbon securing it tightly at the back of her head. She wore a snug fitting smart blue uniform that had the hotel logo on the left lapel of the jacket. She hadn't noticed his arrival so he decided to break the silence. "Hello, I have a room booked. The name is Danks, Inspector

Danks".

"Oh, sorry sir, I didn't see you there. Let me just check our records".

There was a short silence while she had a blank look on her face. Danks had started to get used to this among Martians as they always went into a trance like state whenever they were using their IHU's.

"Yes, you were checked in earlier by a CMPC officer. Your luggage has been taken to your room already. You are on the third floor, room 340. If you could place your thumb on the pad here sir".

Danks obliged and pressed it on the pad. The usual thin blue line then slid down registering his thumb print.

"All done sir. There are similar pads on the wall next to the lifts and outside your room. If you place your thumb on any of the pads it triggers the AI facial recognition and a thumb scan is performed. Only if both of these agree with our records will the doors open".

"This seems rather a lot of security just to gain access to my room".

"The lift and room security are there to make our customers feel perfectly safe in our hotel sir".

"I'm sure I'll sleep peacefully in my bed tonight knowing that" Danks said with a smile.

The receptionist continued, "The two lifts are over there" and she pointed towards the far wall which had two black sliding doors. "Breakfast is from 7am to 10am. If you have any issues don't hesitate to contact Reception".

Danks said thank you and walked over to the lifts.

As the receptionist had said, there were pads on the wall next to each lift. He placed his thumb on the nearest and it was scanned. A few seconds later the lift door opened revealing a clean white interior.

Hung on the lift walls were images of famous locations on Mars. Danks thought that he'd like to see some of them if he got time after his mission was complete.

He stepped inside and an automated voice announced the floor that Danks was heading for. "Third floor room 340" and with that the lift door shut. He could feel the lift accelerate and then it decelerated, finally coming to a halt at his floor.

The door slid open and the lift voice announced, "Third floor. Please turn right for room 340".

He stepped out into the corridor past two other guests who were waiting to catch the lift down.

As the voice had informed him he turned right. He wondered what would have happened if he'd turned left. Would the security system issue an alarm? "Maybe I'll try that one day" he thought.

There were arrows on the walls flashing the direction to his room.

The hotel security system was tracking him on the cameras in the corridor and it was guiding him to his accommodation.

He arrived outside room 340 and placed his thumb on the pad. There was a faint hiss as the door slid back revealing a compact but comfortable looking room. He walked in and found his luggage waiting for him on the floor just inside the entrance.

The bed looked inviting, so Danks lay down on it for a second just to try it out. He was feeling quite exhausted. Prolonged periods in stasis often left people feeling tired even though they'd been in a suspended state. It was something to do with the body's circulation taking time to fully recover.

With a jolt, he suddenly woke up and realised he must have dozed off. The clock was an hour later so he quickly unpacked his gear and he then jumped into the shower as he'd been looking forward to it all day.

While he was showering he couldn't help but think there was something odd about the accident of each of the individuals. It couldn't be a coincidence that they all died in strange circumstances. These sorts of accidents were unheard of with the AI systems controlling the vehicles these days. Why would four of the five people completely disable their AI systems? But all the evidence so far pointed at that being the case.

He dried himself off and returned to the bedroom.

Lying down on the bed he began watching the local news channel until it started to repeat itself. His eyes were beginning to feel heavy anyway, so he switched off the TV and he slid under the soft quilt. It had been a long day and he was exhausted.

"This is so much more comfortable than the stasis tubes" he thought. Soon he drifted off dreaming about the day's events.

Some time later Danks was awoken by noises coming from the corridor. He forced himself out of bed and, with a sleepy walk, managed to get to the door.

Looking at the camera screen he could see someone standing outside but all he could see was the back of their head. He unlocked the door and it slid silently to the side. As it did so, the person outside turned to face him.

There was a moment where neither of them spoke until the man in the corridor asked, "Is everything alright sir?".

"Yes, everything's fine. I heard some noises outside my room which woke me up. When I came over to check what was going on, you were stood outside. Is there something I can help you with?" Danks was trying to suppress a yawn.

"I'm the security guard for the hotel. I was just

patrolling the corridor as the system in my office detected that there was someone moving about in this area".

"Could it have been a guest that was lost?" asked Danks while he yawned.

"I'm not sure sir. The facial recognition for some reason couldn't identify the individual and now they seem to have vanished".

"Don't you have facial and thumb print security identification that restricts access to each of the floors?". Danks was feeling more alert now.

"Yes sir. I'm not sure why the system has failed to identify the person. Anyway, don't worry sir, I will do a sweep of the corridors and if I don't find anything I'll head back and check the system again".

"I'm sure you'll get to the bottom of it.." Danks squinted at the name tag on the guard's shirt, "..Bill".

"Thank you, I'm sure I will. Good night sir".

Danks stepped back into his room and the door slid shut behind him. Pressing his thumb on the panel next to the door he made sure it was locked and returned to his bed.

Danks was too tired right now to be concerned about the stranger in the corridor. But he'd go and check with the security guard in the morning. His main priority was a good night's sleep.

Chapter 29

The following morning Danks got up early. He always hated these first few days on a new planet where he had to get used to the strange environment, the gravity differences and the time zone change.

He ambled off to the shower-room and peered at his reflection in the mirror. A bristly face looked back at him. He badly needed a shave as he hadn't had one since leaving the Earth. Although he was in stasis on the flight, the hairs on his chin still grew but very slowly. It wasn't weeks worth of beard, more like half a day's worth. With a sigh he went for a refreshing shower. Afterwards he dried himself down, donned some underwear and returned to the sink. Staring at his reflection in the mirror he started to carefully shave the stubble from his face.

Danks slapped on some aftershave and returned to the bedroom. He selected a clean set of clothes and threw his dirty ones into a box, knowing they would be collected by the drone cleaners later that night.

Once he felt he was presentable he left his room

and proceeded down the corridor looking forward to a hearty Martian breakfast.

The dining room was a large rectangular shape with images of the Martian surface displayed on the walls. White tables were regimented in lines running parallel with the walls.

A waitress approached. "Good morning Inspector Danks, let me show you to your table". The waitress was using the AI recognition to identify customers.

Danks replied, "That's okay, I'll find my own table. I'm quite picky about where I sit. Oh, and can you bring me a coffee?".

"Of course, sir".

Danks scanned the room to find a table that he felt was in the best place to observe all the other tables. It also had to be positioned so he could see everyone entering and leaving the dining area.

This was an old habit of his and it had proven useful in previous cases when waiting for suspects to arrive or leave.

Selecting a suitable table he sat down. As he did so, the waitress brought over the hot cup of coffee he'd requested and placed it next to him. He thanked her and picked it up.

While drinking his coffee, Danks scanned the room to check out the people already having breakfast. There were two couples who were busily chatting over a coffee, there was another couple that seemed to be having a heated argument and there was a single man sat in the far corner of the room who seemed to be glancing in his direction.

Whenever Danks looked at the man he would quickly look back at his breakfast. It was as though the man was furtively watching him.

Danks saw the man finish his coffee, after which he stood up and left.

The waitress came over with Danks's breakfast. He asked her, "Can you tell me who that man was who has just left the dining area? He was sitting over there". Danks pointed at the vacant table that was being cleaned by drones.

She seemed to stare into space for a few seconds while she consulted the hotel records via her IHU. She replied, "That was a Mr Lynch. He checked in quite late last night".

"What time did he check in?".

"It's shown as 1am in the morning. Is there a problem inspector as I could contact security?".

"No, that's okay".

"Is that all sir?".

"One additional question. Could I have a top up for my coffee?".

"Of course sir". The waitress turned and set off to find a fresh coffee pot.

Danks recalled that the sergeant had mentioned he'd had some dealings with a Mr Lynch. He wondered if this was the same person. He also remembered that the noises in the corridor that woke him were about 1:30am which seemed to be a bit of a coincidence. He decided he'd go and see the security guard straight after his breakfast. Maybe he'd found out who the unidentified person was.

Danks's meal consisted of a couple of slices of bacon and scrambled egg on toast. This was like his usual breakfast back on Earth. The bacon is grown in large culture baths and the scrambled egg like protein is built by bacterial cultures. The only difference was that the bread on Mars was actually ground up mushrooms that had been compressed into a slice. It vaguely resembled a slice of bread but the texture wasn't quite right. However, it did taste good.

A normal loaf of bread is an expensive commodity on Mars because wheat was difficult to grow here. The small quantity that was grown was in large concrete buildings with artificial light. Two meter square trays were used, illuminated with artificial light. The grain had to be kept warm and fed with nutrient rich water which is a limited resource. The buildings could accommodate one hundred trays wide, two hundred trays deep and were stacked twenty trays high.

The wheat had been genetically modified so that it only grew twenty centimetres high and most of that was the wheat head. Any waste from the wheat such as the leaves and stalks would be ground up and used as a source of food for the mushrooms.

There were a limited number of warehouses growing the wheat resulting in its price being high. Only the very rich on Mars could afford real bread.

Mushrooms, on the other hand grew in the dark. They only needed moisture, warmth and some medium for the spores to draw nutrients from. In fact, all Martian biodegradable waste, which includes corpses, was added to the biomass for the mushrooms to feed on. There was no wastage here on Mars as it was a delicate balance surviving in such a hostile environment. The earthly tradition of burying or cremating a body was a luxury that Mars could not afford.

All this recycling helped Mars achieve an almost perfect closed loop. It helped them feed the masses and deal with the inevitable vast quantities of waste that humans generate.

Danks finished off his breakfast although he did think that the 'bread' wasn't quite the ticket even though it was tasty. He missed having real slices of toast. Finishing off the remainder of his coffee, he placed the mug carefully back on the table.

Then pushing his plate away he stood up to leave. At that moment small drones had detected that he was departing and rushed over to his table.

He watched with some amusement as they started to collect everything up including the tablecloth. Another small drone scooted around where he had been sitting vacuuming up any bits of food that may have fallen to the floor.

Before he had left the dining area a new cloth and clean utensils had been carefully arranged on the table ready for the next guest.

After thanking the waitress, Danks strode off in the direction of the exit where he had noticed Sergeant Francis was waiting for him. The sergeant started waving at Danks thinking that he hadn't seen him, but he had.

"Good morning sir, I hope you slept well".

"I did eventually sergeant".

"Eventually, sir?" enquired the sergeant.

"Yes, there was a security guard outside my room investigating an incident last night. I think we should just take a quick detour down to his office before he finishes his night shift".

Danks brought Sergeant Francis up to speed on the events during the night as they made their way to see Bill the security guard.

They stopped outside his office and pressed the communication panel.

A firm voice came from the panel, "What do you want?".

"This is Inspector Danks. I'm here to find out what happened in the corridor outside my room last night".

There was a short pause and the door slid back to reveal a rather plump man, with very short black hair and wearing a gray security guard uniform. He was sitting in an office chair that squeaked every time he moved and there was a screen in front of him. The AI software was selecting camera shots of corridors where people's faces were being analysed. Each face was being compared with the hotel records of guests and workers.

"I'm here to find out what happened at about 1:30am in the corridor outside my room on the third floor" asked Danks. Danks noticed that this wasn't the security guard he had seen last night. He continued, "Where's Bill the security guard from last night?".

"Bill? He wasn't here when I arrived, I assumed he'd left for home early. He does that sometimes".

"Can you find out if he managed to identify the intruder who was in the corridor outside my room last night?".

"There was an intruder? He left no message about that. I'll contact him right away". The security guard tried contacting Bill's IHU but there was no reply. He decided to ring Bill's home. The guard then transferred the video to the screen in front of him so everyone could see.

As he switched it to the screen the call was

answered up by Bill's wife. "Hello George, it's unusual for you to call. How can I help?"

"Hi Katie, can I speak with Bill?".

"I'm afraid he's not here. I thought he was working late at the hotel".

"I suspect he's on his way home right now, I must have just missed him" replied George. "It's quite urgent so can you get him to contact me when he gets in?".

"Sure, I'll remind him to call you back. I'll have to go George, one of the kids has just spilt their breakfast on the floor".

"Okay, bye Katie". George hung up the call. He turned to Danks and the sergeant, "That's worrying. You see, I've been here for half an hour and Bill only lives twenty minutes away".

The inspector turned to the sergeant, "Okay, contact headquarters and get them to locate Bill's IHU".

After a few minutes Sergeant Francis came back with an answer. "He's apparently still here in the hotel, down in the basement".

"Is he responding on his IHU?" asked Danks.

"No, in fact there are no life signs coming from his IHU". Sergeant Francis looked worried.

The security guard's face had gone very pale and he added, "The basement is sealed off from the rest of the building. It's at Mars's temperature and pressure. He couldn't have survived down there without a protective suit".

They all hurried off down to the basement and when they arrived they found a set of protective suits. None had been removed. Danks donned one of the suits that was the right size. Entering the basement pressure chamber, he shut the inner door behind him.

Danks peered through a portal in the door into the main basement area. He couldn't see anything unusual.

To enter the basement he had to initiate the depressurisation before he could open the outer door of the chamber. Once the pressure was low enough he opened the door inwards into the pressure chamber. As he did, the frozen corpse of Bill fell backwards onto the floor of the chamber. He was in a seated position with his back against the door. That's why Danks couldn't see him through the portal as the body was too close to the door.

Danks spoke into his microphone, "Are you guys seeing this?".

"Yes sir" replied the sergeant, "why would he knowingly go into the basement not wearing a protective suit?".

"Sergeant, this is a lot like the other victims as they were unaware of what they were doing.

Report this back to HQ and get the team over here to look for any reason as to why he ended up in here. I suspect there'll be little to go on but there might be something that will shed some light on it".

Danks put the corpse back outside the chamber so that it would preserve any evidence and he shut the outer door. He repressurised the chamber and opened the inner door.

On stepping back into the corridor, Danks removed his protective suit. Turning to the sergeant he said, "Stop anyone entering this area until the forensic team have completed their analysis of the area".

Once they'd sealed it off they returned to the security office.

Danks asked the security guard for an image of the Mr Lynch who had stayed at the hotel that night. The security guard found one and put it up on the screen.

"Sergeant, is that the Mr Lynch you had dealings with before?" enquired Danks.

"Why, yes sir, that's him. He's changed his appearance slightly but I'd recognise him anywhere".

"Is he still in the hotel?" Danks asked.

The security guard checked the hotel records, "No, he checked out straight after breakfast".

"Can you locate him on the m-net sergeant?".

The sergeant went quiet for a minute or two then replied, "It seems he's no longer on the m-net. But he's done that before when we've been trying to apprehend him".

"Okay, sergeant, get HQ to order all officers to watch out for Mr Lynch and bring him in for questioning. I think he has to explain what he was doing here as he's the main suspect in Bill's death. Also, get the hotel records of all the guests and instruct HQ to cross check for anyone else who has a criminal record on that list".

The sergeant sent the request through to HQ.

"We should head over the Bill's place now, as we have to give the bad news to his wife. It might be best we do that in person.

Afterwards, we'll visit Mr Burgess's residence to find out what he was working on and see if we can find out who he was planning to meet at The Free Press. There must be a link between all these deaths. Also, why was Bill's body sitting against the outer door? That's very odd".

"Why is that sir?" asked the sergeant.

"Because he'd probably have been dead before he could step out into the basement area. So I suspect his body was placed there".

They told the guard that they were leaving and headed back to the hotel foyer.

Once they were back in the police vehicle they set the coordinates for Bill's home address and sped off.

"Giving bad news to loved ones is one of the

worst aspects of being a policeman" thought Danks. This wasn't going to be easy.

Chapter 30

It was quite traumatic visiting Bill's wife where they had to break the tragic news of his death. They spent some time consoling her until the arrival of the officers who would help her through this difficult period.

Once the support team had taken over, they returned to their vehicle. They climbed in, removed their pressure suits and settled into their respective seats. The AI steered the vehicle out into the Martian highway heading for Mr Burgess's residence.

They arrived at their destination later than planned. They cruised slowly up outside a grey two storey building. As they came to a standstill outside the main entrance, the usual walkway tube extended out from the building and attached itself to their vehicle. They walked down the tube and into the main foyer.

"This is Mount Pleasant House where Mr Burgess had an apartment. He was in flat 42 on the first floor sir. His widow still lives there".

They headed over to the lift and as soon as they'd stepped inside they told the lift system the flat number.

After ascending to the first floor the doors opened and on the wall opposite the lift was a screen showing the route to flat 42. They stepped out into a long corridor and studied the map for a second or two. It was a straight forward route to Mr Burgess's flat from where they were. They set off in the direction indicated.

The corridor was bright and clean with windows down one side looking out towards the distant mountains. The other side had plain doors with numbers on.

A drone cleaning machine glided past them. It was rectangular in shape, about ten centimetres tall and thirty centimetres long and wide. It was designed so that it could clean right up to the walls.

It manoeuvred deftly around them. Danks made it difficult for the drone as he kept moving his feet. Eventually, it decided it wasn't going to carry on trying to clean around him and it scuttled off down the corridor carrying on with the task it was designed for.

Danks and Sergeant Francis carried on down the corridor. They checked the door numbers as they passed them and eventually arrived outside flat 42. Sergeant Francis put his hand on a pad next to the door. "I've just informed the occupant that we are at the door. The system tells me that the only person in the flat is Mr Burgess's wife Gemma, sir"

After a short time the door slid silently into the wall. Standing in front of them was a young woman. She was slim, tall with long brunette hair and an almost typical Martian pale complexion. She wasn't as tall as the average Martian as she'd lived on Earth until her family emigrated to Mars when she was a teenager.

"Hello inspector, sergeant. I'm Gemma, Jim's wife. I was expecting you earlier".

"Sorry, we were delayed leaving my hotel" replied Danks.

Gemma showed them in and they walked into a room with light blue walls and ceiling. The floor was a picture of a pine forest but taken from the perspective of looking down on it from above. The strange thing was that as Danks walked across it, the image changed as though he were viewing it from the perspective of a drone flying over the canopy. The sergeant also experienced his own view of the forest as he moved about. Danks hadn't seen this type of holographic flooring before.

Dotted around the walls were video picture frames that had moving images of Gemma with Jim when they were on holiday at some of the Martian holiday resorts.

Danks looked down at the floor. His face must

have had a quizzical look on it as Gemma felt she needed to explain the reason for the images. "It's difficult for Martians to visit Earth as the gravity is quite a strain on their bodies. They have to go through a lot of expensive body modifications in order to go down to the surface. But Jim always liked the idea of visiting there to see the forests that are left. He always held out the hope that Mars could one day reproduce them here when the atmosphere becomes more Earth like".

Danks was amazed, "I've seen holographic flooring before but this I find quite fascinating. Walking over a forest like this is astonishing. I like the way when we look down we can see animals walking among the trees and birds flying above them".

"The hologram controlling system is constantly adding features of interest, so the view is never the same. It can even change the seasons in line with those on Earth. This particular hologram is based on the region I think you call Canada. The system has several holographic options. I often adapt it to something that suits my mood at the time. I particularly like the coastal region on the west coast of a place called Cornwall in England. Have you ever been there inspector?".

Danks thought back to the times he visited there on holidays as a young boy. "Yes, it's a place of great beauty. I used to sit on rocks with a fishing rod catching mackerel".

"I have no idea what a mackerel is but it sounds interesting" she replied, "..anyway inspector, how can I help you?".

"I hope you don't mind as we are reopening the case on the accident that your husband was involved in and we'd like to ask you a few questions?".

"I don't mind, but I thought I'd told the accident investigators everything I knew".

"Well, I'd like to go over it again just so I can get everything clear in my mind".

"If you think that my contribution would help, then you had better sit down". Gemma gestured towards some seats in the centre of the room.

Inspector Danks and the sergeant sat down facing Gemma. There was a small table with a glass top between her and themselves. In the middle of the table was a curious sphere that seemed to pulsate slowly with a faint yellow light. Its pulsations seemed to happen every time someone said anything.

"With my arrival here on Mars I'm approaching this investigation from a different angle to the accident investigators. They were focusing on the cause of the accident whereas I'm trying to determine what links your husband's death with some other previous accidents. So, can you tell me who Jim was meeting that day at The Free Press?"

Gemma was silent for a few seconds while she thought back to that date. "I'm afraid I can't remember, but Alice may be able to help".

"And who is Alice may I ask?" responded Danks. He glanced around the room thinking that there was someone else in the flat that they were unaware of.

"Oh, Alice is the AI system Jim was developing at home in his spare time. I find her extremely helpful about the flat. She's the one that controls the holographic images. In fact she controls everything that keeps this flat operating smoothly" said Gemma. "By the way would you like something to drink while you are here?".

"That would be very kind, I'll have a flat white coffee please" replied Danks.

"We only have soya milk in our supplies" came the response from the sphere on the table. It was about the same shape and dimensions as a soccer ball. Before, it was only flashing a faint yellow light but now there was a female face illuminated inside it. To match the face the voice coming from it was clearly feminine. "Would the inspector require sugar adding to his coffee?" came the voice again.

Danks was taken aback by this unexpected response from the sphere. It wasn't like the other AI voices, it was all around and seemed to be inside his head.

"That's Alice" said Gemma, "Her persona is projected inside the sphere but she is throughout the whole flat. She'll organise the preparation of your drinks".

Danks decided he should reply to the question, "No sugar thank you Alice".

"And what would the sergeant like to drink?" asked Alice.

"Oh, can you make me a Martian Ice cap, no sugar thank you" replied the sergeant.

Danks had to ask, "What on Earth, or should I say Mars, is a Martian Ice cap sergeant?" as he'd no idea what it was.

"It's a bit like your flat white sir, but is a chilled coffee with a cream layer and a small drop of dry ice spinning on the surface".

"Ah" he was fairly sure that there was a similar drink back on Earth but he wasn't too keen on it. He'd mistakenly touched the dry ice with one of his lips and ended up with frost bite. "Yes, I think that drink needs safety instructions" replied Danks.

Suddenly a small rectangular drone on wheels came racing through an opening in the wall carrying two drinks.

"The white coffee is the red cup and the Martian Ice cap is the blue cup" Alice informed them.

They both picked up their respective cups, removed the lids and smelt the fragrance rising from their drinks. In the sergeant's case it was mainly carbon dioxide he inhaled.

After Danks had sampled the first sip he said, "Not bad, it's almost like a real coffee back on Earth".

"I've constructed the flat white coffee from the suggested recipe. Are you saying it needs improving?" queried Alice.

"No, not at all Alice, this is perfectly adequate thank you".

There was a noticeable pause before Alice added "When you say 'adequate' do you mean it's not quite right?".

Danks thought he was getting pulled into a rabbit warren with this conversation.

At that moment Gemma intervened, "I think what the inspector meant, Alice, is that the drink is perfect. Isn't that right inspector?".

"Yes, that's what I meant" said Danks in a way that he hoped would end that thread of the conversation. He decided that he'd better steer away from talking about the drinks and more in the direction of the line of enquiries. "Alice, do you know who Jim was meeting on the day of his accident?".

"Yes, I know who it was. It was Maria Anderton. He asked me to send her a request to meet at The Free Press and I booked a table for him for twelve thirty for lunch. He specifically requested a private booth at the establishment".

"Did you know Maria Anderton, Gemma?".

"Not really, she was someone I knew at school, but not very well".

The sergeant felt he needed to add something here, "But according to your school records you knew her very well. Indeed they say you were best friends".

"I'm not quite sure where you're getting your information from sergeant, but I can assure you we were not 'best friends' as you put it".

"Would you say you were enemies then?" added Danks.

"Certainly not. As I told you, I barely knew her".

"So why was your husband meeting her at a bar?".

"I have absolutely no idea inspector. I have nothing to hide" Gemma replied with some amount of concern in her voice.

"We are merely exploring possibilities" Danks replied.

"Alice seems to be clever enough to access their vehicles and cause them to crash. Did you use Alice to do that?". Danks was trying to determine if Gemma had something to do with that day's events.

Alice broke into the conversation at this point. "Inspector, I can assure you that Gemma did not ask me to do anything to harm Jim or Maria".

"But are you capable of doing that?". Danks was certain Alice was capable of many things other than maintaining Gemma's flat.

"Yes, but I would have no reason to harm either of them".

"Okay Alice, do you know why he was meeting Ms Anderton?". Danks thought she may know more than she was divulging.

"Jim instructed me to retrieve the communication logs of the first two people who'd died from the company Cerebralnet.

I extracted them from the Mars central hub where the last couple of weeks of communications for everyone with an IHU are backed up. I then scanned the data looking for anything unusual. I found that there were encrypted bursts of information that were received and transmitted by the two individuals that started a minute before their respective accidents. These bursts continued until their IHUs ceased functioning".

"Don't you need security access in order to retrieve that sort of information from the central hub?" Danks added with some concern.

"Yes, but they use such a simple security protocol. I gained access in only a few seconds" replied Alice.

"Well, we'll skip over that for now. Although I think a review of the security systems is required when we are back at HQ sergeant".

"Yes, I've made a note of that sir".

"Do you know where the information originated from and can you decrypt it?". Danks was hoping to find out who'd sent the encrypted messages.

"The messages cannot be decrypted without having the original encryption keys and I don't have the signal origin coordinates. However, I can find them out but it will take some time to trace the source".

"Can you transfer the coordinates to me when you find them?" said Sergeant Francis.

Alice acknowledged that she would.

"Thank you Alice" said the sergeant.

Danks decided that was sufficient questioning for the time being.

Danks downed the last of his drink. The sergeant suddenly realised he hadn't even started his drink so quickly took a few gulps and put the mug back on the drone, unfinished. Fortunately, the dry ice cube had long since vaporized so he didn't get frost bite.

Danks thanked Gemma for the drinks and stood up to leave.

"I hope you are able to find out the root cause of the accident inspector" said Gemma as she led them to the exit. "and sergeant, I think you should probably check your sources as I can assure you Maria and I only vaguely knew each other. In fact we never crossed paths socially".

Stepping out into the corridor the door closed softly behind them. They then started heading back towards the lift.

"That's odd sir, the online records definitely say they were in the same class and best friends".

"Well, sergeant, that means either Gemma is lying or your source of information is incorrect".

"But if my source is wrong that would mean records have been tampered with on line".

"All I can say is that it wouldn't be the first time that sort of thing has happened".

"Do you believe Gemma and Alice were involved with her husband's death?" enquired the sergeant.

"I'm fairly certain they weren't. I was just seeing what Alice would do. Firstly, she referred to herself in the first person which I find unusual. Secondly, it was really impressive that Alice was actually defending Gemma, don't you think. No AI would normally do that".

"I must agree, that was a surprise. Alice does seem to be quite a unique AI". There was a short pause before the sergeant continued, "where to now sir?".

"I think the next logical step would be to visit Maria Anderton's flat. Looking around her accommodation may help us find something that will shed some light on what she may have uncovered in her investigations of the first two deaths in this case".

Chapter 31

Danks and Sergeant Francis made their way back to the lobby where they'd left the police vehicle outside. Danks was surprised to discover that it wasn't there.

"Sorry sir, I instructed the vehicle to wait for us in the parking bays at the rear of the building. It'll be back here in a few minutes once I've summoned it". The sergeant accessed the police vehicle via his IHU and instructed it to return to the front of the building to pick them up.

Danks could see through the glass wall of the entrance tube the police vehicle leave the parking bay some two hundred meters away. But as he watched he saw it accelerate towards the tube. He was beginning to think that it was cutting it a bit fine to stop when his arm was suddenly grabbed by the sergeant. He was pulling him back towards the foyer.

"Quickly sir, we need to get back to the main building. The vehicle is no longer in my control".

They both began to take large leaps back in the direction of the main building and were nearly there when the police vehicle crashed into the tube.

The glass withstood the initial impact, but cracks started to creep away from the collision point. This gave them some time to race back towards the foyer just as a hole opened in the glass.

The air started to gush out of the tube and the pressure rapidly dropped. Danks started to be sucked backwards towards the hole. The sergeant managed to hold on to Danks's arm while he was clinging onto a post that was just inside the foyer.

Sirens started to sound in the building and a large glass door began to slide down to seal the walkway off.

The sergeant's grip was beginning to fail him. He lost his hold on the post. Both he and Danks were sucked backwards. They came to a sudden halt when they bumped into the glass door just as it sealed shut.

A second later the remainder of the tube shattered sending shards of glass out into the street. Both Danks and Sergeant Francis slumped to the floor exhausted from their exertions to save their lives.

The porter came scurrying over from the reception desk looking most alarmed, "What on Mars happened? I heard an almighty crash and then the door on one of the docking tubes started to shut. Are you both okay?".

The porter looked up and saw the carnage outside where the tube had been. Small sections of it were still there but parts of it were strewn over a large area where it had been blown with the decompression. In the middle of all the mess was the police vehicle. It was wrecked with its front impact zone compacted down to a small wrinkled mass of metal and shattered sections of carbon fibre.

"Yes, we are okay thank you" Danks said with some relief.

"It appears that the auto recall system of the police vehicle malfunctioned" exclaimed the sergeant. "One minute I was instructing it to come to pick us up and the next my instructions were overridden. It's almost as though someone had intervened and taken control of the vehicle. But that would require them to enter the security codes to bypass me".

Danks eased himself back to his feet and brushed himself down. "I have a suspicion that there may be someone watching our every move. I think we might need to take some precautions.

You may not like this sergeant, but could you firstly disconnect your IHU from the m-net?".

Sergeant Francis looked shocked as he'd never broken his connection from the m-net. "I believe I can although I've never done it before".

Danks continued, "Secondly, I want a police

vehicle that's also not connected to the m-net".

"I'm not sure that's possible sir" retorted the sergeant. It was clear that he was feeling a little uncomfortable with what Inspector Danks was asking for.

"Nonsense sergeant, I do that all the time back on Earth. We'll contact Doctor Mason. I'm certain he can cobble something together for us. We'll send him a message from reception here". Danks could feel the panic permeating the air from the sergeant.

"Don't worry sergeant, I'll do all of the driving".

Chapter 32

Half an hour later a new police vehicle arrived with Doctor Mason at the wheel. He pulled up to an undamaged tube that was at the back of the building.

Sergeant Francis and Inspector Danks thanked the porter for his impromptu hospitality and they went over and got into the vehicle. It was a tight fit when all three of them were in it.

"I'm glad you asked for this. I've been dying to test this little bit of retro kit out for some time" Doctor Mason said with excitement.

"I think the term 'dying' doesn't need to be used in this context does it Doctor Mason?" replied Sergeant Francis worriedly.

Danks let out a quiet laugh as the police vehicle began to accelerate away. It whizzed passed the police recovery crew that were hard at work. They were taking detailed holographic images of the whole accident area.

"You don't seem to be very concerned sir that we are in a vehicle that doesn't have IHU control" the sergeant stated with alarm.

"I'm certain that we are in safe hands with

Doctor Mason at the helm". But just in case, Danks pressed a button next to his seat that engaged a safety belt around his waist and shoulders. Sergeant Francis noticed and quickly followed suit.

"I have to get back to the lab as I've made some progress on one of the victim's IHU.

Not all the data was erased, it seems they were not seeing what was directly in front of them. So, I'll have to leave this vehicle with you but you should be able to drive it with no problems. Take care of it as I have only one other like it" Doctor Mason said as he swerved out onto the main highway heading back towards the CMPC headquarters.

"I drive these all the time back on Earth. I'll show Sergeant Francis what to do seeing as he isn't on the m-net any more" replied Danks.

"I haven't been on the m-net for quite some time. I quite like having the excitement" added Dr Mason.

It wasn't long before they pulled into the headquarters where Doctor Mason left them to return to his lab. Danks climbed into the driving seat and placed his hands on the steering wheel. "You're used to guiding the AI in the vehicle from your IHU. This is a real steering wheel. It works in essentially the same way, except you have to turn it using your arms rather than your thoughts. Now let me see if I can remember how to drive this" he said with some amusement.

"You seem very jovial sir considering we've just had a very narrow escape back there" said the sergeant.

"The likelihood of the police vehicle losing control is sufficiently remote that I'm certain now that this is a murder investigation. It appears that someone is getting nervous and is trying to eliminate us. The case is getting much more interesting. That's why I wanted this police vehicle. It's imperative that it's not on the m-net. It makes it more difficult if not impossible to trace".

"..and control" added the nervous sergeant.

Danks felt better now that he was driving. He didn't like anyone else controlling the vehicle as he never liked the way they drove. He was an awful back seat driver.

"Relax sergeant, the AI in this vehicle is still perfectly capable of assisting us drive, it's just not connected to the m-net".

The police vehicle accelerated out onto the highway heading for Maria Anderton's flat which was in the old part of down town.

Chapter 33

It was ten minutes before the route tracker told Danks that he was at his destination. It was awkward getting into their pressure suits within the vehicle. There were no pressurised tubes in these buildings and the vehicle Dr Mason had provided was smaller than the usual ones. So they had to do it the old fashioned way. At least the suits were comfortable and the helmets were manageable.

They depressurised the cabin and stepped out into the dusty street. The buildings stretched off into the distance like the old terraced houses back on Earth. But here on Mars they were box like grey concrete structures. They had flat roofs with rounded edges where they joined the walls. These buildings were designed to withstand the strong storms that swept through the area. Dotted here and there were small portals to allow light into the premises.

As they walked towards the building their feet kicked up clouds of dust and small vortices swirled in their wake that drifted across the road surface before disappearing. The storm was beginning to abate. Behind them the police vehicle resealed its door.

Once at the building entrance, Sergeant Francis pressed his arm, with his ID chip in, against a panel on the main door. After a short pause it slid to one side and they moved into the small cramped space that was the entrance chamber. The door sealed behind them and there was a whistling noise as it pressurised.

A green light flashed in the ceiling indicating the sequence was complete and the inner door opened.

They stepped into a dimly lit hall that was the height of the building. On their left side was a set of tall lockers specifically for pressure suits.

They each selected a locker. Removing their helmets they slid them onto a shelf inside. Then, wriggling out of their dust covered suits, they hung them under the helmet shelf.

Danks closed his locker door and pressed his thumb on a small rectangular panel in the centre of it. A blue light quickly flashed across his thumb and the sound of locking bolts rang out around the hall. His suit was now safely stowed away. He heard the dust removal start up inside the lockers. It would be nice and clean for when he returned.

The sergeant explained, "In the early days, Mars was like the old western towns of North America back on Earth. Suits were regularly stolen. That's why lockers were installed in all the buildings".

They headed towards Ms Anderton's flat which was on the first floor. Number 176 had been sealed off until the case had been officially closed.

As they walked up the wide staircase to the first floor someone brushed past them heading downstairs. They were already in their pressure suit and were wearing their helmet.

"They're in rather a hurry" thought Danks.

The sergeant and the inspector walked next to one another along the corridor. The doors were staggered on either side so that there weren't any two doors directly opposite one another. This was to give people some sense of privacy in such tightly packed living quarters.

After passing numerous doors they arrived at room 176. There was a police lock on the door but it was hanging loose. What was left of a police surveillance drone was lying strewn on the floor opposite the door. One of its limbs was twitching as though it was trying to stand again.

"What's happened here? It shouldn't be like this" said the sergeant. But before Danks could stop him, he started pushing the door open. At that moment there was an explosion that threw both of them into the wall opposite. The window of Ms Anderton's flat blew out and the contents of the room started to be sucked through the gaping hole.

In anticipation of such events happening, the

designers of the building had made the windows small. Also, each flat had sensors to detect any decompression and it would trigger an emergency metal barrier to close across the window stopping the flow of air out of the building.

The shutter in Ms Anderton's flat began to close. But while it was sliding shut Danks and the sergeant were struggling to breathe as the pressure in the corridor had dropped drastically. With a clunk the shutter sealed the opening and everything suddenly went quiet. The wind subsided and the air pressure returned to normal.

Danks struggled to his feet, he was only slightly bruised, but Sergeant Francis had some bad burns on his left arm. Danks crouched down next to the sergeant and checked his wounds. "We'd better get you to a hospital sergeant".

Danks stood up and touched the screen of his wrist watch. A voice responded which echoed in the hall. It asked for a call destination. He spoke into it, "Connect me to the CMPC quickly".

A second later the CMPC responded. "How can I help you inspector?" came the reply.

"I need a medical team at Buzz Aldrin Street, building 2, flat 176 immediately".

There was a pause before the police operator, whose face was displayed on the watch screen, responded with a clear acknowledgement. They replied that the ambulance would be there in the next five minutes.

The CMPC downloaded a code to his phone so he could track the ambulance on a map displayed on his watch.

Danks continued, "Also, arrange for the forensic team who are dealing with Ms Anderton's flat to get here ASAP".

The operator confirmed that they had been informed and they would be on their way immediately.

Danks rang off and crouched down again next to the sergeant. He lay grimacing on the floor with his head pressed against the wall. His face was bloody and he was holding his arm gingerly. Droplets of blood dripped off the end of one of his hands.

"You'll live sergeant. We were lucky that you didn't open the door all the way as it took most of the blast. I wasn't quick enough to stop you, next time let me go first as I've experienced this sort of thing before. My colleague did the same as you once but she wasn't quite so lucky. She ended up in hospital for a month".

The door of the flat was now hanging loose on only one of its hinges. The other was broken from the blast and then the decompression had nearly ripped it off the remaining hinge.

The light unit on the ceiling in the corridor had come out of its fitments and was swinging from side to side. It created strange shadows that swam around the floor and walls.

Danks saw that what was left in the room had been scattered all around and the drawers of the only cabinet had gone. He realised that they had been forced open as the rapid decompression wouldn't have dislodged them that easily. They were normally held shut with a finger print lock but he could see that the fronts had plastic splinters protruding. Something had definitely been used to force them open.

A notification came in on his watch and he glanced down to read it. The message said that the medics had arrived outside. They had flown in and landed on the roadway just outside the building. He could hear them entering the hallway just as his watch started ringing. He tapped the screen to answer. It was one of the medics calling him.

"Hello inspector, we have just entered the building. Where are you?" said the medic.

"We're on the first floor. Turn left at the top of the stairs and we are about one hundred meters down the corridor outside room 176".

Two medics soon arrived and were clustered around the sergeant scanning him. Eventually, when they knew he hadn't any serious internal injuries, they put his arm in a brace and helped him to his feet.

"He has a broken ulna which has punctured

through his skin, also severe burns to his hand and lower arm with lacerations to his face. We'll take him down to our ambulance for treatment".

One of the medics guided the sergeant gingerly down the corridor towards the stairs where the ambulance was waiting outside.

The remaining medic scanned Danks from head to foot while walking around him. After a while, she looked up with a confused look on her face. "I can't seem to find your IHU. It seems to be malfunctioning. Are you feeling okay?" she asked with some concern.

"I'm feeling perfectly fine and the reason you can't detect my IHU is that I don't have one" replied Danks.

"Oh, I see from your ID chip that you are from Earth. That would also explain your stocky build. You'll be pleased to know that you have no detectable injuries. It appears that your stronger bone structure protected you from the decompression more than the sergeant".

"I was also slightly further away when this happened and the sergeant took most of the force" replied Danks.

The medic looked around at all the damage, then turned back to Danks. "A window blowout wouldn't create this level of damage. What has caused this?".

"This destruction was the result of a small

explosive device that had been placed behind that door. You can see the hole with scorch marks around it".

"But who would do something like that?" enquired the medic.

"Ah, now that is the million dollar question yet to be answered".

The medic received a message that she was needed at the ambulance. "If that's all sir, I'm needed back at the ambulance to help with Sergeant Francis".

"Okay, you'd better go and help. I have a few jobs to get on with here. Will you let me know when he gets out of the hospital?". Danks would have to manage on his own now that the sergeant was out of action.

"There won't be any need sir. We have all the facilities down in the ambulance to treat him right here. It will take no more than ten minutes" she said with a little pride in her voice. "We've all the latest equipment in the ambulance".

"That's very impressive, they don't have anything like that on Earth yet. If you need me, I'll be examining the scene for any clues". At that point the medic set off at a brisk pace heading for the stairs.

Danks stepped carefully into the room and tiptoed around the wreckage. He was scanning around for anything significant and checking for more explosive traps.

There was quite a lot of debris near the window. It had fallen there when the emergency window cover had sealed shut.

Danks flicked over a couple of items with a retractable metal rod that he always carried with him for just such occasions. He was looking for anything of interest that may have dropped and been covered by debris. He searched for about ten minutes, but there wasn't anything of significance.

Just as he was about to give up he did a final scan around. Something caught his eye in the corner of the room. There was a printed sheet protruding from the underside of a tipped over chair. It looked as though it had been deliberately pushed into the seam of a cushion. The person who'd set the explosive device had failed to find it.

He carefully pulled the sheet out of the cushion and unfolded it. The print out was a copy of an old article from the Mars Times. It was about a young woman who'd been arrested for accessing a secret technical report on bypassing the controls on the Integrated Head Units.

In the end she was released with no charge as there was insufficient evidence.

The name had been erased because the case had been dismissed and it was illegal to retain someone's name if not found guilty. What it did indicate was that the person had lived in Australia back on Earth.

Danks folded the paper back up carefully and slipped it into a pocket in his jacket. To ensure he didn't lose it he zipped the pocket shut. He thought that a paper printout was a bit old fashioned but at least it couldn't be erased.

He turned to leave and saw the sergeant was standing in the doorway. His arm had a thin transparent plastic covering over where his wound had been. It extended from his hand right up to the elbow. It completely encased his arm and stretched just like normal skin.

"The medics say I have to go back in a week or so to have the 'ab-skin' removed. It's an artificial breathable skin and it acts just like normal skin. It allows the damaged areas underneath to recover.

They also repaired my broken arm with a cement that they injected with a micro surgical machine and my whole arm was clamped so that the break was held together while the glue set. They say it's better than new now".

He stood there flexing the skin by moving his wrist and arm about. "You can see the wounds and burns through the ab-skin but it feels a lot better" he said in fascination. It was just like a child transfixed with seeing a wriggling worm on the soil surface for the first time. Danks was amused at the sergeant checking out his ab-skin.

Now that the sergeant was on the mend Danks

returned to the investigation. "The police forensic team should be here soon and they'll uncover whatever evidence that's left. In the meantime we need to find out who that person was that pushed past us on the stairs".

"I'll call the security operators to see if there are any usable images of the individual on the cameras in the corridor and stairs" replied the sergeant.

At that moment the forensic team announced their arrival in the building with a lot of clattering noises. They had several boxes of equipment that had to be carried up the stairs and down the corridor to room 176.

"Make sure you collect all the material that was sucked outside, we don't want to miss anything.." Danks said firmly to the head of the forensic team, "..and make sure you scan the walls for any hidden compartments".

The compartments were often well hidden and only the owner's finger sliding along the hidden seam on the wall would reveal its location.

Danks asked the forensic team to send their report directly to him in the usual CMPC encrypted format. He then said to the sergeant that they should return to their vehicle and they headed towards the stairs.

Retrieving their pressure suits from their lockers, they squeezed back into them and then left the building through the pressure chamber returning to their vehicle. They climbed inside it and sealed the doors behind them.

After removing their pressure suits they settled back into their seats. Danks started a video call to the company that operated the security camera system and he transferred the call to the vehicle display so the sergeant could join in.

They had to negotiate a mountain of security questions before they were eventually put through to the AI controlling the camera systems. They explained that they needed to view the recent footage for the building they had just come from.

The AI routed the images of the corridor for the period leading up to the explosion. Unfortunately, there was nothing caught on the video images until the sergeant and the inspector appeared walking down the first floor corridor.

"Why are there no camera shots preceding this?" Danks asked the AI.

"The camera feed was broken for thirty minutes prior to this" replied the AI.

"Do you know why that was?".

"No, but when the connection was re-established the video images in the corridor are what you have been shown".

"Do you have any camera footage of the outside of the building at this time?".

"Yes, this is the recording we have".

An image appeared showing an individual

exiting the building in their pressure suit.

"Can you identify that person in the suit?" Danks frustratedly asked the AI.

"Unfortunately, there are no clear views of the person's face. However, the vehicle did have an identification chip".

"From that can you determine who the vehicle belongs to?".

"The vehicle isn't owned by an individual. It's registered to the company Cerebralnet. The last known user of the vehicle from their information page was a Mr Lynch. Is there anything else I can help you with?".

"No thank you" and with that the screen went blank.

Danks dialled HQ. "This is Inspector Danks, can you do a trace for me?".

"Can't the sergeant do that for you inspector?" said the officer at HQ.

"No as he's taken himself off the m-net for the time being".

"Oh, okay, certainly sir" said the officer.

"Have any officers found Alex Lynch yet? He was in prison for assaulting Sergeant Francis and was released a few years ago".

The call went quiet for a minute. "There have been no sightings of Alex Lynch and we are unable to locate him. It seems he is not currently on the m-net".

"Yes, we know that" replied Danks. "Okay, has anyone been over to Mr Lynch's residence yet?".

"According to the records, no officer has been assigned that yet".

"Well, get Officer Robertson to head straight over there and find out if he's there. If he is take him back to HQ. We need to find out why he was at my hotel, where he was when we arrived here at Ms Anderton's apartment and why he's disconnected from the m-net".

"Yes sir" came the reply from HQ.

Danks terminated the call. "Why has no one been over there?" he thought to himself.

Danks then turned to the sergeant, "In the meantime we'd better pay a visit to Cerebralnet and interview this Doctor Taylor".

Danks put the destination into the navigation and he accelerated the vehicle off in the direction of Cerebralnet's head office.

Chapter 34

Danks pulled the police vehicle up outside a large white building. It had the words Cerebralnet gleaming across the top of the exterior. Just below the sign read the words 'the only way to get ahead' which he thought was a strange use of the words as the IHU's were inserted into people's heads.

As soon as he'd stopped, the usual walkway tube extended out to them. The tube clamped onto the exterior of the vehicle but in doing so it give it a sharp jolt.

"That must be because the vehicle isn't connected to the m-net. It's not communicating with the system in the building controlling the tube and probably isn't getting the information about how far it is from the vehicle. Are you sure this is safe sir?" said the sergeant with alarm.

"Yes it's safe sergeant. That sort of thing doesn't happen back on Earth. Maybe the sensors on the tube are not functioning correctly".

Once the walkway tube was attached, the door opened and Danks stepped out into the tube.

"This is their main building sir. I won't be able to accompany you as a message has just come in on the CMPC comms pad from headquarters. It seems that something has happened to Officer Robertson. They haven't specified what at the moment".

"Okay sergeant, I think I can handle it from here. Don't worry about picking me up I'll get a taxi back to headquarters". Danks walked to the end of the tube and stepped into the main foyer.

Doors slid quietly together behind him and the tube then retracted from the police vehicle.

Danks watched as the sergeant gingerly drove off with a slight swerve in the steering every so often.

"Hmm, it looks like the sergeant is getting used to Dr Mason's modified vehicle. Although it appears the AI is trying to correct his driving. The question is will he cope with driving the retro vehicle once he's in heavy traffic" he thought. He saw that the sergeant was hesitating at joining the highway.

At that moment his wrist watch rang. It was from HQ. He tapped the face of the watch to accept the call and Dr Mason's face appeared on it.

"Hello Dr Mason, have you anything new to report?".

"Hi inspector, I'm afraid I've some bad news. That IHU that still had some video information on has been erased".

"How did that happen?" asked Danks trying to

hide his annoyance.

"I connected it to the m-net to analyse the images and as soon as I did something from the network came in and erased it. By the time I realised what was happening it was too late".

"In a perverse way that somehow doesn't surprise me. I'll explain when I'm next back at HQ. I have to go as I have an appointment here at Cerebralnet" and with that he terminated the call.

Danks walked over to the reception desk. Leaning towards the receptionist he began, "Hello.." and noticed the name badge on the person's jacket. "..Katherine, I'm here to see Doctor Taylor she should be expecting me. My name is Inspector Danks".

"Hello inspector, she has already been informed that you've arrived" she replied.

"How did you know it was me?".

"The AI image recognition system in this building tracks people via their facial features and matches it up with their IHU or ID chips. It scanned your ID chip as you entered the building so I knew it was you before you arrived at my desk".

"That's interesting, what would have happened if they didn't match up?" he asked inquisitively.

"We've never experienced anything like that. But if that were to happen I think our security guards would be alerted and the individual apprehended very quickly.

Our security system has been updated with your details. You have clearance to enter certain restricted areas of the building. If you would follow the drone it will take you to Dr Taylor's office on the top floor".

The drone was about three feet tall with two spindly legs. It had two hemispheres on the front side of its body that acted as its eyes and they swivelled like the eyes of a chameleon.

It was stood next to the reception desk and when Katherine pressed a virtual button on her screen, the drone sprang into life. It started moving forward and Danks had to walk briskly to catch up with it.

He shouted, "thank you Katherine" and she nodded in appreciation. She thought it was nice to have a visitor who was polite for a change.

The drone stepped onto an escalator and Danks followed. He felt quite unnerved that this small machine was guiding him through the building.

After a couple of floors, the drone began marching down a corridor and came to a halt outside a door that was entirely made out of opaque glass with a brain emblem etched into the surface.

Danks caught up with the drone and came to a halt next to it. The opaque glass door slid back revealing a large room with a single desk on the far side of the room with a chair in front of it. There were a couple of settees against one of the walls and a long table with chairs around it for meetings.

A lone figure was standing behind the far desk staring out of the window over the red landscape towards Olympus Mons in the distance.

Danks suspected that the individual was deep in thought as they didn't seem to notice that he'd entered the room. He cleared his throat to catch their attention. The person turned slowly, their silhouette was black against the red background. It was a very feminine hour glass figure that was accentuated by the fact that she was wearing a pencil skirt and a top that was a snug fit around her waist.

There were no lights on in the office, so the reflected orange-red glow from the outside was the only source of light filling the room.

As the silhouette walked towards him it created a long shadow that stretched across the room towards him. He heard her say, "Good afternoon inspector, I'm Doctor Taylor. I'm the Chief Technical Officer and the Chief Executive Officer at Cerebralnet or at least until a new CEO is elected".

As she approached he could make out the fine detail of her face. Danks thought that Doctor Taylor had a unique kind of beauty. She had an attractive face with blue eyes that seemed to shine when she looked at him. She had long rich coloured auburn hair and her body was beautifully highlighted by her close fitting clothes. She wore expensive looking shoes and she walked as though she was a model on a catwalk.

Her movements caught his attention and he found it difficult to concentrate on what his next question was going to be.

"Can I get you something to drink?" she purred.

It seemed an age before he answered as it was as though he was spell bound by her voice.

Danks pulled himself together when he became acutely aware of the silence and blurted out, "Yes please, I would love one. Could you make it an Earl Grey tea as they can't make a decent cup of tea back at HQ? Something to do with either no one drinks it there or the drink machine has the wrong programming on how to make it".

She approached her desk and waved a hand over a small pad on the surface. "Katherine can you arrange for a lemon tea and an Earl Grey to be brought to my office?".

"Certainly" came the response.

She turned towards Danks and sat on the edge of the table that seemed to accentuate her physique even more. "I thought this meeting was with two officers from the CMPC?".

"Unfortunately, Sergeant Francis has been

called away on an urgent matter".

"Ah, I see. So, I'm just left with you".

Danks felt a bead of sweat run down the side of his face. He quickly wiped it off with a tissue that he pulled from his pocket.

"Now, inspector, I'm not quite sure why you needed to see me. I've had to cancel an important meeting to accommodate you".

"I'm sorry you've had to do that. I assure you it's quite important for our enquiries" he responded.

"So, what is it that I can help you with?" she looked pensively at Danks.

Danks's throat seemed to go dry. "Where was that damned cup of tea?" he thought to himself. After clearing his throat a few times he forced some words out through the dryness. "With the recent unusual deaths of individuals, some of whom were employees here at Cerebralnet, I would like to find out what those people were working on here?".

Dr Taylor seemed to mull the question over a while. "All of them were managers or directors and didn't really work on any projects. However, they were aware of what we were and still are working on. They were kept informed as to the progress on a weekly basis". She shifted her sitting position on the table. "We work on the way data is processed and displayed to the IHU user. Each department develops detailed routines that can be tested on a computer model. But ultimately it has to be tested with the help of a user's IHU".

"Do you do any research into viruses?".

"Of course not inspector. We specialise in IHU implants and the associated software".

There was a short pause while she stood up and walked around to her seat behind the desk and lowered herself majestically down into it. "We don't initially use a live brain. We have a system here where the brain is simulated with each of the departments latest work pulled together in this virtual brain. Only once all the tests have been completed and passed the rigorous requirements can we proceed to the next stage. We use the guinea pigs or maybe I should call them volunteers for the final testing".

Danks was a little surprised to hear Dr Taylor referring to the human volunteers as though they were just guinea pigs. It did seem to be rather cold and calculating. He also thought she'd realised that and became friendlier suddenly. He continued with his questioning. "Have you noticed anything unusual recently with any of your employees?".

"To be quite honest, inspector, many of our software engineers are bordering on the insane anyway. So asking me to notice anything unusual is like asking if a baboon is out of place in a tribe of baboons".

Danks also thought what a strange way to refer to her work colleagues.

Just then a four legged drone, which looked a lot like a medium sized dog, entered the room with the much needed tea. They were on a tray that was neatly balanced on, what Danks thought looked like, its head. As it moved towards the table near Doctor Taylor, the drone raised the tray and gently slid it onto the table surface.

Once the tray had been delivered the drone turned and trotted out of the office, just like a dog, to perform its next task.

"I assume you don't want sugar with your tea as sugar is quite an expensive item here on Mars".

"No sugar thanks".

"Do you want milk? I should point out that the milk is generated from a genetically modified bacterium that secretes something akin to cow's milk. I rather like it, it's got something that is difficult to describe. Some people are a bit squeamish about it".

Danks couldn't bring himself to having bacterium milk even if he'd wanted it. Although he did think how could it be any different from having milk from a big lumbering creature like a cow?

"I don't have milk with Earl Grey, but thank you anyway" he replied.

Dr Taylor handed Danks his cup. She then

returned to the other side of her desk where she sat down on the luxurious seat and swivelled around on the seat to stare out of the window.

Danks lifted his tea to his lips. He took a sip and felt the warmth of the liquid in his throat. It wasn't as hot as he usually liked it, but then, here on Mars, the atmospheric pressure inside the buildings was lower than on Earth. This meant water boiled at a lower temperature. At least it was warm enough.

"Can I ask if you knew a Maria Anderton at all?". Danks didn't let on what he knew about her as he wanted to see where the conversation would lead.

"The name sounds familiar. Let me check our records".

Dr Taylor sat up from her reclined position and swept her hand over her desk screen several times. Each time she selected a name from a pull down menu. After a short while she leaned back on her chair and replied. "She came in to have her IHU checked because she was having some problems".

"And what were those problems?".

"Well, they were just minor glitches that just needed small adjustments to meet her requirements" she replied. "Some people like to have some quirky features added to the usual installation".

"So what were these adjustments that were

carried out and was she fully informed of what was being done?" continued Danks. He felt it very important to fully understand what had happened to Maria as all the facts were needed in order to reach a conclusion.

"We record all consultations and modifications performed on our customers for legal reasons. I can recover the records of Maria if you want me to?" she said and then she took another sip of her drink.

Danks nodded his head. "Could you forward these to the police HQ so we can analyse them?".

"Certainly, but I don't think you'll find anything useful. It's all quite mundane really".

"All information is important in order to build the correct picture of events in a case. Surely, you as a scientist should know that".

She seemed to hesitate, but then she leaned forward and started typing on a virtual keypad in front of her for a few minutes. Eventually she leant back, "I've forwarded the files to Sergeant Francis".

Danks thanked her. "Does everyone with an IHU come here for treatment?".

"No, only certain individuals who require a more detailed treatment. Most updates are done remotely and it's up to the user if they want to accept the changes".

"But I thought you said Maria had only minor

problems and that her IHU just needed a fine adjustment? Surely by coming here that meant she had a more serious issue with her IHU".

"Not really, she had requested specifically to see me".

"Really, then why didn't you remember her straight away?".

"I'm very busy and see many people so it had slipped my mind".

"So why do you think she wanted to see you in particular?".

"I have no idea as her problem was nothing out of the ordinary. I did suggest she saw the company IHU consultant but she was quite insistent".

"You talked directly with her on the IHU link?".

"Yes, and from the readings I was getting over the link there wasn't any reason for her to come to see me. However, she insisted that there was something she wanted to discuss in detail".

"And what exactly was it she wanted to see you about?".

"I'm not entirely sure. After examining her there was nothing wrong with her IHU. I did the new uploads that she wanted and she then left feeling more confident that everything was okay".

"Are these new uploads included in the information you sent Sergeant Francis?".

"Naturally, I've included everything that we have on Maria".

"Did she talk about anything else while you were treating her?".

"Nothing significant, it was mainly girl talk".

"Are you sure it was all girl talk? Her friend, Mr Upton, seems to think she was investigating the deaths of the Cerebralnet employees".

"Really, she didn't mention that she had a friend she confided in".

"Do you have the recording of the meeting?".

"Not for that meeting".

"I thought the company policy was to record all patient meetings?".

"It is, but this was bypassed for some reason. The video and audio were supposed to be recorded by one of the assistants. But apparently there was a fault on the data stream from the room at the time".

"Who was it that was supposed to be recording this meeting?".

"According to the logs it was supposed to be Tim Wang".

"Can I talk to him?".

"Not really as he hasn't been into work for quite some time now. He's currently registered as absent. You need to check with Katherine on reception as she was trying to contact him".

"Can we locate him with his IHU?".

"Possibly but you need to check with...".

Danks cut in to complete the sentence, "...with

Katherine?".

Dr Taylor looked slightly annoyed at his interruption, "...no, I was going to say 'with reception' but I suppose that equates to being the same thing".

"Has Mr Wang been registered as a missing person with the CMPC?".

"No as he's a contractor and we don't keep tabs on them. Now why don't I give you a virtual tour of Cerebralnet and introduce you to some of the engineers working on our new developments" she said with what appeared to be a sudden enthusiasm.

She handed him a pair of what looked like dark sun glasses. "You'll need these to do the tour as you don't have your own IHU".

As he placed the glasses on, he could see the room clearly but from a different location. He took them off and looked at them. The glasses were completely black on the outside but on the inside there was an image of the room. As he moved them up and down the image followed where he was pointing the glasses. He slipped them back on and scanned around the room. He could see Dr Taylor standing and he could see himself sat in front of her.

"All you have to do is stay sat where you are and I'll guide you around the building".

Their virtual presence proceeded out of the

room and turned right down the corridor. Danks noticed a reflection in a window and it was an image of a drone. So the images projected back to him were from the eyes of a drone as it moved around the building.

Dr Taylor controlled where they went with her drone and his followed close behind. However, he could control where his drone looked by turning or tilting his head.

They moved swiftly down the corridor and then turned sharply right and went through a small doorway that was specifically designed for drones so they could move freely between rooms.

As the drones passed through the door, Danks saw that they'd entered a room where there were several people sitting at large 3D terminals. They were manipulating blocks with their hands and fitting the virtual blocks together.

The drones stopped and Danks could hear Dr Taylor's voice. "This is where each child's IHU is constructed to their parent's specifications. The IHU is made up from memory blocks, transceivers and a sophisticated neural network webbing. Once implanted in the child, their own body builds upon this webbing to allow all this to integrate into their brain.

Through the webbing, the user can access the transceivers and memory blocks. This gives them a greatly enhanced memory and the ability to access the m-net. Once fully integrated the user can control all these processes simply by their thoughts".

"Do you have an IHU Dr Taylor?" asked Danks.

"No I don't as I lived on Earth in my youth".

"I'm sure that these enhancement features are quite useful. However, what about someone externally gaining access to the IHU?".

Dr Taylor was quiet for a short time before answering. "I'm not quite sure I understand you".

Danks decided to be a little more blunt. "Could a person be manipulated or controlled through their IHU? A bit like in the early years of computers where scumbags would download viruses or trojans into other people's computers to disrupt or control them".

"There are numerous barriers in the way preventing someone gaining access. The individual can block them easily as they would quickly become aware of an external illegal access".

At that moment something caught Danks's eye in the corner of the room. He was sure he'd caught a glimpse of a shadow moving across a wall through a glass door on the far side of the room. It had a large warning sign on it saying that it was sealed and no one could enter.

Danks turned around to face Dr Taylor. "What's behind the sealed door?".

"That door is a relic from the first colonisation

of Mars. It's from the days when they used the old fashioned nuclear fission reactors to generate the electricity they needed".

"Does anyone go in there?".

"No, it's strictly forbidden because it is unsafe. It was built into the side of the cliff that this building is connected to. The old tunnels are unstable and have high levels of radioactivity".

However, Danks was convinced that he'd seen something moving in there. "Can our drones go in so we can have a look around?".

Dr Taylor moved rather awkwardly on her seat then replied, "I don't think that's possible as the door's sealed".

"Can we have the seals broken and get the door open?".

"I don't see why you would want to do that as there is nothing to see in there except radioactive cylinders. The contamination may escape if the seals are broken and the tunnels could collapse".

"Why, exactly, does Cerebralnet still have this here? Why not brick it shut?"

"It's because when the company first started in this building, it was cheap to rent and these tunnels came with the original building. Anyway, we must end this tour as I have a prearranged meeting that I can't cancel".

A moment later Danks's virtual glasses were removed and Dr Taylor was standing over him holding the glasses. "I'll arrange another appointment with you, but as I said I have an urgent meeting".

Danks got up from his chair. "Maybe next time I can talk to some of the engineers and we can take a look inside that sealed off area?" he said.

"I'll talk to our safety department and see what they say" she replied.

As she showed him out they stopped at her office door. "This drone will escort you back to reception inspector" and with that she pressed the close button.

The door slid shut behind Danks and he was alone with the drone in the corridor. Through the glass he could see her return to her desk. "Now that seemed like I was cut off rather quickly" he thought to himself. The drone lead him back to reception.

"Before I leave Katherine, what is the current status of locating Tim Wang?".

"There is no further information. His IHU is not registering on the m-net".

"Where was his IHU last located?".

"It went off line when he was on his way home".

"Can you tell me, was it the same day that Dr Taylor had a meeting with Ms Anderton?".

"Well, yes, it was. That does seem to be rather a strange coincidence don't you think?".

"Not really Katherine. I feel this fits into the jigsaw rather well". Danks continued, "Could you do me a favour and order me a taxi?".

"One has already been booked. In fact it's waiting for you right now". She pointed in the direction of the walkway.

"You're extremely efficient. Thank you".

She nodded in appreciation.

When he arrived at the end of the tube, he waved goodbye to Katherine and climbed into the taxi that was waiting for him.

As it pulled away from Cerebralnet and started to accelerate he could see Dr Taylor watching him from her high up office window. Just as he began to focus on her, a cloud of Martian dust blew past and when it cleared she was gone.

Chapter 35

When Danks returned to the CMPC HQ he was given the bad news that Officer Robertson had died.

"What happened sergeant?".

"For some unknown reason Officer Robertson removed his helmet before he'd entered the building where Mr Lynch was believed to be living. I just don't understand why he would do that" replied the sergeant. He couldn't get his head around the fact that he'd lost a colleague and a friend.

Danks asked Sergeant Francis to get all officers to give top priority to finding Alex Lynch and Tim Wang.

Danks drove back to his accommodation with the sergeant in the passenger seat. They drove in silence as it was hard to accept that the CMPC had lost a good officer.

On arrival at his hotel, Danks climbed out and the sergeant moved over into the driving seat.

"Now you are sure you'll be okay driving this retro vehicle sergeant?".

"I'm sure sir. Although the annoying AI keeps

adjusting my driving. Anyway, I'll see you in the morning inspector".

Danks watched as the sergeant accelerated slowly off into the distance with a cloud of red dust rising in his wake.

After such a traumatic day, what was required was some food, a strong drink and a shower in that order.

Danks needed some quiet time to think this case through. He entered the hotel and headed straight to his room.

The hotel had stocked the fridges in the guest rooms with a few simple meals. Danks selected one and heated it up in the microwave.

While eating it, he reviewed all the videos the commissioner had given him. There wasn't anything new he could see that was of any use. After his meal he prepared a strong drink.

Danks needed a shower. His clothes were covered in Martian dust through getting in and out of the pressure suit. He carefully removed them and placed them in the laundry box that was to be collected by drones during the night. The following morning they would be returned clean and ironed ready for the new day.

Danks picked up his drink and took a long gulp. It was just what he needed. As he put his glass down there was a buzz from the doorbell. He quickly wrapped a towel around his waist and went over to the door.

Looking at the image of the person outside on the door screen Danks was surprised to see that it was Dr Taylor. He opened the door. She was standing in the corridor wearing a tight fitting dress that emphasised her hour glass figure. Her clothes were a matching red with red stiletto shoes. Her lips were a luscious red. She breezed in past him without saying a word. He caught the fragrant scent of her perfume as she glided past.

"This is a pleasant surprise Dr Taylor I wasn't expecting to see you. I'm sorry, you've caught me about to have a shower. But how did you get past the hotel security?".

She slowly turned and replied, "I told reception we were friends and I wanted to surprise you. Anyway, I thought I'd come over so that we can get better acquainted. Maybe over a drink? Our meeting was cut short and let's dispense with the Dr Taylor, call me Nikola".

Danks felt a strange surge of feelings that he hadn't felt for some time. "That sounds like an excellent idea. Why don't you make yourself a drink Nikola while I just have my shower. That Martian dust seems to get everywhere" he replied.

As she walked to the drinks dispenser unit, he hurried off to have his shower.

Danks felt relieved to be under the hot shower washing all the grime of the day off. His feelings were beginning to settle down when suddenly Dr Taylor stepped into the shower next to him. She was naked and his first thoughts were that she was even more beautiful than he had imagined.

"You disappeared off to the shower so quickly, I thought maybe I should join you" she purred. She moved closer and kissed him. Her hand slipped up behind his head to hold him. His mind was buzzing with excitement as he folded his arms around her waist and pulled her closer.

Danks slid his hands down her back until he reached the bottom of her spine. He carried on until he felt the fullness of her buttocks in both of his hands and he squeezed them tight.

Moving his finger between the cheeks of her bottom, she seemed to respond with a slight moan as she pushed her tongue deeper into his mouth.

Putting his other hand over her belly button, he slowly moved it down between her legs. He felt her take a short breath as he began caressing her. She relaxed as he gripped her buttock tighter with a hand.

She felt his fingers pressing firmly against her. Her lips became soft and her tongue stopped moving as she let herself succumb to the pleasures.

With the warm shower water running down her back and with him caressing her she tensed up in a spasm as her climax washed through her body.

She pulled away, stepped out of the shower and

lay down on a towel that she'd already set out on the floor. He followed her out and lay down on top of her. His head was dizzy with the smell of her perfume, the warmth of her body and the sensuousness of caressing her skin.

She was moaning quietly as he made love to her. With their bodies entwined, they kissed deeply until his climax surged through him.

They lay there for some time kissing. Then he got up and helped her to her feet. "I'll just finish off showering, put some clean clothes on and we can have that drink you mentioned earlier" he said with a smile.

She walked out of the room to collect her clothes and get dressed. He jumped back in the shower.

He finished showering, grabbed a towel to quickly dry himself and went to the bedroom to dig out some clean clothes. As he was about to return to the living room, he heard the door of the apartment close. He thought that he must have left it open and went out to check. He was surprised to discover that Nikola was no longer there, she had left.

Chapter 36

The following morning Danks got out of bed later than he'd wanted. He headed to the shower room where he leaned on the basin and stared at his bristly face reflected in the mirror. "Time to have a shave" he muttered to himself. He washed and shaved then returned to his bedroom where his clothes were waiting after being cleaned overnight.

Once in the small kitchen he made himself a hot coffee.

Danks couldn't help but think why did Nikola come over to see him and then leave without saying anything?

Why had she decided not to stay for that drink after the good time they'd had last night?

The TV flashed that there was an incoming call. Danks answered it and Sergeant Francis appeared on the screen. "Ah, sergeant. Any news on Alex Lynch's or Tim Wang's whereabouts?".

"Nothing yet sir, but there is some progress over at Harry Ramsdale's crash site".

"Okay, what is it?".

"The site investigator is suggesting we go over there. Unfortunately, it's a full day's flight. I'll pick you up so we can head over to the CMPC aerodrome. I'll be there in twenty minutes sir".

"You'll find me in the dining area" replied Danks.

"Okay, sir" and the sergeant rang off.

Danks dashed off for his breakfast as he didn't want to be travelling all day without having something to eat.

Just as he was finishing his breakfast, the sergeant arrived. Danks thanked the waitress and both he and the sergeant left for their trip to the South Pole region.

Thirty five minutes later Danks and the sergeant arrived at the aerodrome. Once inside the pressurised dome they clambered out of their vehicle.

Dr Mason was already there and he seemed glad to see them as he was hopping from one foot to another with a big smile on his face. "You're going to love this. I've prepared the special CMPC aircraft as you asked. It's got no m-net connection. It should be exciting to fly. I've only tried it once" he seemed to be envious that he wasn't coming along.

Danks was an accomplished pilot back on Earth and quickly familiarised himself with the aircraft with Dr Mason's help. "Right sergeant shall we head off".

"With respect sir, I think I would be more use

staying here. I can then carry on investigating Alex Lynch's and Tim Wang's whereabouts. Also.." the sergeant seemed a bit hesitant.

"Go on sergeant, spit it out" Danks urged, but he had a feeling he knew what this was all about.

"..well sir, I'm a bit nervous about flying in an aircraft without an m-net connection".

"That's okay sergeant, I understand. Maybe you're correct. You can update me when I'm back".

Dr Mason added, "You're missing an exciting ride".

"I think I've had plenty of excitement with your road vehicle" the sergeant replied with some relief.

Danks climbed into the aircraft and sealed the door behind him. He taxied the aircraft towards the aerodrome exit as the sergeant and Dr Mason waved him off.

Once out of the aerodrome, the aircraft took off vertically. Danks pushed the joystick forward and there was an exhilarating sensation of acceleration. He swept the craft around before straightening it up. The heading was the South pole of Mars.

Danks had the coordinates of the crash site. He punched them in to the AI navigation and the aircraft banked to follow the new route. As it flew along he couldn't help but notice how barren the scenery was as it passed by. Out here there were no signs of habitation.

After a couple of hours the aircraft was getting close to the edge of the southern icecap. The AI system warned him that he needed to increase his height as the ice ridges were approaching on his current heading. He took the aircraft higher. He didn't want to have a similar accident to Harry Ramsdale.

The aircraft was now flying about two hundred meters above the ice sheet below. Danks could see the delicate fingers of the white snow ridges extending out over the red landscape.

As the aircraft flew on towards the crash site, the ground below eventually turned completely white. Danks was now flying over the southern icecap. He thought how beautiful, how desolate and yet how deadly.

The sun was setting and Danks still had a couple more hours of flying before he arrived at the destination. He could see red streaks across the sky above him where the sun's rays scattered off fine dust in the upper atmosphere. He leaned forward and turned on the lights which illuminated the ice sheet below.

Every so often deep ravines would flash by in the lights. Danks could just make out what he thought were caterpillar tracks winding their way across the ice sheet below him. There were hardly any people out here. It was only the very rich who wanted to escape the clamour of the cities and who could afford to have a remote residence in this location. "The night sky views must be spectacular. This was probably what the rich people were after living out here" he thought.

The AI system warned Danks that he was approaching his destination. He was just thinking he should contact the station at the crash site when a voice came over the communication channel.

"Unknown aircraft, please identify yourself. We have picked you up on radar and yet you are not visible on the m-net".

Danks responded quickly, "This is Inspector Danks flying the CMPC aircraft K4 requesting permission to land".

"Ah, I was wondering if anyone was coming from the CMPC. Glad you've made it inspector. I'm Anne Wilson I'll switch on the landing lights for you".

Suddenly he could see the station and the landing site was lit up in the blackness ahead.

The station consisted of four units.

The first unit was the accommodation.

The second unit was the canteen and the communal office.

The third unit was where the machinery was kept to keep the station running. It had the processing plant that extracted drinking water from the station's liquid waste. Solids were compressed into cubes ready to be processed by the mushroom farms. Carbon dioxide was extracted and recycled to produce the oxygen to breathe. It also generated the heating, lighting and pressurised the air for the station.

The fourth unit housed the nuclear fusion reactor which was the beating heart. Without it they couldn't survive for long out here in this frozen wasteland.

The station could support a maximum of ten people. With Danks's arrival, it would be a tight squeeze at the maximum personnel count.

Danks deftly brought the aircraft to a halt above the landing site. Slowly he descended until he felt the landing gear engage with the ground and the information on the panel in front of him indicated it was safe to turn off the engines.

The communication channel rang out again, "I will meet you in the main cabin at the station inspector. I've turned on the lights on the pathway to show you the way here. Please don't stray away from the path as there are precipitous drops on either side".

Danks exited the aircraft in his pressure suit. He walked down the ramp and stepped onto the ice and the door of the aircraft closed behind him. He was alone on the icy surface with only the pathway lights eating into the darkness that surrounded him.

The station was some two hundred meters away from the landing site. The Martian wind kept buffeting him with the occasional snow flake blowing past illuminated in the lights of his helmet. He was glad there were hand rails as the path got particularly narrow in places.

He followed the lights and occasionally he could see down into deep crevasses that were on either side of the path.

After several minutes of struggling against the conditions, he arrived at the station. The entrance door was at the end of one of the units so he moved towards it.

The station stood above the ice on long legs to keep it away from the cold ice. Danks climbed the stairs to the door and opened it to enter the station. Once he'd stepped inside, he closed the outer door and pressed a red square on a screen on his right hand side that had the word 'pressurise' flashing within it. Air whistled into the small cabin and when it was fully pressurised the red square turned green. He removed his helmet just as the inner door opened.

"Welcome inspector, I'm Anne Wilson. You've arrived rather late. I assume you want something to eat".

"I certainly do and after that some rest. It's been a long flight out here".

"I was thinking we could make a start inspecting the crash site in the morning" she replied.

"That sounds great". Danks removed the rest of

his pressure suit and hung it up.

"I'll show you where the dining room is" and Anne led the way.

After a small but sufficient meal, Anne showed Danks to his bedroom for that night.

"Sorry inspector, but we don't have a lot of room here in our temporary accommodation. It's been brought in over the ice to the crash site by snow trucks".

"I think I saw some of the caterpillar tracks on the ice as I flew here" replied Danks.

She stopped outside a narrow door. "This is your room for the night. It was my room so I'll be bunking up with one of the other ladies as she's two beds in her room".

"That's very kind of you. You know I could have slept in the aircraft".

"But that would be even more uncomfortable".

"Well, all I can say is thank you again. I'll see you tomorrow".

"Good night inspector" said Anne and then she retired to her temporary sleeping quarters further down the slender corridor.

Danks opened the narrow door into the tiny bedroom. His first view of the accommodation made his heart sink. Hung on the wall was the bed that folded down and nearly filled the width of the room. There was a small basin with a tap at the far end of the bed and not much else. There was a communal toilet just down the corridor. He squeezed through the door entrance and closed it behind him. "Ah well, at least it's for only one night. The others here have to endure this until they've completed the recovery" he thought.

Danks lay on the bed and watched some TV for half an hour. Then read for a short while until his eyes were getting heavy.

Standing up from the bed he turned to use the basin and had a wash. Afterwards, he unrolled the sleeping bag that he'd got out of an overhead cupboard and he laid it out on the bed. As he undressed, he folded each item and put them back in the same cupboard. Then climbing onto the bed he slid into the sleeping bag. It was quite restricting but he managed to zip it up and shifted around until he thought he'd found the most comfortable position. Eventually, he drifted off into a shallow sleep.

Chapter 37

In the morning there was knocking on Danks's bedroom door that dragged him out of a deep sleep. He managed to unzip the sleeping bag so he could stretch over and partially open the narrow door. Anne Wilson was standing in the corridor. "Good morning inspector, I thought I'd better come and see if you were awake".

"Sorry Anne, I must have overslept. Give me ten minutes to get ready and I'll see you in the dining area" he said sleepily.

"Okay" said Anne and Danks closed the door. He eased himself out of the sleeping bag and began getting ready.

When he arrived at the canteen he realised how small it was. The night before it had felt bigger as it was empty, but now it was jammed full of people. There was only room for two small tables and they were both occupied.

"We can get some food and take it to the communal office inspector".

"That sounds like a good idea" he said.

They collected their food and had to squeeze their way past several people before they could exit the canteen.

The communal office was a little larger than the canteen and there were some spare seats where they could sit.

While eating Anne said, "We'll descend into the ice fissure this morning so you can see the crash site for yourself".

"Sounds dangerous!" responded Danks.

"Not really, we've installed a lift to take us down to the site. However we have already discovered some information about Mr Ramsdale. We recovered his body a few days ago and managed to access his IHU".

Danks anticipated the response, "Don't tell me, it was completely erased".

"Not quite. The IHU was blank except for a few seconds of video just before the crash".

"That's interesting, what was recorded?".

"I'll show you" and with that she pointed to the screen on one of the office walls.

A video started showing what Mr Ramsdale had seen as his aircraft descended down into the crevasse. Danks heard the audio of Mr Ramsdale saying, "What the hell.." and then the video went blank.

"The recording stopped at that point because the aircraft hit the bottom of the crevasse. It seems Mr Ramsdale suddenly came to his senses and tried to pull the aircraft up but it was too late".

They finished their breakfast and Anne continued, "We can head down to the crash site now".

They left the office heading for the station exit. Putting on their pressure suits and helmets they stepped out of the station into the forbidding cold of the south pole.

Arriving at the lift they manoeuvred themselves into the cage. Anne shut the wire mesh door behind them and started their descent.

After about five meters Danks could see the gouges of the wings of the aircraft as they hit the sides of the crevasse on its doomed dive.

Anne pointed at the marks, "This is the point where we'll lose contact with the m-net so it might be a bit of a shock for you. It took me by surprise the first time I experienced it when I came down here".

"I won't find it disturbing Anne, as I don't have an IHU and my aircraft isn't connected to the m-net".

"Really? That would explain why you didn't appear on our m-net system last night".

"Did Mr Ramsdale's IHU recording start at this point?".

"Yes, I was going to say that it was roughly here in his descent".

"That would explain a lot" said Danks as another piece of the jigsaw could be added to the case.

They arrived at the bottom of the crevasse and stepped out of the lift cage.

The lights attached to the side of their helmets illuminated the way ahead. On the walls above the fuselage were deep gouges showing where the aircraft had slid down just before it came to a sudden halt. Danks walked past the fuselage looking for any clues.

As Anne neared the front of the aircraft she said to Danks, "We found Mr Ramsdale's body over here inside the cockpit".

Danks moved towards where she stood and peered into the cockpit where the body had been. There were signs of frozen blood splattered around the headrest in the cockpit. He noticed an area of blood that looked as though it had been scrawled with a finger on the cockpit control panel.

"We had to apply a special stain to highlight where the frozen blood was otherwise you wouldn't have been able to see the detail with all the ice crystals".

"How long do you think Mr Ramsdale could have survived after the crash?".

"It wouldn't be for long as the front windscreen shattered a few seconds after the impact. The instruments indicate a sudden decompression. With the rapid pressure decrease he would've asphyxiated and his blood would've started to boil within his skin. The temperature would drop and his body would eventually freeze solid. Not a pleasant way to die".

"Would there be sufficient time for him to write something if he knew his IHU had failed?".

"I suppose so. He may have detected that it'd stopped recording. We think he must have touched the back of his head as there was blood found all over his right hand. It's possible that he may have realised at that moment that he hadn't got long before the windscreen blew out".

"Would you say that smear of blood was the start of the capital letter 'A'?", Danks pointed at the area on the control panel.

"We had thought that his hand had done that accidentally as he slumped forward, but yes, I can see that it does resemble a letter 'A'. Do you think it could be significant?".

"It could be. The prime suspect at the moment is an Alex Lynch. Maybe Mr Ramsdale was trying to tell us who he thought had caused his accident. There are some officers trying to locate Mr Lynch at this very moment".

"Can you find him via the m-net?".

"No as he's disconnected himself from it".

They inspected the site for a couple more hours for further evidence but there wasn't anything Danks thought was noteworthy. The important thing was that letter 'A' scrawled on the control panel. He took some images of the area for his records.

They both returned to the lift and started to head back to the surface. On the way up Danks said, "I would suggest that you and your colleagues disconnect from the m-net until further notice".

"Why? Do you think we are in danger?" replied Anne with alarm.

"I believe it'd be safer for all of you".

The lift stopped at the surface and they returned to the station.

"Now that you have seen the crash site we will remove the remaining wreckage and take it back to headquarters for further examination. We've already laser scanned the site and it's stored on the headquarters main frame if you need to study it further inspector".

"Thanks. But just in case, I suggest that you keep a copy on an isolated system so that it can't be tampered with".

"Do you think someone could do that?".

"It's already happened back at HQ with an IHU Dr Mason was working on".

Collecting his belongings from the room he'd slept in, Danks shook Anne's hand and said his farewells as he had a long trip back. It would be gone midnight by the time he'd arrive back at the aerodrome.

He left the station in his pressure suit and found

his way back to his aircraft along the treacherous path. Once he was inside he removed his protective gear leaving it in a heap by the door and he jumped into the pilot seat. Booting up the system he prepared for lift off.

"Safe trip back inspector" said Anne over the communication channel.

"Thank you Anne, see you back at HQ" and with that the aircraft lifted off gently. Once he'd gained sufficient height Danks pushed the joystick forward and to the left. The aircraft swept around and over the station, heading northwards towards the CMPC HQ.

The trip was long and thankfully uneventful. Danks mulled over the new information. It was now looking certain that this Alex Lynch was behind all the deaths. It was paramount that they apprehended him as soon as possible.

Some time later, Danks arrived back at the HQ aerodrome and taxied into the hangar. It was late, so he climbed into the last remaining specially modified vehicles of Dr Mason's who'd left it there for him the day before. He positioned himself in the driving seat, set the coordinates for his hotel and pushed his foot down on the accelerator.

Leaving the aerodrome he drove out onto the dark but empty highway. "It should be a nice and quiet drive to the hotel" he thought.

By the time he got to his room it was two in the morning and he was exhausted. He quickly got ready, climbed into his bed and, as soon as his head hit the pillow, he fell into a deep sleep.

Chapter 38

Danks was dreaming that the TV was making a ringing noise and he was trying to ignore it. But then he woke up. With bleary eyes he saw that there was a real call coming in. In the centre of the TV was a flashing phone symbol. It meant someone was trying to contact him so he sat up in bed and answered it. An image of Sergeant Francis appeared on the screen. "Good morning sergeant. I assume it is morning" Danks said half yawning.

"Good morning sir, although I'm not sure about the 'good' part".

"Why do you say that sergeant?" as he yawned again.

"We've found Tim Wang, however you won't like it sir".

"Don't tell me, he's dead". Danks shook himself out of his tiredness.

"I'm afraid so sir. A citizen was searching an area about five kilometres north of the city for old meteorites. In the process he came across an arm that was protruding from the soil surface and he reported it to the CMPC straight away.

When we uncovered the body the AI identified

it as Tim Wang. The reason we couldn't locate his IHU was because there was a bullet hole in his pressure suit helmet. It went through the back of his head destroying the IHU.

While we were there, we also discovered two more bodies that had been buried in the same crater. They were identified as Officer Jameson and Officer Adamson. They too had both been shot in the head destroying their IHU's". The sergeant went quiet for a moment and then continued. "That's not all sir. Tom Upton's body was found hanging in his office yesterday.

According to the forensic report there was no evidence of foul play. It concludes that he must have hung himself".

"Okay sergeant, make your way over here and bring Dr Mason with you so he can pick up his other modified vehicle. Then we should head over to Cerebralnet headquarters as I think it's important that we see inside that restricted area in their building".

"It'll take me about twenty five minutes to get there sir. I'll call when I arrive at the hotel".

"I'll be here in my room" and then Danks terminated the call.

Danks got dressed and prepared a small breakfast in the kitchen as he wouldn't have time to go down to the dining area. During his breakfast there was a buzz from the door. "Was this another unexpected visit from Nikola?" he thought.

Danks switched the TV over to show the door camera, it was Sergeant Francis. "Funny!" he thought, "the sergeant was going to call when he was coming over. Maybe he forgot. Anyway, he's got here earlier than expected".

Danks decided to let him in rather than make him wait. He instructed the door to open and it slid to one side allowing the person in the corridor to enter. He swivelled his chair around to face the door. However, it wasn't the sergeant that entered the room, it was a masked person who promptly raised a gun.

Danks tried to dive towards a nearby table but at that instant he heard a muffled bang. There was a sharp pain in his neck. He tried to raise his hand in response. The room became blurry and he felt dizzy. To stop himself falling he made a grab for a table top but missed. He slid down the side of it and collapsed to the floor. Sprawled on the ground he thought, "Well is this how it's going to end?".

As he lay there motionless, he saw a pair of red, dust covered boots approach. But then darkness descended and he passed out.

Chapter 39

As Danks regained consciousness, he struggled to focus. His vision was blurred but he could make out that he was in a well lit room and there was a faint humming noise from some machinery in the background.

The left side of his face was lying on something soft and lifting his head he saw it was a cushion. Scanning around he concluded he was probably on a sofa. He tried to push himself up but found his hands were tied behind his back with electronic handcuffs. His feet were similarly bound. He managed to swing his legs off the sofa and by moving his head from side to side on the sofa back he was able to get into an upright position.

His vision was settling down and he could make out the silhouette of someone standing with their back towards him at a console. He squinted to improve the image he was seeing.

The silhouette turned out to be a woman in a tight catsuit. She had long auburn hair which cascaded down her back, a bit like Nikola's. Her figure was an hour glass shape, a bit like Nikola's. He began to think this was too much of a coincidence when she turned around. It was Nikola!

"So you're awake. You've been unconscious for over an hour".

That would explain why he was feeling so hungry and needing to go to the toilet.

"Where am I?" Danks said in a quiet and hoarse voice. He cleared his throat and asked again.

She replied, "I don't think you need to know that.

You're proving to be rather a nuisance. If only you'd got an IHU I could have arranged a suitable ending for you".

"What have you done with Sergeant Francis and why did you shoot me in my room?" he said croakily.

"That wasn't me, it was Alex. He only drugged you with a dart gun. All I did was monitor your TV signals going to your room. During the sergeant's call to you, I thought it was a perfect time to send Alex in place of him. When he rang your doorbell I replaced the door camera feed with a video clip of Sergeant Francis. That fooled you into thinking he'd arrived early".

Danks realised why he was feeling dizzy, it was the side effects of the drug he'd been darted with. "So..", Danks cleared his throat again as it was dry, "..Alex and you were involved in the accidents of your co-workers".

"They were idiots. They were trying to control me and the money I needed to complete my father's project. They started to suspect I was misusing the funds and threatened to cut the supply off".

"So that's why you killed them?".

"I wouldn't say that. They killed themselves with a little help from me" she said with a satisfied look on her face.

"I'm guessing you hacked into their IHUs but how?".

"Very good inspector, you're not quite the PC plod that I thought you were. I've been working on the IHU software for some time and my father had deliberately left a security flaw in the hardware. He knew that one day he, or rather I, could exploit this feature that allowed me to gain control of any individual. I can project any images or thoughts into that person's mind".

"So you took control of your victims. That, in my book, means you killed them".

"'Kill' is a bit of a strong word, let's just say I gently nudged them in the right direction" she said with an evil laugh. "When you first arrived at Cerebralnet I gave you a little nudge with the walkway tube just for a laugh. It would have been sweet to destroy your vehicle with you in it but the safety system wouldn't let me do that".

"So, that was you and not a sensor issue" he

said.

"Yes it was me. Unfortunately, I was unable to control you as you didn't have an IHU".

"Why are you doing this?".

"I may as well tell you as you'll be dead soon and won't be able to tell anyone".

"Lucky me!" said Danks with dash of sarcasm which seemed to miss the mark as Dr Taylor continued.

"My father started the IHU project, as you know, back on Earth but it was banned when problems started to happen".

"You mean children started dying".

"That's the price of progress inspector" she said in a cutting voice. She switched back to being calmer, "anyway, the Mars authorities saw potential in his work and he moved out here.

However, after making breakthroughs and everything was working well, the board of directors at Cerebralnet forced him out. He died shortly afterwards because he was a broken man. Apparently he stepped out of an airlock with a protective suit on then removed his helmet. I was only a baby at the time and after the funeral my mother made the decision to return with me to Earth.

When I graduated from university I decided to come back to Mars and pick up the work my father had been doing. I managed to uncover his log books online at Cerebralnet and that's how I found the loophole in the security. He'd planned it all along so I decided to use it.

I was funnelling money into this side project and was developing a system that could not only control one person but large groups of people. That way I could govern the whole of Mars".

"You do know that you sound just like some despots from history such as Hitler and Stalin?".

"Someone has to bring order to disorder".

"Presumably you use that console to take control?".

"Right again, I put on this headset so I can see what I've programmed the console to project into their minds via their IHUs".

"So, with Matt Hitchen, who died when his vehicle drove into the Coprates Chasma canyon, you projected an image of the road ahead. I'm guessing you made him think it was a straight road and he simply drove over the edge without knowing it".

"That's right, you're in the wrong job inspector. I did similar things for Charles Lowe and Harry Ramsdale.

As for Mr Ramsdale, he came to me saying he was going to divert my funds elsewhere. But, with a little help from me, he conveniently flew his plane into a crevasse. I got him to disengage the AI system and then made him think he was flying horizontally but he was actually in a dive".

"So why did Maria Anderton have to die. Was she getting too close?".

"She was an interfering bitch. She'd gathered sufficient information to nearly work out what had really happened. I suspected that she had an inkling that I'd removed Matt and Charles, but she didn't know how I'd done it. She came to quiz me about it as you know. I fortunately found out that she was meeting with that Jim Burgess who I knew had uncovered more than he should have. So, it proved convenient to kill two birds with one stone as you might say.

You see, Jim Burgess had taken himself off the m-net but he'd forgotten to take his vehicle off it too, so I knew where he was. Ms Anderton didn't know about me controlling the IHU's so I took control of her. I nudged her and her vehicle in the direction of Mr Burgess. It was a particularly pleasing result when they were both eliminated".

"I'm certain you tried to frame Mr Burgess's wife with their murders".

"Yes, it was quite simple to modify and distort the truth with her school records. I was hoping the CMPC would add two and two together and come up with three" she seemed to smile at that thought. "Unfortunately, it didn't fool you".

"Presumably you were unable to gain access to Alice, Mr Burgess's AI system to control her?".

"Right again inspector. No matter what I did that annoying system wouldn't let me access it.

When I've finished with you I'll make sure Alice is terminated. We can't have AI systems thinking for themselves.

I located the sergeant at Mrs Burgess's apartment and realised that you'd probably been talking to that Alice machine. So, I thought it was time to get rid of you and the sergeant.

Stupidly I should have waited until you were both in the police vehicle. But I was a bit too impetuous and I took control of the vehicle ramming it into the walkway tube. I thought that would be the end of your meddling. Sadly you both escaped". She paused then said, "I assume that was when the sergeant left the m-net as I couldn't trace him after that?".

"Yes, I had a feeling someone was tracking us and the m-net was the most likely route".

"Clever of you to also find a vehicle that wasn't on the m-net".

"That was courtesy of Dr Mason".

"Ah yes, I've not been able to find Dr Mason on the m-net recently" she said in an annoyed tone.

There was a short pause before Danks swapped tack. "While at Ms Anderton's flat I came across a hidden old newspaper article. A young woman had been arrested for trying to access a secret report on bypassing the security protocols on the IHU's. I'm guessing that was you?".

"Yes, it was. As I told you, the report had been written by my father so I saw no reason why I couldn't access it.

After that I had to change my identity and reinvent myself. It cost a fortune to change my ID chip and my face so that the AI systems wouldn't recognise me. I even had my DNA slightly modified. The process was extremely painful.

You wouldn't know this but I used to have black hair and after the DNA treatment it gradually turned auburn. I must say, I rather like this new look".

Danks thought it was a good look as well but he wasn't going to tell her that. "So what's your real name if it's not Dr Taylor?".

"I don't think you need to know. Nobody knows that other than my mother".

He continued with another question, "Is that why you sent Mr Lynch to clear out her flat?".

"When I thought you were getting too close I sent Alex over to remove all evidence she had. But he obviously failed as you found that article. I'll have to reprimand him later for that".

"What about Tim Wang, did he see and hear more than he should have when he was recording your meeting with Maria?".

"Yes, he came to tell me that he would forward the recording to the police authorities unless I paid him to keep quiet. I persuaded him to go home and I'd sort out the money.

Annoyingly, Mr Wang had disconnected himself from the m-net so I got Alex to escort him home. He fortunately came to a sticky end in a remote crater where your nosy sergeant found his body.

If only the sergeant had continued to remain on the m-net I could have arranged for you both to have had a tragic accident". Her voice was filled with venom.

"What about Officers Jameson and Adamson, did you kill them and have them buried in the same crater as Tim Wang?".

"No, that was Alex. Apparently they followed him to a cave system near Olympus Mons. He took it upon himself to eliminate them. I didn't think he needed to bother as they weren't making any progress in finding out what had happened".

"And what about Tom Upton, was he an annoyance?".

"Ah, yes, I heard about that. He was a minor nuisance. However, I wasn't involved with that either. It was just a happy coincidence. It seems he couldn't get over the death of Ms Anderton. Your visiting him stirred up memories, so one might say you and the sergeant killed him. However, I would have got rid of him at some point anyway" she said with an evil smile. "The reason I let you and the sergeant continue with your investigations was that I wanted to see how good your reputation was. I must say, you did seem to piece together some things relatively quickly. So your reputation does have a small amount of truth in it.

Anyway, once I've sorted the problem of what to do with you I will deal with the sergeant via other means. I'm sure Alex will assist me in that area".

"Has Mr Lynch forced you into doing all these bad things?". Danks was hoping beyond hope that she would show some remorse or a glimmer of redemption. Either that or she would at least come to her senses.

"Of course not. He's a stupid man just like you. He loves me and he thinks I love him but actually I use that to manipulate him into doing what I want. He is just a tool that allows me to arrive at my final goal. Getting rid of Tim Wang is an example of how obedient Alex is".

At this point it dawned on Danks that Mr Ramsdale wasn't trying to scrawl an A for Alex. It was the start of an N for Nikola. Unfortunately, he must have died before managing to complete the first letter. "So Mr Ramsdale tried to communicate to us that you were the one controlling him by trying to scrawl your name with his own blood".

"Did he really? I didn't know that. I lost contact with his IHU as he dived into the crevasse. I thought that would be the end if it. I did manage to erase his IHU just before he crashed".

"Yes, you erased his IHU, but it started recording again after you lost contact with him. Unfortunately, he wasn't able to tell us your full name but he did write one thing on the console".

"So, he survived long enough to record some information and scrawled something to help you. But only you know it was me and you'll be terminated soon".

"Tell me, why did Bill the security guard have to die? Did he find out Mr Lynch was the unrecognised person in the corridor?".

"He caught Alex snooping around your floor and realised that the AI system hadn't recognised him. He tried to detain Alex. That's when I got 'Bill', as you call him, to take a walk into the hotel basement with Alex assisting him. I controlled him from this very console". She patted the console as though it was an obedient dog.

"I wondered why he ended up sitting against the door. Presumably Mr Lynch placed him there?".

"How annoying. I told Alex to just leave him in the pressure chamber. But I guess he had some perverse sense of humour and must have propped him up just inside the basement. His body must have slumped back against the door before it froze".

At this moment Danks remembered he needed to visit the toilet even if he was about to die. "If you are going to kill me would you grant a dead man a final request. Could I visit the men's room so I can go to the toilet?".

"I suppose I should allow you that final wish after that bit of fun we had the other night. Although, it was purely a means to an end for me. Besides, I wouldn't want you to relieve yourself in here and ruin the carpet".

She swept her hand over the console and selected a name from a list that appeared projected above the console. It was Alex Lynch's name, the very person Officer Robertson had been tasked to find before he died.

She spoke into the microphone that she was wearing. "Alex, get down to the control room. I have a job for you" and then she swept her hand over the console again to terminate the call. She continued, "I usually try and eliminate people myself but when they take themselves off line I can't get at them. That's where Alex comes in useful. He has been a loyal servant to me but at some point he'll have to be sacrificed for the cause".

"We've been hunting for him for some time".

"Ah, yes, he came close to solving my problem with you and the sergeant by nearly blowing you both up.

Alex then had a problem with an Officer Robertson but I sorted that for him. Sadly the officer carelessly removed his protective helmet before he'd entered the building that Alex's flat is in".

"He was a good officer with a family. Didn't you think about that before you killed him?".

"He was getting in the way" she said with anger.

It seemed to Danks that Dr Taylor was revelling in the power she was wielding. He was familiar with this sort of despot and their complete disregard for life. "This woman must be stopped, but how?" he thought to himself.

At that moment Lynch entered the room and Dr Taylor gestured in Danks's direction. "Take the inspector to the men's room then bring him back here".

Lynch pointed a handset at Danks and the ankle restraint fell to the floor. He grabbed him by the arm, yanked him to his feet and pushed him in the direction of the exit.

Chapter 40

Danks was thrust through into the men's toilet as though the door wasn't there. It made his face smart and Lynch seemed to get some pleasure out of it.

"I thought I'd managed to get rid of you and that annoying sergeant the other day but somehow you both survived the explosion". He shoved Danks towards a urinal and let go of his arm. "I would've loved to see you both get sucked through the window onto the Martian surface".

"I'm sure you would've" Danks replied sarcastically.

For a second Danks stood in front of the urinal thinking Lynch would undo the handcuffs but in the end he had to prompt him. "Unless you want to help me unzip my pants and get the old todger out, you'd better release my hands".

Reluctantly, Lynch removed a handset from his coat and pressed a button. One side of the handcuffs was released so his hands were free.

While Danks was relieving himself he asked, "Are you in love with Dr Taylor?".

"What's it to do with you?" Lynch snapped.

"Well, she told me that she'd have to sacrifice you for 'the cause' at some point".

Lynch seemed to get angry at that. "You're talking through your backside. She loves me and I love her. When all this is over I have plans for both of us to live happily together here on Mars".

As Danks zipped his trousers back up he carried on trying to annoy Lynch. "Well, she and I had a really good time the other night. She couldn't keep her hands off me".

That did the trick. Lynch lost control and leapt at Danks. The inspector was ready and instinctively swung his right fist up with the handcuffs on. It struck Lynch on the underside of his chin. Lynch momentarily staggered back but then his eyes widened and lit up. It was obvious the red mist had descended. He rushed at Danks with his arms out as though he was going to tackle him to the floor. Danks felt himself thrust back and they both slammed into the wall. For a second Danks was winded.

Lynch lifted Danks up the wall by his throat. The inspector was finding it hard to breathe. He had to do something quickly. With his left fist he punched the right side of Lynch's face hard. Lynch staggered backwards and fell to the floor. Danks slid down the wall and managed to land on his feet. He moved away from Lynch keeping the wall to his back.

Blood ran down the side of Lynch's face from a cut near his eye. He wiped the blood off with his hand.

Danks said, "Stay down or I'll put you down again".

Lynch started to stand and rushed at Danks again with his head down. However, Danks was expecting this as so many criminals don't like being told to stay down. He quickly stepped to his left and grabbed the out stretched right arm of Lynch. Using Lynch's own momentum he threw him against the wall. There was an almighty bang and blood ran down the wall where his face had collided with it.

As Lynch turned around looking stunned, Danks hit him with a right punch to the solar plexus. Lynch crumpled forwards winded. Danks had his opportunity and followed through with a left punch to Lynch's right temple. He fell to the floor with a heavy thud and was out cold.

Danks stood there for a few seconds while he regained his breath. The slam against the wall had knocked the wind out of him. "Good job I went to all those martial arts classes" he thought.

Danks searched Lynch's pockets and found the handset for the handcuffs. He released his other hand, pulled Lynch's hands behind his back and secured them with the handcuffs. Dragging him into one of the cubicles Danks sat him on the toilet. He closed the toilet door behind him and locked it.

"Now you just wait there while I go and have a little chat with Dr Taylor" he said smiling to himself. He exited the men's toilets and crept back towards the control room where he'd last seen her.

Chapter 41

Danks realised that the control room was in the radio active 'NO ENTRY' area of Cerebralnet. It was the door he'd seen on the drone tour. He pushed it open and entered the corridor. "So much for it being sealed" he thought. He remembered seeing a moving shadow the last time he was here. That was when Dr Taylor had cut the tour short. It must have been Lynch's shadow he'd seen that day.

Danks quietly crept down the dimly lit corridor. He reached the entrance to the control room and looked inside expecting to see Dr Taylor at the console. There was no sign of her in there.

Suddenly, a hard object hit the back of his head and he fell into the room.

Lying on the floor he watched stars floating around in front of his eyes. He rubbed his head where he'd been hit but saw that there was blood on his hand afterwards. "That wasn't very smart letting someone sneak up on me" he thought to himself.

"Get up" demanded Dr Taylor.

"You know you could've just asked me to enter

the room rather than hit me over the head".

"Yes, I could've, but where's the fun in that?".

She kept a gun aimed at him as he struggled to his feet.

"Did you really think I'd let Alex take you to the toilet without me watching everything through the security cameras?".

"I thought you might have used Mr Lynch's IHU to watch me get my tackle out".

"Oh get over yourself. Besides, his IHU is off line. The other night was purely business. I just wanted to see where you were in your investigation. While you finished off showering and were getting ready I had a quick look around. I found nothing that indicated you were making any progress in the case, so I left".

"I wondered why you'd got dressed so quickly. I thought we were going to have a drink. Probably a good job you didn't stay as you'd probably have poisoned it".

"Enough" she said, "Head for that door over there". She pointed with the gun towards a red door with a warning sign on it. It said 'Radio Active Area'.

Danks pushed the door open. He could see down the dimly lit corridor.

She pushed him in the back with the barrel of the gun forcing him down the passage way.

They walked in silence down the corridor.

Motion sensing lights turning on as they moved down it. Not all of the lights were working and some only flickered but there was sufficient light to see where they were heading.

As they approached the end of the corridor, Danks could see the edge of a deep crevasse that cut straight across the end of the passageway.

To the left was an old disused lift that descended down the side of the crevasse. He started to walk towards the lift.

"No, I want you to walk to the edge and look down" said Dr Taylor with some annoyance. "You won't be needing the lift".

He stepped to the edge and could only see darkness below. "HQ will find out that it was Mr Lynch that abducted me from the hotel. So they'll trace him to here" Danks said nervously.

"No they won't. I disabled the AI and security systems at the hotel for the whole time it took Alex to extract you. So no one knows you're here and your dead body will never be found at the bottom of this crevasse. Only Alex and I come down here" she replied with some pleasure. "Do you know it's where they stored all the radio active waste in the early years? It's said to be one hundred metres deep. It doesn't take long to reach the bottom, especially if you don't use the lift". She seemed to revel in that statement.

At the edge Danks tuned to face her, but she

then shoved him in his chest with the barrel of the gun. He started felling backwards as his feet slipped off the edge of the crevasse. He flailed around with his arms hoping to catch hold of something. As he fell, a jagged rock protruding from the wall of the crevasse halted his descent and he clung on desperately.

Dr Taylor peered over the edge expecting to see him falling but instead saw he was clinging to the side of the crevasse wall. "Why won't you just die?" she said with some venom in her voice. She pointed the gun at him and he closed his eyes resigning himself to the worst.

But just then there was the muffled noise of a projectile being fired. He opened his eyes to see Dr Taylor drop the gun. She seemed to be shaking and then she stumbled forwards. Her footing slipped off the crevasse edge.

He saw the look of horror on her face as she fell past him. He stretched out a free arm in an attempt to save her but to no avail.

Chapter 42

Sergeant Francis peered over the edge of the crevasse and saw Inspector Danks clinging to a solitary rock about four feet below.

The sergeant looked around and found some old discarded cable that must have been used for the lift. He dropped it down to the inspector. He grasped it tightly and the sergeant pulled him up.

He dragged Danks away from the edge of the crevasse. They lay there for a few seconds recovering their breaths and let their heart rates recover.

"I thought she'd killed you sir. I arrived just as you fell into the crevasse. I only meant to taser her. I didn't think she'd go over the edge".

"Thank you sergeant I'm so glad you turned up when you did. It's unfortunate that she fell into the crevasse".

"Unfortunate indeed" said the sergeant.

"How did you know where I was?".

"Before I went over to your hotel, I received a message from Alice saying she had some useful information. What she'd discovered was that there were some anomalous signals that were sent to

Officer Robertson just before he took off his pressurised suit helmet. Alice told me it took a little while to isolate them but eventually found their origin. Anyway, to cut a long story short it pointed to here in Cerebralnet. This delayed me getting to your hotel.

I tried calling you but I got no answer. When I arrived at your room I found that you weren't there. There were dusty footprints on the carpet and I remembered you saying you wanted to head to Cerebralnet. So, I took a gamble and decided to come straight here. The building was still dark and there were a couple of security guards in the foyer. They said they'd last seen Dr Taylor down in this section only an hour earlier so I came down to investigate".

"Well I'm glad you did sergeant. It's a good job you followed my advice and disconnected from the m-net as she would probably have killed you".

Danks, now recovered, got to his feet and they both walked back up the corridor.

As they were returning to the control room the sergeant asked, "Just out of curiosity sir, how would she have killed me?".

"You wouldn't know, but she'd found a way to interfere with anyone's IHU and via it she could control them. She was syphoning money away from the company to finance her research. It was all directed at making a system to control large numbers of people at any one time. If she had succeeded she would've taken complete control of the planet".

"That's scary, I guess I'll have to remain disconnected from the m-net".

"Not necessarily, sergeant". Danks stood next to the console that she'd used for controlling her victims. "Destroy this console and everything is back to normal. Probably best to get Dr Mason to come over with the strictest orders to take it permanently out of action. In the meantime, we must restrict access to this area until he's dismantled it completely".

Just then some officers scurried in and the sergeant told them to cordon off the area until further notice.

"By the way, you'll find Mr Lynch handcuffed in a cubicle in the men's toilet. He won't be in a happy mood.

Arrange to have him taken back and put into a cell. We'll charge him with the murders of Tim Wang, Officer Jameson and Officer Adamson. Also, the assault of an inspector and I'm sure there are several other charges we can pin on him".

The sergeant and the inspector then left the control room heading for the building's exit.

Danks needed something to eat and he'd seen a place nearby called the Martian Maypole. Maybe they could get something there.

Chapter 43

A few days later, Danks had packed his bags and was looking forward to returning to Earth.

Sergeant Francis had come over to drive him to the space terminal where he'd catch the space-lift.

"Hi sergeant, thanks for offering to take me to the spaceport. I could've got a taxi you know".

"It's my honour sir".

"I guess we don't need to be so formal now, call me Tristan".

"Okay sir, I mean Tristan. Please call me Stuart".

"So, what has happened since I was last in at HQ?" asked Danks.

"Dr Mason said the console was interesting and complex, but he's managed to put it permanently out of action".

"What about retrieving Dr Taylor's body?" Danks said with some sadness.

"We sent some drones down to the bottom of the crevasse. Well, this is the funny thing, no matter how much they searched they were unable to find her body. There were slide marks down the cliff face and there was rubble where her body should have ended up.

One thing the drones did find was that there were lots of tunnels leading off in all directions. It seems the early settlers used them to shelter from the harsh environment and there were old bits of equipment down there.

The area was later used as a dumping ground for the radio active material. The drones tested for radio activity but the whole area is clear of radiation. It must have all been removed a long time ago.

Some of the officers are now going to descend down into the crevasse and do manual searching. If she survived I'm sure we'll find her".

"I hope she has survived as she should be brought to justice" said Danks.

"You know Tristan, I find this whole case has tainted Mars" the sergeant said sadly.

As Danks picked up his bags he said, "Well, now that the console has been decommissioned all this will soon be forgotten" and they left his accommodation for the last time.

Back in the hotel lobby they strolled down to the police vehicle. Danks placed his bags carefully inside it closely followed by himself and the sergeant.

Danks sat in the driver's seat and the vehicle door closed behind them. He grabbed the steering wheel, pressed down on the accelerator and sped off towards the spaceport.

Danks glanced back at the building that had been his residence for the last few weeks and he was glad to be leaving. The bad memories were being left behind.

"You know Tristan, I have my IHU re-enabled. I could do the driving".

"But where's the fun in that Stuart?" replied Danks.

After, what the sergeant thought was a scary journey along the Martian highway, Danks pulled into the pressurised area in front of the spaceport. He climbed out and collected his bags. The sergeant slipped over into the driver's seat.

"Have a pleasant journey back and thank you for all your help Tristan" said the sergeant.

"No problems Stuart, it was a pleasure working with you. I'm sure we'll meet again some day and remember, disconnect from the m-net occasionally for some excitement".

"I will".

Danks turned and walked down the tunnel into the spaceport.

He watched as the sergeant sped off into the distance.

"Was Stuart driving manually?" he thought with a wry smile.

He walked over to the check-in desk to hand over his bags where he watched them disappear down a shoot. A drone would pick them up and take them to the correct cargo pod. The pods would be flown up to the space docking port in time for the spaceship departure.

The check-in desk issued him his e-ticket which he transferred to his wrist watch. An automated voice told him where to queue for the next space-lift.

He joined the back of the queue for the lift. The doors were already open and people were filing in. He sat near the doors, which is where he always liked sitting, and buckled himself in.

Just as the lift doors started to close, he caught a glimpse of a woman among the people queuing for the check-in desk. He thought for a second that it was a familiar figure. Her hands and part of her face seemed to have coverings on them like the ab-skin that the sergeant had with his injuries. She wore a hat that covered most of her hair but some of her long blonde hair hung down over her shoulders.

Danks didn't think anything more of it as he was heading home. At that moment the lift doors closed and it started to accelerate upwards. He thought back to the woman in the queue and said to himself that there must be lots of women with figures like that.

After a couple of hours journey they arrived at the space docking port. He released himself from his chair, grabbed the side railing and used it to guide himself down the corridor.

Arriving at the boarding door of the interplanetary spaceship he showed his e-ticket. The steward registered it and indicated the direction he'd have to go to find his stasis pod.

Gliding down the corridor and squeezing past other passengers, he arrived at his stasis pod. He swung his legs up to the pod and slid in feet first.

Once inside the pod, he made himself as comfortable as possible and closed his eyes ready for the stasis sequence to start. He reflected on the events that had passed in the last few weeks here on Mars. There was a lot of explaining he had to do when he arrived back on Earth not only to his superiors but also to his wife.

Being distracted from the job in hand by an evil woman, he'd nearly paid the ultimate price as a result. Maybe he was getting too old for all this but if he gave it up he would miss the adrenaline rushes whenever danger was near.

The stasis sequence started and he was entering the long suspended sleep for the journey, but just as he drifted off his last thoughts were "I'm looking forward to seeing Earth again. But wait, I think I recognise that woman…"

The End

The Blood Covered Earth
Inspector Danks mysteries
Book 3

Chapter 44

"This is sooo cool" thought Inspector Danks. It was his first holiday in years and it was at the prestigious Perigee Hotel.

Danks was thinking it was the most amazing hotel he'd ever stayed in. He was lucky that his friend Andy was paying for the whole trip. He'd said that Danks deserved it for solving a case in which he'd been the prime suspect. He was relieved that the real criminal had been identified and captured. So, as a thank you, he'd offered Danks this holiday of a lifetime and he'd jumped at the chance.

Danks had become very cranky lately due to the stress. He'd been working solidly without having a break, other than for food, drink and sleep. It had inevitably led to his peculiar behaviour recently.

Andy was supposed to have accompanied him on this 'lads' holiday but he'd been called away on urgent business at the last minute.

So here Danks was, on his own, on a week's holiday in this exceedingly expensive hotel. He was hoping to completely unwind here from all the pressures of work.

It had been a particularly difficult year. His wife had died in a freak accident just over a year ago. After the funeral he'd dived headlong into his work in an attempt to block out the difficult memories of those days.

Danks's boss had commented that he should take some down time. But he ignored that suggestion and promptly started taking on some of the toughest cases.

The last few weeks on Earth had been particularly difficult. Danks had been threatened by a Mafia boss who then sent a gang of thugs to eliminate him. Thankfully, with the help of his sidekick Sergeant Turner, he'd managed to neutralise the gang leader in the ensuing fight. Once that guy had been taken out of the equation, the rest of the motley crew decided they were fighting a lost cause and scattered. The sergeant and inspector were left licking their wounds.

At least they'd managed to arrest the gang leader and the Mafia boss. They were now languishing in separate police cells. The gang leader was being charged with attempted murder of two officers. The Mafia boss was being charged with smuggling illegal drugs to the outer colonies and attempted murder of police officers. They were both awaiting their trials.

What Danks needed was to recuperate and there was nothing better then recharging the old batteries in such a wonderful location.

Danks didn't have to do much to order a drink here in the hotel. All he had to do was simply select a drink from the menu on the table beside him and within a minute a drone would turn up with it. A drone had just delivered a glass of ruby red beer to his table as he sat watching the world go by, literally.

The Perigee Hotel was in orbit around the Earth. It was roughly the shape of an old wagon wheel with a central hub, but with multiple rims. The hub was the reception and the spokes were the lifts going down to the living areas. The whole structure rotated around the hub creating a centripetal force akin to gravity. The force increased the further out from the centre you travelled. Lifts ran up and down the spokes ferrying guests and staff to the rings.

Danks had read in the brochure that the hotel wheel was twenty meters wide with a radius of two hundred meters. It also said that each ring consisted of two floors and each floor was three meters tall. "That's plenty of headroom for me to stand up in" he mused.

The brochure had a diagram showing that there were seven concentric rings around the centre of the hotel. The first ring started at seventy four meters from the centre. The artificial gravity on the floors in that ring was nearly the same as on

Mars. This was a comfortable area for the Martian visitors. The outer ring, at two hundred meters radius, had an artificial gravity close to that of Earth. This was ideal for Earthlings.

Some Martians, who had stockier builds, would gradually move to the outer rings. This was if they were wanting to acclimatise themselves to the Earth's gravity for a planned visit to the surface. But for most Martians the Earth was out of bounds as their physique couldn't withstand the increased loading on their bones. There were medical treatments to increase their skeletal strength but that took a few weeks to have an effect. Predominantly not many Martians wanted to visit the Earth, they just liked to look down on it from the safety of the hotel.

Danks's room was in the outer ring. The floors were numbered from the centre outwards so the fourteenth floor was where his accommodation was to be found.

That particular floor was perfect for him. He felt comfortable here with this artificial gravity. At least he didn't need a cover on his beer glass like he did in places such as Mars and Titan.

Chapter 45

While Inspector Danks was relaxing he thought back to when he first arrived at the hotel.

He was looking out of a side window as the space-shuttle approached the hub. This is where the passengers would disembark into the hotel.

He could discern a circular tube like structure clearly protruding from the central hub of the hotel. As the shuttle approached, he felt he was being thrust about in his seat as it fired small jets to adjust its approach.

Through his window he could make out that the shuttle was gently and carefully manoeuvring towards the end of the tube.

Danks could see that the tube wasn't rotating. He knew that without the rotation being cancelled, the shuttle wouldn't have been unable to dock with the hotel.

There was a small jolt as the tube and shuttle connected. He heard the clamps tighten around the fixing latches. The ship was now securely attached to the hotel.

There were only seven guests arriving on this

trip with him. Danks released himself from the straps in his seat. He started to drift upwards and he had to stop his movement as he was about to bump his head on the ceiling.

Pushing gently against his seat he moved out into the aisle. The other guests were ahead of him and were drifting towards the exit. He floated after them as they started to leave the shuttle.

Danks glided out into the tube. It was ten meters long and he was using handrails on the sides to pull himself down to the hotel.

Reception was a cylindrical room at the end of the tunnel. He found it quite disorientating as he entered. The whole room was rotating. He couldn't get over what a strange sensation it was. Just before he entered reception an attendant told him to catch hold of a handrail. He did and he started to gently rotate with the hotel.

Once he'd settled into the motion of the hotel he was greeted by a well dressed woman. Her long black hair was tied back and wrapped into a tight bun at the back of her head. It was hotel rules that all guests and staff had their hair secured back otherwise it would bring a new meaning to flyaway hair. Fortunately, Danks's hair was short so he didn't have a problem.

The female attendant was wearing an all in one suit that was the standard company issue. All guests and staff had to wear them. Dresses and kilts in zero-g were not allowed as they could cause some embarrassing and disturbing moments.

She informed him that her name was Susan and that she would be guiding him to his accommodation.

Inspector Danks noticed that she was wearing a pair of magnetic boots that looked out of place with the rest of her attire. He was familiar with these types of boots on previous trips in outer space.

She used them to clamp her feet to the floor which stopped her from drifting about, unlike himself. He felt a bit foolish as his legs were floating around aimlessly.

She held out an arm and caught him with a surprising amount of ease.

After some dextrous manoeuvring she'd managed to bundle Danks into a nearby lift.

"She's probably an expert at Tetris too" he thought.

While he was being woman-handled he was trying to suppress a feeling that he was just a bale of hay being thrown onto a haystack.

Once she'd secured Danks into his seat in the lift, she sat next to him and clipped herself in. They had to wait a few minutes while other guests and their guides joined them in the same lift. Once everyone was fastened in, the lift door closed and they started their descent.

They left the central hub and entered one of the spokes leading down to the outer rings. From here there were spectacular views of the whole Universe around them. The blue disc of the Earth hanging in the blackness of the sky. This precious jewel where life could exist without all the pressurised suits and buildings to protect the fragile human body. Danks couldn't help but think, "Why were there so many stupid people who didn't appreciate how lucky they were living on such a rare and beautiful blue gem. All they can do is either destroy the environment or one another or both". The only part not visible was the Sun as it was blotted out. If it wasn't it would be blindingly bright and hot inside the lift.

Susan acquainted Danks with the structure of the hotel.

Floor zero was the reception area. That was the area that Danks had just come from. On that same floor was an area sectioned off for guests to enjoy the microgravity experience.

They could play games like the hugely popular zero-g football. Players wore small backpacks that fired jets of air to control their position in the game. This was one of Danks's favourite sports. He enjoyed watching it on TV. Maybe this was his opportunity to try it for himself while he was here.

Susan continued briefing Danks by saying that

each ring was made up of two floors. The upper floor was usually for storage, restaurants and the staff accommodation. The lower floor was for the meeting rooms, gym area, saunas, spas and guests' accommodation.

As they passed through each ring, she explained what the facilities were on those floors. All facilities were available to Danks as he was a premier guest. He could sample any of them on any floor.

On their slow journey down towards Danks's accommodation, he could feel the artificial gravity gradually getting stronger.

Ring one had floors one and two. The artificial gravity on these floors was roughly equivalent to that on Mars. Martian guests started their stay on these floors.

For the next six rings the artificial gravity increased up to the final seventh ring. This last ring matched Earth's gravity and was perfect for Earthlings.

Danks noticed that each even numbered floor was divided into two sections across its width. One half was the accommodation with a main central corridor and the other half was the facilities available to guests such as gyms.

Guests could use the corridor for recreational walking as well as accessing the lifts, accommodation and the facilities.

Susan pointed out that the lifts were the only way to move between floors.

Eventually they arrived at floor fourteen where Danks's accommodation was located. He felt so much better on this floor. Susan stepped out of the lift and he followed behind, gazing at the amazing views.

She slipped off her magnetic boots, carefully placed them in a small cupboard next to the lift and then picked a pair of shoes out of the same cupboard. Once she had slipped them on she continued the tour.

Susan gestured towards a glass wall that separated the main corridor from the facilities area. Danks was amazed that the sports facility on his floor was a swimming pool. He couldn't wait to try that out.

"As you can see, this floor has the endless swimming pool" she said. Danks could see people already enjoying it.

"Your main restaurant is on the floor above. All information about each floor can be displayed on the screen on the lift wall for your convenience".

Danks thought all her speeches must have been rehearsed as she'd been talking none stop since they'd left reception.

"Automatic doors in these glass walls allow you access to the sports areas". They strolled past one door that had just opened for a guest who was

clad in their swimming trunks as he entered the pool area.

Dotted along the pool were cubicles. After finishing their swim a guest would step into a cubicle. It would first shower them down with clean water and then dry them with warm jets of air.

The accommodation rooms were on the other side of the corridor from the pool. No expense had been spared on the accommodation of guests.

She waved her hand over a lock symbol next to the door and the door slid into the wall revealing Danks's accommodation. This was going to be where he was to spend his week of bliss.

"This is the hallway" Susan said as she started walking down it. Danks followed closely behind her.

"On the left is your bedroom with an en-suite".

Danks had a quick glance in and saw it was a king size bed. "Brilliant, and it comes with a coffee making drone. Can't wait to try that out in the morning" he thought. But then he realised he'd fallen behind and had to scurry after her.

"The hallway leads you to the living room".

He caught up and stopped next to her as he stood transfixed at the view.

"In here, inspector, you have panoramic views of the universe". She did a sort of sweeping action with her arm so as to emphasise the huge vista in

front of them.

"I think I'll lounge on that chaise longue sipping my Vodka Martini while soaking up that amazing sight" he said in awe.

"I'm sure you'll have a great time with us inspector".

She reminded him that there was no key for his door as the facial recognition would detect him. All he needed to do was swipe his hand over the lock symbol to enter or leave his accommodation.

His memories of his arrival in this wonderful place were still vivid in his mind.

But right now, this was his first full day and he was comfortable here under this sunlamp. He was trying to build up his 'suntan', or should that be 'lamp-tan' he thought. He had a cool beer on the table next to him and looking out of the side window he could see the majestic beauty of the blue disc of the Earth drifting past.

Chapter 46

Danks had done a single lap of the 'never ending' pool, or at least that's how the advertising blurb called it. Afterwards, he'd hauled himself out and was lying on his deckchair.

He thought back to when he was just about to start his first swim, he'd stood facing the side of the pool and all he could see was it curving up to his left and right. It had the illusion of disappearing into the ceiling as it curved up and away from him. But he knew that it was circular and the two ends met above his head some four hundred meters above him. He'd stood there at first just taking in the sight.

Danks felt that one benefit of the pool was that everyone swam in the same direction. There was no need to turn around as there was no end! It was nothing like the swimming pool at his local gym back on Earth.

Danks had been looking forward to swimming here. It was so much more civilised. There weren't those aggressive jerks that appear out of nowhere, like a speed boat ploughing through the water coming the other way. That just didn't happen here. Anyway, most of them were swimming in the adjacent lane. The rope with floats that separated the lanes was held in place with stiff rods that were attached to the bottom of the pool. This stopped anyone straying into the other half of the pool.

"What bliss" he thought.

Susan had told Danks that the other inner rings had either circuits for running or endless velodromes. Maybe later in the week he'd catch the lift up to those floors and try them out. But right now he was desperate for a second swim.

Danks jumped into the pool next to his deckchair for his second lap. It was bracing after lying under the sunlamp for so long. He had to tread water at first until his muscles had gotten used to the temperature. Once accustomed he set off swimming in the correct direction. He knew it was the right way as there were arrows on the bottom of the pool to show swimmers the correct direction. Lifeguards quickly stopped anyone if they got it wrong.

With every other stroke Danks could see out into the star studded blackness. After quite some time, his arms were beginning to ache but he was determined to complete the task. It felt like he'd swum the channel by the time he'd done a lap. He recognised his deckchair and he swam until he was level with it. It had taken him longer than he thought but at least he'd managed to complete a second lap.

His swim had followed the curvature of the hotel which was a completely new experience to him. He'd ended up back where he'd started his swim at his deckchair over a kilometre later. He decided that two laps of the pool was sufficient for his first full day. By his last day he was planning to do as many laps as possible without stopping. In his mind, he'd concluded that he'd have to call them laps rather than lengths as there wasn't an actual end to define a length.

Danks wasn't a great swimmer but his friend Nicky, down his local pool, used to make him feel like he was a tortoise idly bobbing about in the water. Tortoises are not good swimmers unlike their cousins the turtles. Yes, Nicky was a turtle and he was a tortoise.

He was proud that he'd managed to finish two laps considering how out of shape he was. Okay, he'd stopped for a break after one lap, but he didn't care. It was an achievement that made him feel good.

Now he'd finished his swim for the day, he thought he'd pull himself out of the pool like a bronzed, muscular swimming athlete. Well - in reality he hauled himself out onto his stomach a bit like an overweight walrus. He was exhausted.

"I hope all this exercise is worth it" Danks

thought. He lay by the poolside grimacing as his muscles ached and he was also trying to collect his composure.

Managing to roll over onto his front, he then, with some effort, got up onto his hands and knees and did his best tortoise impression as he made his way to his deckchair. Rolling into it he stretched out his heavy right arm and folded his fingers around his glass of beer. Lifting the drink to his lips he took a sip and thought, "Refreshment at last".

Since his wife had passed away, he'd put a lot of weight on in the intervening year. While she was alive she always made sure he had a good diet. But now he'd completely gone to pot and he'd stopped going to his martial arts classes.

"My first beer of the day" he thought as he had a second sip of the rich flavours of his drink.

Scanning around the pool he noticed a woman sitting not too far away from where he was slouched. He realised that maybe she'd been watching him do his tortoise impression and he was convinced that she was smirking.

"I must make myself look a little more presentable" Danks thought, so he pulled in his belly and sat up straight. Slouching didn't look good even if he felt comfortable.

"There, that'll show her what a manly specimen I am" he thought.

In the end, he decided the best course of action was to concentrate on his beer and not his belly so it returned to its slightly rotund shape.

The best tactic now, he decided, was not to look her way and so he turned his head to gaze out of the window. Staring out at the stars drifting by he settled himself back into his comfy seat.

A few seconds later a voice interrupted his appreciation of the spectacle.

"Excuse me, it's Inspector Danks isn't it?" came a voice from his left.

Danks pulled his attention away from the star studded sky. "Yes, that's me" he replied. He was just thinking, "is this someone who's got a grudge against me because I've put her husband behind bars?".

"You probably don't remember me" the lady continued.

Danks looked at her again and blinked a few times and it then dawned on him. "Hello it's, erm, Gemma isn't it?". He wasn't quite sure as she had changed significantly from when he first met her back on Mars.

"Yes, inspector. You do recognise me. I'm here on holiday and I noticed you swimming in the pool. You looked very impressive".

"Oh well, I wouldn't say that. I'm more of a doggy paddler" he replied, although her comment did wonders for his pride.

"We Martians find swimming rather challenging as water is a scarce commodity back home as you know. Maybe you could teach me one day?".

"I would love too" he said, although he was a little daunted as he'd never taught anyone before.

"Anyway, it's been quite a while since we last saw each other" said Gemma.

"I guess it's been about three years since I was on Mars". Danks had tried to work it out quickly in his head.

"Yes, it's been three years and one month". Gemma had obviously kept count.

"I thought you Martians found this level of gravity uncomfortable?".

"Yes we do, but I've been here for nearly two months. I've been gradually working my way down from the first floor to here and I'm almost acclimatized now. Strengthening my bones and muscle has taken a while but my resilience to the increased gravity is much better now".

"They're quite dramatic measures. You're very committed. That's probably why I didn't recognise you at first!" he replied with some amazement in the changes to Gemma.

"So, isn't it very expensive to stay here two months and why are you putting yourself through all this pain?" he added.

"Well, it turns out Alice, back on Mars, is an expert in predicting share price fluctuations and has accumulated quite a large amount of money. So, that's how I can afford it.

As for the pain, you may recall that Jim and I always wanted to see the forests of Earth so I'm here to do that in his memory".

"Ah yes, I remember Alice and the holographic images of the forests in your flat. That's very adventurous of you to visit Earth. I hope you have a great time".

Danks then had an idea. "I tell you what, I'm just about finished here. What would you say if we met in the bar on the floor above in about one hour. I need something to eat and I'd be honoured if you would join me. You could then update me on what you've been doing in the last three years".

"That would be wonderful. See you later then" she replied. She returned to her deckchair picked up her belongings and headed off in the direction of her room.

Danks jumped to his feet and grabbed his few belongings. Finishing the last of his beer, he dashed off towards his accommodation. He was keen to look presentable for Gemma as he felt he had to redeem his cool image instead of the slouching one she must have formed of him.

What he needed was a shower and to spray on some body deodorant. Then dig out his best and only suit.

Chapter 47

The bar was quiet when Danks walked in. He was right on time. Looking in a long mirror at the bar entrance, he checked that he was looking reasonable in his suit. He smoothed out a few creases in his jacket where it had been folded in his holdall and straightened his tie. He wanted to look good for Gemma.

There was only one couple at the bar when he arrived. A waitress came over and asked if he'd got a reservation.

"No, but can you see if there's a table for two free?".

"Certainly sir, let me just check". She touched a screen on the pedestal in front of her. It lit up and she flicked through a list of reservations. "You are in luck sir, there is one free".

She showed Danks to the only table that didn't have a reserved sign projected onto the table top. He sat down and scanned around the almost empty bar.

Five minutes later, he was sitting looking at a tall glass of chilled light blonde beer that a drone had placed in front of him only a few seconds earlier. The room was busier now as people were being shown to their tables. He'd just taken his first sip of his drink when Gemma appeared at the entrance to the bar.

His first thought was she looked radiant standing there in her slim dress and her hair cascading down to her shoulders. She was scanning the room, so Danks stood and waved at her in an attempt to catch her attention. She saw him and waved back. As she started in his direction she signalled to a lady standing behind her to follow. He wasn't prepared for an additional guest at the table.

Gemma and her friend breezed over to where he was sitting. They were both very similar in build, but the friend's facial features were slightly different and her hair was blonde, whereas Gemma's was brunette. "Could they be sisters?" he thought.

"Hello Gemma, I didn't know you were bringing a friend. I'll get an extra chair". Danks waved to the waitress that he needed another chair and she instructed a drone to deliver one to their table. The drone picked up a spare chair, scurried over and placed it where Danks had indicated.

"Here's the seat - erm? I don't know your name!" he said. He held out his hand and they shook.

"I'm Alicia. Nice to meet you in person

inspector. Gemma has told me a lot about you and I feel I already know you".

Danks felt flattered.

He gave Gemma a kiss on her cheek and they then sat down. He replied to Alicia, "I'm sure what she has told you is greatly exaggerated. Certainly on the swimming front" he smiled.

"Oh, okay. I'll readjust my expectations of you" responded Alicia.

Danks was taken aback and felt a little deflated. He decided to change the subject. "So, Gemma, is Alicia your twin sister as you look very similar?".

"Oh, no. She's a close friend who is accompanying me on this holiday".

"I didn't see Alicia with you at the poolside".

Alicia answered, "That's because for some strange reason Gemma is trying to swim. I, on the other hand, have no desire to attempt it. I know I'd sink to the bottom. Besides, I was back at the room recharging my batteries".

Gemma interjected, "Metaphorically speaking".

He saw Gemma glance at Alicia. He got the impression that she wasn't happy with Alicia for her reply.

Danks tried to lighten the conversation. "Everyone can float. It's just getting over their initial fears that's the difficult part".

"I'm not everyone" Alicia replied firmly.

Gemma decided to divert the conversation away

from swimming. "Shall we order food and some drinks? I think I know what I'd like to have".

Danks was caught off guard as he hadn't even checked the menu. Scanning down the list he chose the first item that looked reasonable. He didn't want to feel a fool by taking ages to select an item.

On previous outings with colleagues, he got so wound up with people who couldn't decide what they wanted to eat. He often ended up drumming his fingers on the table and thinking "For fuck sake, pick something, anything!".

He entered what Gemma and he wanted into his wrist watch and then looked at Alicia enquiringly. "Have you made a choice yet Alicia?" he asked.

"Oh, I won't be eating. I filled up back at our room" was her reply.

"Would you like a drink?" he said thinking she was going to just have a liquid meal.

"No, thank you. It would disagree with me" she answered sharply.

Danks was a bit nonplussed with Alicia's replies.

He ordered their meals by doing a swiping action across his watch in the direction of the bar.

"Now back to the conversation" he thought. "So, Gemma, where did you two meet?".

"We've known each other for quite a long time. Well before you arrived on Mars".

"And how much longer are you here in the hotel?". He was hoping they'd be here for a while longer as he enjoyed Gemma's company.

"Oh, this is our last few days as I've been given the okay by the medics. I'm now strong enough to go down to the surface. We are so excited" Gemma looked at Alicia and she nodded in agreement.

"We catch the shuttle down to a place called Vancouver. We're staying there for a few days to see the sights. Then we head up to a place called Banff where we are booked on some tours into the forests. Then we're flying to Sydney. From there we're visiting New South Wales and Queensland Australia before heading home". Gemma was clearly looking forward to the holiday down on the surface.

"Sounds like a fantastic holiday" replied Danks.

"Anyway, lets talk about you inspector. What have you been up to?" Alicia enquired.

"Ah, I don't know how much you've heard. So I'll start from when I left Mars. I'm not sure you know this, but as I was leaving on the space-lift there was a woman boarding the same spaceship back to Earth as me. I didn't think much of it at first until I was about to enter stasis. It was then that I realised who she was".

"And who was she?" Gemma asked interestedly.

"It was none other than Dr Taylor. Of course

that isn't her real name. I haven't been able to find that out yet. When we arrived back at the spaceport orbiting Earth I awoke from stasis and hurried to intercept her. Unfortunately, she had been awakened some time before me. It was then that it was discovered that two pods were missing from the emergency escape area. One was found on Vancouver Island but the other was never traced".

"Did you manage to catch her" Alicia asked.

"No as the trail went cold. I continued my investigations until the station commander said it was time for me to move to another case. It was actually more of an order really. So, it's been put on hold until some new information turns up".

"Sergeant Francis told us that Mr Lynch was found guilty of the murder of those two officers and Tim Wang. It seems he and Dr Taylor got away with the murder of my husband and the others" said Gemma sadly.

"Unfortunately yes" Danks sympathised.

"We also heard that he'd managed to escape from prison on Mars". Gemma sounded almost annoyed.

"Apparently so and he hasn't been located". Danks couldn't understand how he could've escaped prison in this day and age.

"I heard that he'd managed to leave Mars undetected" Alicia added.

"More than likely, as there was one passenger who travelled on the journey from Mars to Earth that has since been found to have been using a false identification. The facial recognition software had been tampered with and that's why I believe he wasn't acting on his own" replied Danks.

"I understand that the tampering occurred remotely, from either the Earth or the Moon" stated Alicia.

"How do you know that?" asked Danks as he was unaware of that information.

Gemma stepped in, "As far as I'm aware it was hearsay back on Mars". Danks was sure he saw Gemma give Alicia a stern look.

Fortunately, the waitress arrived and broke the awkwardness. She took their meals off the top of the drone that had carried the food to their table. Danks waited until she had placed the meals in front of them both before he asked for another drink for him and Gemma. The waitress and the drone returned to the bar to complete his order.

While they ate Alicia watched them in silence.

Danks found it difficult to eat being watched by Alicia, so he continued with his résumé. "I solved several new cases back on Earth, but then my wife was tragically killed in a freak accident. The subsequent investigation simply said it was a one in a million chance. That didn't make me feel any better".

Both Gemma and Alicia offered their condolences.

"Anyway, I threw myself into my work for the following year. Then my boss pulled me into his office to tell me I was getting crankier than normal and I was easily irritated by other people. He suggested I took a break. I realised he was correct when I found myself shouting at him. That was rather embarrassing. So, that's why I'm here. I'm trying to unwind".

"Well I think you deserve it" Gemma replied in sympathy.

They finished their meals and Alicia said she needed to return to their room.

Gemma and Danks continued having drinks at the bar. It felt good to unwind with Gemma. They had a lot of laughs. Time seemed to fly by and then Gemma noticed it was getting late.

"I think I should return to my room and see how Alicia is getting on. So, goodnight and thank you for treating me to a very pleasant evening" Gemma said with a slightly slurred voice.

"Shall I escort you back to your room". He thought she might need help as she did seem quite tipsy.

"No, I'll be fine".

"It was a most enjoyable night Gemma, we must do this again soon. Maybe I'll see you at the pool again tomorrow". Danks had thoroughly enjoyed the evening and was hoping that their friendship would continue to blossom.

He watched as Gemma left the bar and she waved as she disappeared around the corner.

It was time for him to hit the sack too. So he finished his drink and signalled goodnight to the waitress. Patting the drone on its top thinking it was its head, he left the bar and walked in a wobbly manner down the corridor towards the lift.

Chapter 48

"Oh, my head. I think I drank too much last night" Danks said to himself. He'd had a rough night's sleep.

He groaned as he headed off to the en-suite where he started preparing himself for the day ahead. He'd half shaved his face when he heard his wrist watch ringing in the bedroom. Dashing out of the en-suite he threw himself onto the bed and answered the call.

Sergeant Turner was on the other end. "Hello inspector - Oh, have I rung at the wrong time?".

"No, Helen. I got up a bit late as I bumped into an old friend last night".

"Late night then! Did you have a good time?".

"Yes, it was great fun. Although I've got a hangover this morning. Anyway, you didn't ring me to quiz me about my late night session. How can I help you sergeant?".

"You know you wanted to be informed if something came up on that old case you were working on".

"Which case was that?".

"You know, the one you worked on when you

were sent to Mars. Well something a bit odd has turned up".

"Okay" he said in a slightly dubious voice. He wasn't expecting anything exciting.

"A woman was arrested in Sidney last week. The AI system in the shop identified her as shop lifting".

"Okay" he sounded slightly more interested.

"The typical DNA test was performed on her as her face wasn't on the records. The system identified her as being a near relative of that Dr Taylor you were looking for".

On hearing this he sat bolt upright. "How close a relative?".

"It's difficult to determine because, as you know, Dr Taylor had her DNA slightly modified. Taking that into account the system reckons the woman is possibly her Aunt".

Inspector Danks was excited. At long last there was a glimmer of light in the case. It sounded like he could reopen it.

"Okay, send me the details". He was keen to check out this new piece of the jigsaw.

"I was only ringing to inform you of the latest info. I wasn't intending that you chase this up. You're supposed to be on vacation after all". Helen was concerned that she'd potentially ruined Danks's holiday.

Reluctantly she sent the details through to

Danks.

"Okay, I've got that, thanks. I'll let you know if I discover anything Helen".

"Don't work too hard on this Tristan. You're on holiday remember".

"You know me Helen. I'll be completely laid back about it".

"Yeah, I believe you but I don't think the commissioner would".

"Ha Ha. I'm sure he'd disapprove as he was the one who insisted I came on this holiday. Anyway, thanks for the info and I'll see you soon" and Danks rang off.

He went back to the en-suite to finish shaving.

Keen to check out the new details he got dressed quickly and dashed off for his breakfast.

While eating he read through the report that he'd displayed on the screen in the table top. Her reason for shoplifting was that she was running short of money. She rented a two bedroomed flat in a Sydney suburb. Someone had offered her cash if she lifted certain items from a particular shop. Unfortunately, she was spotted by the AI and caught. She was put on probation as she had a dependant back home and he thought that it was probably an old parent. He decided to call her when he'd returned to his accommodation.

When he got back to his room, he sat on his bed and dialled the number in the report. It was ten a.m. in Australia right now so he wouldn't be getting them out of bed he hoped.

As someone answered he flicked his wrist watch call in the direction of the TV on the wall. An image appeared of a mid-sixties woman.

"Hello, who is it?" said the woman who answered in an annoyed tone.

"Hello Mrs Halliwell, I am Inspector Danks of the Interplanetary Police Agency".

"What would the IPA want with me?". She sounded even more irritated.

"I'm calling to ask you about a relative of yours. A Nikola Taylor?". But as he said this there was the sound of a crash in the background and a child started crying.

"Hang on a minute while I sort out Freya" the woman said.

Danks saw Mrs Halliwell walk to the other side of the room and pick a small child up. She came back comforting her.

"I'm afraid I don't know that woman. You must have the wrong address". It looked like she was about to terminate the call, so Danks had to act quickly by probing a bit further.

"Her DNA profile indicated that you were - erm, related". She stopped just before she shut down the transmission.

Danks had realised that he had stuttered his sentence because he'd noticed the child's hair. It was an auburn colour.

"I don't have any relatives other than my daughter and I haven't seen her for the last year.

She turned up here out of the blue about three years ago. At first I didn't recognise her because her face and hair had changed. Something to do with having her DNA modified. I don't understand young people these days wanting to do something like that. I took her in and helped her get better.

She had some protective plastic bandage on her arm and face to help it heal she said.

Anyway, a month later she found out she was pregnant. Some bastard had left her in the lurch. I reckon the bloke who got her pregnant must have done that to her face and arm".

Danks didn't know what to say. But fortunately Mrs Halliwell carried on. "A year after she had the baby she vanished leaving me to bring up Freya on my own". She sounded quite annoyed at Dr Taylor.

"Your granddaughter has beautiful hair don't you think?". Danks could see it was the same colour as Nikola's.

"Yes, it is. Funnily enough there's no one in the family that has hair that colour. It's apparently due to the DNA treatment Eleanor had".

"And how old is your granddaughter?". Danks was getting a funny feeling about this.

"She was two years old a few months ago".

Danks couldn't believe what he was hearing but he continued, "I'm guessing that you used to live on Mars?".

"Why, yes. How did you know that? We left shortly after Eleanor was born because her father committed suicide. The bastard left us in the lurch".

Another piece of the jigsaw had magically dropped into place. He now knew who Dr Taylor really was. Also, could this child be his daughter. He was stunned.

He had to clear his throat before he could ask the next question. "Do you know the whereabouts of Eleanor at the moment?".

"No, otherwise I'd tell her to bloody come back and help me look after Freya".

"Would you object if I arranged for an officer to come over and take a DNA sample of Freya? It would help us in our investigations". It wouldn't but he felt he had to find out definitely who the father was.

"Is there any money in it for me?".

"I'm sure we can come to some arrangement". He felt guilty that if this was his daughter then he should help them out. "Okay, I'll arrange for someone to contact you and thank you for your help Mrs Halliwell. Bye Freya". He waved at the child and she waved back. He terminated the call and flopped back onto his bed.

His head was spinning. Was it from the night before or from these new revelations?

His next thought was to contact Sergeant Turner. He dialled her up and flicked the video to the TV. "Hi Helen, can you do me a favour?".

"It depends on what it involves" she sounded dubious.

"Can you arrange for a DNA test of the child that lives with Mrs Halliwell?".

"A bit unusual, but yes. Why do you want it?".

"I believe she may be the daughter of Dr Taylor whose real name is Eleanor Halliwell".

"Blimey, how did you discover that?". Helen sounded amazed.

"With some lucky questioning I guess. It turns out that Mrs Halliwell is her mother not Aunt. Can you let me know the results on the child ASAP?".

"Okay, I'll get straight to it" and she ended the call.

Danks sat for a few minutes while he collected his thoughts. It had already proved to be a significant day.

"Right, I guess I'd better return to my exercise regime" he said out loud to himself.

He changed into his swimming costume and left his room. He had a spring in his step and was ready to take on at least three laps of the pool today. But only if his body would let him.

Chapter 49

Danks was coming up to the end of his first lap when Gemma and Alicia appeared next to the pool.

"Hi Tristan" called Gemma above the noise of the pool. "We've come to say goodbye as we're leaving today and heading down to the surface".

He stopped at the edge and hauled himself out and grabbed his towel to dry himself. "I didn't think you were going so soon" he couldn't help sounding a little disappointed. Gone was the chance of seeing Gemma again.

"Yes. The doctors have brought it forward as they believe I'm ready. So we decided to jump at the opportunity". Danks was sure he detected some sadness in her voice.

"I hope it meets your expectations down there. It's the end of spring in Canada so there may be some snow still lying about".

"We'd love that as we've never seen snow in its natural environment" Gemma said with some excitement.

"I'm sure it will be an aesthetically pleasing sight" added Alicia.

"Well have a great time. It was fun meeting you both here. It's made my trip all the more enjoyable. Remember, keep up the swimming, if that's possible on Mars".

"I will" she said.

Danks embraced Gemma. Alicia extended a hand and he shook it.

Danks watched them leave and get into the lift. He returned to the pool feeling a little sad as it had been fun seeing Gemma, although Alicia seemed a little distant. He did have a few suspicions about Alicia, but then he thought, "Nooo, I must be mistaken".

Danks thought he'd do one more lap and then it'd be time for some refreshment while looking out of a viewing window.

About an hour later he was sipping his drink just as he saw the shuttle leave that Gemma and Alicia were aboard. It passed by in the distance and drifted across the Moon's crescent that was shining bright in the jet black vastness of space.

"It won't be long before they are enjoying the sights, sounds and fragrances of the forest" he thought. He returned to his drink and watched out of the window as the universe rotated around his world.

Even though he was trying to relax, he couldn't shake off that tight feeling in his neck and shoulders. He wasn't used to all this swimming, so he decided he needed a massage. He grabbed his things and headed over to his accommodation to change.

Leaving his room he jumped into the nearest lift, secured himself into a seat and entered the floor destination. Slowly the lift moved upwards through the restaurant floor, then out into space along the spoke like structure. He had spectacular views of the Earth and the Moon.

Dotted around the black sky he saw glimpses of other hotels and shuttles heading to and from them. In the far distance he could make out the space docking port that he'd arrived at some three years earlier from Mars.

Travelling up in the lift he left his cosy Earth like gravity and entered a world that was a little easier on the body. It wasn't bad, it just felt different. Floor eleven's reduced gravity was only slightly less than on his floor but the difference was still noticeable.

Arriving at his destination floor, he scrambled out of the lift and followed the signs for the Spa. On entering the reception he casually asked if they could squeeze him in for a massage. He thought that was quite a clever use of the word 'squeeze' but the bronzed muscly guy behind reception had probably heard it all before.

Inspector Danks tried to appear as though he did this sort of thing regularly. However, his bravado was shattered when the reception guy rattled off a list of different types of massages that he hadn't even heard of. Danks didn't have a clue as to which he wanted. He just wanted a massage to iron out those knots in his neck and shoulders.

Danks had to come clean and told the receptionist that all he wanted were the aches and pains easing out of his upper body. The guy gave a wry smile and then recommended the basic one. A couple of towels were pushed towards him over the reception counter along with an electronic tag which showed which massage room he had been assigned.

"I've allocated you in our system to Tina. She's one of our best masseuses but she's just finishing with a customer at the moment" said the receptionist. "She'll be about ten minutes".

Danks didn't fancy waiting that long so he asked for a different masseuse.

"Okay, Sarah has just become free, shall I change your appointment to her?".

"Yes, that would be great". Inspector Danks picked up his towels with the new tag and headed in the direction of the massage rooms.

"You're in expert hands inspector. Just relax and enjoy the experience" shouted the guy behind reception as Danks set off down the corridor.

He arrived outside the room with the number that his tag indicated. Putting his tag on a pad next to the door triggered it to slide out of the way. Inside the room it felt almost tranquil with the low lights and the soft music. He was sure there was some sort of fragrance in the air as his nostrils seemed to appreciate it.

"Come in. If you could take your shirt off and then lie on the massage table". The masseuse took the tag from him and laid it on a pad on the table. "Ah, I see from the tag that you are Inspector Danks. I hope you are having a good time with us". The inspector said he was enjoying it so far.

He'd been given the impression that massages were supposed to be good for the body. So he was going to give it a try at least once.

Lying flat on the massage table he tried to relax. The masseuse's hands were soft but firm. He could feel the tight knots in his shoulders get gently smoothed away with those expert hands.

He was feeling that this was just what he wanted. His eyes were closed and at last he felt he was relaxing. The music, fragrance and light level were achieving the desired effect. He was becoming drowsy.

Suddenly, there was a scream from down the corridor. He lifted his head at first hoping it was just a one off. The scream came again and the massage came to an abrupt end because Danks jumped to his feet.

"I'll be back in a minute" he said and left the

room at speed to find the source of all the commotion. One of the masseuses was standing outside a room crying. Danks ran over to her. She pointed into a room opposite.

The room was dark just like the one he'd come from. It had similar background music playing. Stepping into the room he could make out that there was someone on the massage table. The person wasn't moving. Danks put his fingers on their neck, there wasn't a pulse. There was a fragrant flannel over the man's face. "Was this put there before or after he died?" he thought.

A few seconds later a medical team bustled into the room and pushed Danks out into the corridor. They started to try and revive the person. Ten minutes passed before they came out. Quite a crowd had formed to see what all the commotion was about.

Danks approached the medical team leader. "I'm Inspector Danks. Did you manage to revive the man?".

"Regrettably not sir. We can't understand it. It's like he had a heart attack but none of our attempts to restart his heart worked". The lead medic looked quite bemused.

"May I take a look?" requested Danks.

"Sure, we'll be getting a team to remove the body and take it to the morgue in a few minutes".

"You have a morgue in the hotel?". Danks

sounded surprised.

"Oh yes sir, we have about two deaths a year. It's usually men who have come here with their young wives or girlfriends. Their bodies aren't as young as they think". The medic then answered a call on his watch, it was to arrange for the body to be removed.

Danks entered the room again and did a quick scan of the corpse observing anything that looked out-of-sorts. There seemed to be contusions on his arm that he'd noticed were there before the medical team had pushed him outside. They resembled marks he'd seen on other corpses. It was as though the person had been held down very hard. "Could that be a sign of a struggle?" he thought. He took some pictures of the contusions and left the room.

The masseuse was sitting on a chair being comforted by a couple of colleagues. Danks asked her to wait while he put his shirt back on. He couldn't conduct an interview improperly dressed. This wasn't a beach in California!

Once he was ready he took her into an empty room and sat her down on a chair opposite him. He handed her a glass of water and she took a short sip as her throat had gone dry.

"Now, I'm Inspector Danks. I want you to tell me everything that just happened. But first, tell me your name?".

"I'm Tina" she replied between sobs.

Danks realised that she was the masseuse he'd been initially assigned to.

"I was given a guest to massage. In fact, it was supposed to be you, but then at the last minute it was swapped to Mr Wright. I did the usual and asked him to lie down on the massage table. I put the scented towel over his face. The fragrances help people to relax. But then I received a message from reception saying that I was needed urgently. I told Mr Wright to just relax and that I'd be back soon. I then hurried off to see what they wanted".

"Why were you needed at the reception that was so urgent?" enquired Danks.

"That's what's so strange. When I got there they said they hadn't messaged me".

"How long were you away from the room?".

"I couldn't have been away for more than three minutes".

"So when you returned what happened?".

She seemed to hesitate as she was finding it difficult to talk about it.

"I opened the door and went into the room. I asked if he wanted his shoulders massaging first but I got no reply. At first I thought he'd fallen asleep but he didn't respond when I started the massage. It was then that I realised he was -" she took a deep breath, "he was dead". She put her face into her hands and she started sobbing.

Inspector Danks put his arm around her shoulders to console her.

Tina's manager came in, helped her to her feet and guided her out of the room. As they were leaving she turned to Danks and said, "We'll see that she has some time to recuperate from this terrible incident".

"She'll need to have some counselling too" suggested Danks. "Something like this is a big shock to a person".

Danks left the room just as the team were carrying the body down the corridor. A plastic blanket was draped over the body. There were still a few people hanging around who were morbidly interested.

Danks stopped the head of the team. "Any idea when the autopsy result will be available?".

"Probably tomorrow as we have a forensic pathologist on site. The lab's on the first floor. The person to see is Dr Wagner. It'll probably be the usual cause".

"And what is the 'usual cause'?" Danks had an idea what the guy was going to say.

"Some of our guests lead stressful lives. They have bad diets and when they aren't used to doing hard physical exercise it can, in some cases, result in a fatal heart attack".

"I think I'll wait for the lab report before making my final judgment" replied Danks. Were

Mr Wright's contusions due to some sport? Danks wasn't convinced.

He watched them troop off down the corridor until they'd disappeared.

Should he carry on with his massage? Finding the corpse had put a spanner in the works. He abandoned the idea as he was no longer in the mood. Gathering up his belongings he said sorry to the masseuse and left to catch the lift back down to his floor. What he needed right now was a few long cool drinks. Preferably ones with alcohol in.

Chapter 50

The following morning Danks was woken by the sound of his wrist watch ringing. Sitting up he answered the call. At the same time he flicked the video image towards the TV. Sergeant Turner appeared on the screen.

"I hope I didn't wake you inspector".

"Good morning sergeant. No, it's time I got up anyway. I have to get an update from a Dr Wagner about a death that happened at the hotel yesterday".

"I thought you were supposed to be on holiday?".

"So did I". Danks smiled back at the sergeant.

"Sounds like a busman's holiday to me".

Danks brushed his fingers through his hair in order to make himself feel a little more presentable. "So sergeant, what have you found out?".

"We managed to get a sample of the child's DNA. For some reason the grandmother seemed to think she was due some money".

"Ah, yes. I'll sort that out". Danks was a bit embarrassed about that. He'd arrange for some money to be sent to her after the call.

"Anyway, you were correct about the child. By the way, should I say Dr Taylor or Eleanor Halliwell?".

"Let's stick with Dr Taylor for the time being" replied Danks.

"Well, Dr Taylor is the mother of the child".

"And who does the report say is the most likely father?". Danks felt nervous about the potential answer.

"The report says they scanned the whole male data base and found only one strong match".

There was a pause while the sergeant finished reading the report. "Oh, my giddy Aunt!".

"What is it sergeant?". Danks was on tenterhooks as to what the answer would be.

"There must be some mistake sir. The report identifies you as the father". The sergeant looked shocked.

"I don't think there's a mistake. There was one night when Dr Taylor and myself got together. But in my defence it was before I became suspicious of her role in the case".

He liked the idea of being a father and yet this woman was a monster. But was it ethical for an investigator to have a one night stand with a suspect. Although he didn't know that she was a suspect at the time.

After a few seconds of silence the sergeant

decided to say something. "What should we do next?".

"Can you find out if Mrs Halliwell knows what form of transport her daughter used when she left? That might give us a chance in tracing her".

"Okay, I'll get onto that".

"Keep me posted as to what you find out".

"Bye - 'daddy', I mean inspector!".

"Very funny sergeant" he said with a dash of sarcasm.

Danks rang off and he slumped back onto the bed. "I'm a father, but the mother is a complete mad woman. What will happen to the kid? Her mother has disappeared and even if we find her she'll have a long prison sentence ahead of her" he thought to himself. His mind was bouncing lots of questions around in his head.

He threw the duvet to one side and rolled out of bed. "En-suite here I come" he said as he waved his hand at the door sensor and it slid to one side. He needed to prepare for the day.

This holiday had started out really great, but now he was beginning to get bored with the lamp-bathing. His whole working life had involved danger and excitement. Now that Gemma and Alicia had left there just didn't seem to be that fun any more. It had evaporated when they had left. He needed to focus on the old Dr Taylor case again as it was getting interesting.

Donning some clothes he went to the restaurant for his usual breakfast. He plumped for the full English and afterwards he felt he'd eaten too much. "Maybe I should change it to something less filling next time" he thought.

After finishing his coffee, it was time to give Dr Wagner a visit. He left the restaurant heading for the first floor.

Seating himself in the lift he told it to take him to floor one. The door closed and their slow ascent began. One good thing about this holiday, he thought, was that he enjoyed the views of outer space as the lift moved up the spoke to the upper rings.

The lift voice announced his arrival at floor one. Remembering that this floor was like walking on Mars he restrained himself from leaping out.

Outside the lift were some cupboards that contained weighted boots so he put a pair on. They allowed him to walk a little more normally on this floor.

He walked over to a reception desk that was conveniently situated nearby. "I want to speak with Dr Wagner, is he available?".

"Who shall I say is calling?" came the reply from the person behind the desk.

"Inspector Danks".

The receptionist took a few seconds to locate Dr Wagner and then spoke into his microphone. "Dr

Wagner, there's an Inspector Danks here to see you".

There was a pause while Dr Wagner was obviously communicating with the receptionist. "Okay, I'll tell him". The receptionist tapped the side of his headphones which disconnected the call. "He's free now. If you go down this corridor about twenty meters, you'll find him in room seven on the right".

Danks repeated the room number back to the receptionist just to confirm he had heard it properly.

As he walked down the corridor he checked the room numbers as he went past them. He stopped outside room seven. As he did so the door slid quietly to the side. There was a green dim light emanating from the room. He moved inside with some trepidation. He was prepared for anything.

"Ah, inspector. I'm glad you could find my office. I'm Dr Wagner". The doctor was sitting down at a desk about two meters away. He stood up, but he didn't seem to increase much in height. He had the statutory white lab coat on. He had long white hair which blended well with his lab coat and he had a small set of spectacles on the end of his nose.

Usually people have their eyes corrected but obviously Dr Wagner had decided not to have it done. Inspector Danks didn't know why as it was painless and only took a couple of minutes by the opticians. He'd had it done several years ago himself.

"Now I'm guessing you are here to ask me about Mr Wright, no?".

Danks wondered why Dr Wagner had used a negative at the end if his sentence, but that was digressing. Could he detect a slight German accent?

"Yes, how did you know?" replied Danks.

"Simple deduction as he's the only corpse I have in the morgue at the moment". Dr Wagner seemed to find that funny as he sniggered after he'd said it. The snigger was more like a pig snorting thought Danks.

"Okay". Danks often found pathologists have a twisted sense of humour. Maybe because their audience doesn't give any feedback. He decided to press on with the questions.

"Have you determined his cause of death?".

"Yes, this was a very interesting case. I've not seen anything like this here in the hotel before. It's nearly always heart attacks. All that rumpy-pumpy going on you know".

Danks was thinking, "This guy has been alone far too long in the morgue". He decided to ask the next question anyway. "What was interesting?".

"Ah well, I did my usual tests thinking it was the same old thing but they were negative. I did a scan of his heart, but there was hardly any sign of heart disease. So I thought I'd try and see if it was sepsis but it wasn't that …".

Danks interrupted Dr Wagner as he didn't want to hear the full history. He wanted to find out what had killed Mr Wright. "Can we cut to the chase Doctor?".

"Oh, yes, yes. The reason he died was that he received an injection of a highly concentrated botox toxin. Few people realise it's one of the most toxic substances known to man and yet they have it injected into their bodies. There they are, having it pumped into their lips and faces. The silly people should have more sense".

Dr Wagner stopped and dragged himself back to the original subject. That bee in his bonnet had caused him to start ranting and he realised he'd lost his train of thought. The doctor continued. "Anyway, I digress. The botox was injected straight into his carotid artery. You can see the faint puncture wound in the holographic image of his neck. It was so small I nearly missed it". The doctor zoomed in on the region on Mr Wright's neck. "He was dead within a couple of seconds".

"What about the contusions on his arm?". Danks believed that it was related to this lethal injection.

"Ah yes. The marks on the arm appear to be that he was held with a tight grip while the injection was administered".

"Did you manage to get a DNA sample of the other person?".

"No. The person was wearing surgical gloves as there was some residual powder where they'd held the arm".

"Could one person have done this?".

"Difficult to say. One person could have done it or maybe two".

Danks realised he'd missed being murdered by a whisker as he was supposed to have been Tina's client. "Thank you doctor".

"Should I inform the authorities that someone has been murdered?". Dr Wagner seemed to be excited at the thought of doing something different as his job was usually quite mundane.

"No, I'll do that" replied Danks.

Dr Wagner's smile disappeared on hearing that, as he was looking forward to doing it.

Danks left the morgue and went straight to the lift. Leaving the weighted boots in the cupboard he'd got them from, he seated himself in the lift.

"Floor eleven" he commanded. It was time to visit the spa again to get more information

As he descended he thought, "This murderer was after me. It appears that Mr Wright was in the wrong place at the wrong time. No pun intended. This holiday has just become much more exciting".

Chapter 51

Several minutes later, Danks had arrived at floor eleven and was standing at the spa reception. "I'm investigating Mr Wright's death. Can you give me access to the video recordings for that day in this corridor?". Danks scanned his ID chip to show he had the authority to view the logs.

"Certainly sir, for what time period?".

"From when I arrived until the medics arrived".

"Okay". The guy behind reception recovered the time info from Danks's ID chip and then pulled down a menu that had the security camera recordings. He entered the time period and flicked the video recordings across to Danks's watch. "You should have them now".

Danks checked and they were there. He thanked the guy and he returned to the lift. Descending back to floor fourteen he was heading for his accommodation. Back in his room he went straight over and sat down on the end of his bed.

He tapped his watch and scrolled to the video recordings from the spa. He reviewed each of the camera recordings on his TV.

Whenever someone appeared on the video, the

AI facial recognition registered them and it overlaid their name on the screen next to the individual.

He saw several people enter and leave that section of the corridor. Mr Wright arrived and entered the room. Then, a few minutes later Tina left. She had only just walked a short distance away from the room when a new person arrived. Their face was covered with a mask and there were surgical gloves on their hands, just as Dr Wagner predicted. The AI facial recognition was unable to identify them. They entered the room.

About a minute later Danks saw the suspect leave the room. They looked furtively down the corridor towards reception and then walked in the opposite direction. The videos followed the person down the corridor until they stepped into a lift and the door shut behind them. About a minute later Tina arrived back from reception and that's when everything hit the fan.

"The way people walk can sometimes be very specific to an individual" though Danks and he was sure he'd seen that particular gait before. But he just couldn't put his finger on who it could be.

Danks needed to get his hands on the logs for that lift. He left his room and caught the lift back to reception in the hub. Arriving at the desk he recognised that the person behind it was Susan the guide who'd shown him around when he first arrived.

"Hello inspector. I heard about the incident yesterday. I hope it hasn't spoilt your stay with us".

"No it hasn't. In fact it's made it more interesting" came his reply.

"How's that sir?". Susan seemed surprised.

"I do enjoy mysteries and this is one of them" he smiled at her. "To help me further with my investigations, there is something you can help me with. Can you replay the video footage of lift two between three thirty, when Mr Wright arrived at the spa, and four o'clock?".

Susan scanned through several menus on her desk and then swept the information to the screen on her right. The lift showed a couple of guests getting in and out at first with the usual names linked to their image. Then the suspect appeared with a pixelated face.

"Stop the video. Why has that person got a pixelated face?" requested Danks.

Susan brought up the AI controlling the images. "AI can you explain why that person has a pixelated face?" she asked.

"An instruction was entered by an employee to remove the facial features of the individual for the period that you are viewing" came the reply from the AI.

"Who was that employee?" asked Danks.

"That has been erased" replied the AI.

Danks saw that the suspect had alighted at the hub floor.

"Susan, can you show me the video from reception in the hub for that lift?".

A second or two passed while she found the clip. She flicked it to the screen and the new video started. The same person with the pixelated face floated out of the lift and travelled up the tube to a waiting shuttle.

"Do we have any video coverage inside the shuttle?" asked Danks.

"I'm afraid we don't. That shuttle is owned by a contract company used for ferrying staff down to the Earth's surface" replied Susan.

"Do we have a list of staff that boarded the shuttle?". Danks was desperate to find out who it was.

"Yes, I can show you all the images". Susan selected the boarding passes for everyone on the list and flicked it to the screen. Images of people who'd left the hotel on leave that day and who'd boarded that particular shuttle started scrolling up the screen.

Danks checked each image as they scrolled past. He read the names of each of the staff members that were displayed under their image. Would there be a name he would recognise?

"Stop!" shouted Danks. "Go back an image.

What are the records on that employee?".

The AI responded, "He came with an exemplary record from his previous employer. Hard working, courteous and helpful".

Susan looked a little dumbfounded.

"Have you got something to add Susan?". Danks had seen that she was looking astonished.

"Yes, actually. I found that he never really felt he was part of the team. Whenever I talked to him he was rude and sneering. He worked the last couple of weeks on floor fourteen and he was receiving treatment to help his body get accustomed to the gravity level. Also, he'd received a couple of reprimands in his short eight weeks here. I'm quite surprised he hadn't been asked to leave".

"That doesn't surprise me" said Danks.

Susan was shocked for a second before asking, "Why, do you know him?".

"Yes, he's not Mr Johnson as his ID suggests, he's a convicted criminal. His real name is Alex Lynch. I'd recognise him anywhere".

"But how did he evade the AI recognition and all our security checks?". Susan sounded surprised.

"I suspect that someone helped him. There is a certain associate of Mr Lynch who is perfectly capable of that. What I don't understand is why he would come here?".

Danks thought that it wasn't just to kill him as

he didn't even know he was coming here until a week ago.

"Well, it's a good thing he's gone" said Susan with some relief.

"Why is that Susan?".

She hesitated as it was a company policy not to tell guests of certain private functions taking place in the hotel. However, these were exceptional circumstances. "Well, there is a meeting of delegates from all three main colonies. It's happening here in ring one this week. They all arrived yesterday".

Danks had many questions running through his head. "Could it be that his main purpose was to target the meeting? But why would he leave right now? Why try and kill me?".

Danks decided he should check that level out. "Contact your security department and get them to meet me on floor one outside lift two in ten minutes. Do you know who is in the delegations?".

"I only know it's mainly politicians and the commissioners of each of the colonies".

"Thank you. You've been a great help".

Danks floated towards lift two and managed to clamber inside with some help from a conveniently located hand rail.

Securing himself into a seat as the door shut, he called Sergeant Turner back on Earth. Her face appeared on his wrist watch screen. "Hi Helen, I'm sending you all the details on a Mr Johnson. He should have arrived back on the surface yesterday from this hotel. It's his first time on Earth so he may be disoriented or struggling with the gravity".

"Why are we after him?". Helen was a bit distracted as she was currently dictating a report when he rang.

"His true identity is Alex Lynch".

"What, the guy you got convicted on Mars?".

"Yes, the very one. He broke out of prison a while back and somehow managed to escape from Mars. It appears he created a new identity and was living on the Moon until he came here to the hotel as an employee".

"We don't have an extradition treaty with Mars so we can't deport him" said the sergeant as she thought it would be futile to arrest him.

"That's true, but he's now a suspect in the murder of a Mr Wright here at the hotel and that is in our jurisdiction".

"Okay, I'll start looking at the arrivals from the hotel for yesterday".

"Thanks Helen. Be careful, this guy is dangerous. If my hunch is correct he might lead us to Dr Taylor".

The lift came to a halt on floor one just as he finished the call.

Chapter 52

Danks had to wait a few minutes before the security contingency arrived. It was only one guy.

"Where are the rest of security?" asked Danks. He was somehow expecting there to be more than one person.

"I'm the whole of the security team sir. There isn't a big call for security on this exclusive hotel. It's not like we're going to get a huge number of yobbos arriving in reception". He had a bit of a snigger when he said that.

Danks saw his point and shrugged his shoulders. "Ah well. You'll have to do. We have to search this floor and the floor below".

"What are we looking for sir?".

"I'm not sure, anything that is out of place. Something that you feel seems odd. I know that isn't much to go on but all I can say is that I've a hunch that something isn't quite right. So let's get on with it".

They began checking all the vents in the corridor. As they came to a room they would check thoroughly inside it. They repeated that process for the whole of the floor. Eventually, they'd covered everywhere and nothing unusual was found.

"Right, down to the next floor". Inspector Danks was hoping for more luck there.

They travelled down to the floor below and began the same meticulous search.

As they continued their hunt they eventually arrived at the main hall where there was a gathering of the delegates. They were the politicians and commissioners from the colonies.

As they entered the hall a tall burly bouncer confronted them. "Do you have an invitation to this meeting?". The bouncer stood looming over them. He was trying to look as big and menacing as possible.

The security guard wasn't prepared for this. In fact he was sure the original job description didn't include being challenged by big burly blokes. He'd only been in the job for two weeks.

Danks replied, "No we don't, but I'm Inspector Danks".

The burly bouncer seemed to look even more menacing. "I don't care if you're Inspector Pants or not. No invitation, no entry".

The bouncer went to grab them both by their collars as he was planning to eject them. He caught the security guard and lifted him up so his feet were no longer touching the ground, but missed the inspector.

Danks reacted quickly and caught the bouncer's out stretched arm. With a lightning fast movement he gripped it and twisted it over. He then rammed the bouncer sideways against the wall with his free hand on the bouncer's throat.

One side of the bouncer's face was pressed against the wall. Miraculously he still managed to maintain his firm grip on the security guard.

"I'm here on an investigation and you're not going to get in my way are you?". Danks had lowered his voice and was whispering angrily in the bouncer's ear.

"Tristan, are you and the bouncer checking out the quality of that wallpaper?" a cheery voice said from behind him.

Danks released the bouncer's arm, turned him around to face him and straightened his lapels. The guard was still dangling from the end of the bouncer's outstretched arm.

"We were just having a quiet discussion on the merits of decent wallpaper and examining the fine workmanship, weren't we?" he said with a smile while looking at the bouncer who nodded in response.

Danks turned around knowing who it was as he would recognise that voice anywhere. "Well, nice to meet you again Commissioner Gilbert. I wasn't expecting to see you here today" Danks said in a cheery voice.

"Nor I you. It's okay, I'll vouch for the inspector". The commissioner waved a hand at the bouncer.

The bouncer was still holding the security guard some thirty centimetres off the ground. He resembled a rabbit that had been grasped by the scruff of the neck by a child. Danks thought he'd better help him out. "Commissioner, the security guard is with me. Could you get Yogi Bear to release him?".

The commissioner signalled to the bouncer to let the man go. The bouncer seemed a bit miffed as he was looking forward to throwing someone out, anyone!

Danks was scanning around the room while talking to the commissioner and he spied Sergeant Francis on the other side of the room. "I see you have the sergeant with you".

"Yes, he's here to help with the tricky matter of looking after the politicians. They tend to be rather a slippery lot of characters.

Did you get a promotion after the sterling work you did back on Mars?".

"Fortunately not. I'm happy where I am". The problem with a promotion is that he'd end up in an office job which Danks would've hated.

The commissioner signalled for the sergeant to come over.

"Well I never, Tristan. What a pleasant surprise

seeing you here. Are you here to accompany the Earth politicians and commissioner?".

Danks felt aggrieved that he hadn't been told of this meeting. Maybe it was because he'd been a bit tetchy with his bosses recently at work. "No, you might find it hard to believe but I'm here on holiday" said Danks with a smile.

The commissioner and sergeant looked at each other then back at Danks.

"Shouldn't you be enjoying yourself rather than gate crashing a dry meeting like this?" replied the commissioner.

Danks agreed in his head, but he also felt there was a reason why Lynch had been here. His instincts kept telling him there was a more sinister reason for him being in the hotel.

"The escaped criminal Mr Lynch from the Dr Taylor case has been seen here in the hotel. I believe he's been working here for a few months now under a false ID. I know he's already murdered a guest but I suspect he was here for a specific reason and I believe it's something to do with this meeting. We could all be in great danger". Danks had changed his tone to a more serious one.

The sergeant asked, "Do you think he's trying to kill more people?".

"He's an agent of the Syndicate and I don't believe he was working here just for his health".

Inspector Danks started scanning the room.

"Do you know what we are looking for?" replied the sergeant.

"It could be anything out of the ordinary and more than likely concealed" said Danks.

All four of them split up and began searching different sections of the room. They checked under the tables and chairs. Danks was searching along the head table where many of the meeting organisers would be sat. As he moved along it he saw a vent cover that was directly behind the chairman's seat at the table. It wasn't quite flush with the wall so he knelt down next to it. Putting his fingers along its edges he pulled at it and it pinged off with surprising ease.

Danks could see there was a box shaped object about an arm's length inside the vent conduit. Reaching in he was able to gently pull it forward. Once at the front of the vent he lifted it out carefully placing it on the floor in front of him. He could see it properly now.

There were two concentric rings of LEDs. The inner ring of lights were turning off sequentially in a clockwise direction with a period of a second between them. Once all the lights of the inner ring were off it would trigger one of the outer ring lights to turn off. At the same time the inner ring would all turn back on and then the whole process would repeat.

It was clear it was counting down, but to what?

From the lights still lit in the outer ring Danks estimated that there wasn't much time left. He decided he needed to act quickly. But where could he dispose of such an item in a short time? There were no doors he could just throw the box out of. He had to get it out of this room at least. Then he'd have to think of something after that.

Danks picked the box up carefully and he started to move towards the exit. The bouncer looked nervous as he opened the door to let him out.

From Danks's estimation, there were now only about two minutes left. He had to get it to one of the lifts.

He moved as fast as he thought he could safely manage towards the lift.

Time was running out.

The last outer LED had gone out.

Only sixty seconds left.

He wasn't going make it to the lift before the countdown reached zero.

He was concentrating on not dropping the package as he raced forward. But suddenly a hand snatched it from his grasp. The person was moving faster than he was or could. They arrived at the lift, quickly placed it inside and sent the lift down into the spoke travelling towards the rings below.

Danks could make out that the person had their hand on the lift control panel on the wall.

Moving over to a viewing window, he was just able to see the box moving at speed outside the hotel. Somehow the package had been ejected from the lift. Moments later there was a small flash and a cloud of gas emanated from the box. It quickly dissipated.

Danks let out a sigh of relief as the danger had passed. He approached the person to ask who they were but got a shock as he already knew them. She turned to face him, it was Alicia.

"Hello, inspector" she said.

"Alicia, what are you doing here? I thought you'd gone down to the surface".

"That was the initial plan inspector. However, Gemma insisted I stay behind to keep an eye on you".

"An eye on me?" Danks said out loud. He felt he didn't need looking after. But then she had just saved his life.

"Yes. You were clearly in danger from that weapon" stated Alicia.

"Well I'm glad you were here".

Just then Sergeant Francis and the security guard arrived.

"What happened? Did you manage to get it out of the hotel?" enquired Sergeant Francis.

"Yes with Alicia's help" replied Danks. "After all that excitement I think I need a drink. Will you and Alicia join me?". Danks was looking at the sergeant when he said it.

"I'd love to" replied the sergeant.

"I'm not really-". Danks interrupted Alicia.

"I have a lot of questions to ask you Alicia. Come and talk to us".

"If that's what you want". Alicia gave in to his request.

The security guard muttered that he had a mountain of e-forms that had to be filled in after that eventful period and headed back to his office.

Danks, Sergeant Francis and Alicia set off towards the bar.

Chapter 53

Two large drinks sat in front of Danks and the sergeant at a table in the bar on floor one.

Danks drank some of his beer. It felt really refreshing especially after he thought he was going to die only a few minutes ago.

"Are you going to join us Alicia?" the sergeant asked her.

Danks thought he'd better jump in here. "She won't sergeant. I've been wondering for a while now why you -", he looked at Alicia "- didn't drink or eat when you, Gemma and I met up. Also, some of your mannerisms".

The sergeant looked perplexed.

"So I'm I going to come straight out with it. Are you an android Alicia? In fact, are you Alice from Gemma's flat on Mars?".

There was a surprised look on the sergeant's face. "Sir, I'm sure Alicia is offended by you saying she's an android when it's obvious she isn't".

"Actually, sergeant, Inspector Danks is partially right" replied Alicia.

The sergeant couldn't believe his ears. Was he

to take it that the woman sat at the table with them was not a woman. He felt the situation was really weird as he had found her very attractive.

"Yes, I am an android. Alice designed and built me as a companion to Gemma. When the body was complete she downloaded a copy of herself into it. So although you are right that I was Alice at first, from the point of download I became a separate entity. Alice is still back at Gemma's flat on Mars".

"I noticed that you seemed to be controlling the lift through a link. Is that why you had your hand on the panel?" asked Danks.

"Yes. I stopped the lift at the halfway point and opened the door to outer-space. The package was thrown out with the decompression".

The sergeant had a question. "Was it a bomb?".

Danks responded, "It was a sort of bomb. It had a small explosive inside it but that was to release an aerosol spray of highly concentrated botox into the air. The aerosol would have been distributed throughout the whole of this ring via the ventilation system. Everyone on the two floors would have inhaled it and been dead in minutes".

"How did you know it was botox?". The sergeant couldn't fit all the pieces together.

"It all started a few days ago when I decided to take a massage but at the last second I switched to a different masseuse. Lynch must have known which room I was in but didn't know Mr Wright had taken my place. Mr Wright was found dead and the pathologist determined he'd died with a single botox injection into his neck. It appears he was trying to kill me. Maybe he was seeking revenge for me sending him to prison". Danks felt good that he was getting under the guy's skin.

The rest of the night they spent reminiscing and laughing. Alicia listened and contributed to the conversation even though she only came into existence two years before. However, she still had the memories of Alice from the period before her 'singularity'.

Laughter was something Alicia couldn't understand. It seemed that some orders of words caused humans to go into convulsions. She wasn't sure it was good for them.

It was late in the evening and Alicia notified Danks that she had to return to her room in order to recharge.

Both Danks and the sergeant agreed it was late, so they decided it was time to grab some sleep. The sergeant headed off to his room that was on that same floor while Alicia and Danks proceeded to the lift.

"I assume it's safe to use this lift now" Danks asked Alicia.

"It is perfectly safe for you humans as the package detonated outside the lift".

He knew that Alicia would have been totally unaffected by the botox, so her actions were purely to save him and the other guests. He was impressed.

They arrived at their floor and Danks said good night. Alicia acknowledged.

"It had been an interesting day" thought Danks as his head hit the pillow.

"Let's see what tomorrow brings" and he quickly drifted off into a deep sleep.

Chapter 54

When Danks woke up he realised he'd overslept. Getting ready quickly, he dashed off for his breakfast as he was famished.

Waiting at his table was Alicia. "Did you oversleep inspector?" she said with, what Danks thought sounded like, sarcasm.

"Yes. I forgot to set my alarm last night. Maybe because we celebrated until late". He was searching for an excuse that sounded good.

"I seem to have been unaffected by the celebrations" replied Alicia.

He thought, "That's because you don't drink!".

Alicia continued, "I could wake you at a specific time if you wanted me to".

"No that's okay. Anyway, you don't sleep do you?".

"Actually, I do. During recharge I enter a period where memories are reorganised and I do experience dreaming".

"That's interesting" said Danks as he munched on a mouthful of scrambled egg on toast.

His plans for today were swim, sunbathe, swim and then have a refreshing drink. In that order.

Danks thought that Alicia looked as though she had something to say.

"Alicia are you feeling okay?".

"I'm in a dilemma. I am in possession of some information but I don't want it to spoil your vacation".

He thought to himself, "Do I really look that bad that everyone thinks I need some rest from my work?".

"Well, I've nothing planned for today". He was lying of course, but he was thinking Alicia usually had something interesting to say, "so you'd better tell me".

"Well, I've managed to trace the source of the signals that were used to pixelate the face of Mr Lynch in the videos".

There was silence for a few seconds. Danks thought Alicia wasn't going to tell him. So he prompted her.

"And that was from?". He was all ears at this point.

"The origin was from the main settlement on the Moon. I can't locate it more accurately than that".

"Why didn't you tell me last night?" retorted Danks.

"I only discovered it this morning during recharge".

Danks called up Sergeant Francis. "Hey, Stuart. Alicia and I are catching a shuttle to Earth's Moon.

She has traced the source of a signal that pixelated Lynch's face. Do you fancy tagging along?".

The sergeant's face seemed to light up. "Would I? I certainly would as I'm getting bored here pampering stupid, spoilt politicians. Anyway, Commissioner Gilbert did gave me permission to help you".

"Okay, get your belongings together. We'll catch the next shuttle to the lunar surface".

Several hours later they had boarded a shuttle for the Moon. Their destination was the main settlement called Lunaville.

Chapter 55

The shuttle landed on the Moon and came to a halt. Drones attached themselves to it and manoeuvred it off the runway into a clear dome on the lunar surface. Once inside, the entrance door closed and the dome was pressurized. The shuttle came to rest next to a platform and a walkway was extended out until it pressed up against its hull.

Once in place the exit doors were opened and the passengers began to disembark. Danks tried to look cool by strolling along the walkway, but in reality it was more of a bunny hop. The only person not bunny hopping was Alicia, she had the foresight to wear her weighted boots.

This was Danks's first time landing on the Moon and he remembered what one of the earliest pioneers had said. He repeated it, "the Eagle has landed". If he had enough time he'd have to visit the museum dedicated to Armstrong, Aldrin and Collins. "Now those guys were truly brave" thought Danks.

At the immigration desk Danks presented his ID chip and the border guard scanned it. The guard looked at his screen and scrutinized the readings.

"What is your reason for visiting inspector?" came a rather curt question.

"We are in pursuit of a couple of criminals and our investigations have led us here".

"You do realise that you're outside your jurisdiction here on the Moon. So you won't be able to arrest anyone" said the guard sternly.

Alicia stepped forward and replied, "The sergeant here has jurisdiction as there is a mutual agreement between the Moon and Mars". She pointed at the sergeant who fortunately had his Central Mars Police Council uniform on. The border guard looked taken aback as he knew she was correct.

Alicia scanned her ID. It was a fake one but she ensured that the system wouldn't detect it. The sergeant followed closely behind her. He did a brief salute to the guard as he passed him.

The border guard watched them leave, then turned his attention to the next person in the queue.

"You're a mine of information Alicia. It's a damned good job you came along" said Danks and slapped her on the back.

Danks and the sergeant rented a pair of weighted boots each from a nearby shop. They were just like Alicia's. It was very busy in the shop as the new arrivals were all clambering to hire a pair. The boots helped people to walk more easily on the moon.

They then left the shop and stepped onto an escalator that was inside a clear semicircular tube. Danks was awestruck at the views of the lunar landscape just before they started the descent below the surface.

Reaching the end of the escalator took some two minutes. But to keep the travellers interested, there were video advertisements at regular intervals on the walls as they travelled downwards. Danks couldn't help but watch the adverts on the journey. The videos were so interesting that before he knew it he was at the end of the escalator. Danks stepped off it and walked the short distance to the platform of a monorail. It was going to ferry them from the moon-port to the heart of Lunaville.

Boarding the monorail they found three free seats that were together. They sat down and Danks looked out of his window. He was amazed at the view as they left the moon-port. There was a large expansive cave system. All the walls, ceilings and floors were concrete lined. The concrete was made from the crushed Moon rock that was excavated to make the caves. This also kept the costs down for transporting any materials from Earth. He also noted that the buildings were made from the same material and they were deliberately built from the floor to the ceiling of the caves to give the roof extra strength.

The monorail smoothly decelerated as it pulled

into the station at the centre of Lunaville. Grabbing their bags they stepped out onto a grey featureless platform. Most of the passengers alighted here, so the platform was quite crowded and noisy.

Near the station was a pod hotel. These were cheap and basic, but fulfilled all their accommodation requirements.

After checking in at reception, they headed down the main corridor to locate their sleeping pods. It wasn't long before Danks was standing outside one of them. Looking in he thought it was a bit of a comedown from his previous living quarters. At least there was more room than on the interplanetary spaceships.

There was enough room for a bed, a small screen, their luggage and not much else. Sergeant Francis found his pod and tried it out. He found it was a little short for him so he'd have to sleep with his legs bent.

At the corner of each block of sleeping pods was a communal wash-room. They were basic but they were sufficient for Danks and the sergeant's needs.

They dumped their bags into their respective pods, shut the outer door and scanned their palm prints to lock them. Alicia had no palm print, so she had to link to the hotel computer to lock hers.

"Right, what do we do now?". Sergeant Francis was excited as to what Danks had planned next.

"Can you locate the signal now we're here?" Danks asked Alicia. He was hoping Alicia could make progress now they were nearer the source.

"All I've discovered is that it originated from a square kilometre in this area" replied Alicia.

Danks was feeling a little deflated. The lead had gone from hot to tepid in the blink of an eye.

He reasoned that the next possible plan of attack would be to see their counterparts at the Lunar Police Headquarters or LPHQ. Maybe he could persuade them to use their AI facial recognition system to see if it could locate either Mr Lynch or Dr Taylor.

Lynch had gone down to the Earth's surface but that could be just a ruse to throw them off the scent.

Returning to the monorail station, they boarded the next train heading towards the LPHQ.

Chapter 56

The monorail pulled into the station that was opposite the LPHQ. Danks led the way with a spring in his step. He was hoping for a friendly reception. The sergeant put his hand on Danks's shoulder to hold him back.

"Maybe I should handle this sir. I have a few contacts here at the LPHQ. I liaised with this department several months ago".

The LPHQ building blended in with its surroundings. The only distinguishing feature was a main door made of white glass with the letters LPHQ embossed across it.

The sergeant led the way, crossing the road that was in front of the building. Once inside the sergeant strolled over to a screen set into the wall opposite the main doorway. When he spoke to the screen it flickered into life and the face of the AI assistant appeared on it.

"How may I help you?" it asked with a slightly monotonic voice.

"That could do with some improvements" Alicia said quietly. Danks was sure he could sense the disdain in her voice.

"I'm Sergeant Francis of the Central Mars Police Council, can you put me through to Lieutenant Price?".

The sergeant was hoping the guy would remember him. He tried combing his hair with his fingers in an attempt to make himself a little tidier. A few moments later the screen swapped to Lieutenant Price.

"Stuart, you didn't tell me that you were dropping in down here. Come through to my office. It's room four down the corridor on your right. I'll buzz you through the security door".

They made their way over to the door and when it buzzed they pushed it open. The corridor was dark with light streaming out of office windows on either side. Moving down the corridor they arrived at room four. They knew it was the right one because Lieutenant Price was standing outside it waiting for them.

He vigorously shook Sergeant Francis's hand. "Stuart, nice to see you in person at last and who are your colleagues?".

"This is Inspector Danks from Earth and this is Alicia from Mars. She's assisting the inspector". The sergeant added that so as to give her a reason for being there.

Alicia replied, "Actually, I've been tasked to protect the inspector".

"Have you really. From what I've heard about

the inspector, I'm surprised he needs someone to protect him". Lieutenant Price seemed to not quite believe what he'd been told.

"She's very knowledgeable and a great help to me" added Danks.

Lieutenant Price ushered them into his office. He dashed around his room tidying up strewn weighted boots, helmets and empty coffee vessels. He put the vessels on the windowsill behind his seat and pulled down the blind to hide them.

"Right, you must be here for a reason or is it just a holiday?" enquired Lieutenant Price.

Inspector Danks answered, "We're here on a case I've been working on for some time. We are following up on a lead that has brought us here. There may be a suspect or suspects hiding somewhere in this neighbourhood. Sadly, the trail has gone cold and this is where you could help get us back on track".

"That sounds like fun" added Lieutenant Price with some excitement. Life on the Moon was relatively quiet for the police.

"Is it possible to get your AI facial recognition system to see if it can find either of the two suspects in this case?". Danks kept his fingers crossed that the answer would be yes.

"What are these suspects supposed to have committed?". Lieutenant Price was waiting to enter the details into his console.

Sergeant Francis added, "The first character broke out of prison on Mars. He was serving life for multiple murders and he's also a prime suspect in the murder of an individual on the Perigee Hotel. The second character has evaded capture and is wanted for murder on Mars. So, we're hoping you can help".

"Sure, give me the pictures of the individuals". Sergeant Francis had the images stored in his Integrated Headset Unit. Martians had the IHU put into the visual cortex from an early age giving them enhanced memory and communication skills. It was a simple matter of transferring the images and other vital information on the criminals to Lieutenant Price's computer system.

Lieutenant Price's computer received the images and he entered it into the facial recognition software. A short time later some results popped up. "Right, the last recorded sighting of Mr Johnson, also known as Mr Lynch, was when he boarded a shuttle about two months ago. It says the shuttle was heading for the Perigee Hotel. As for Dr Taylor the AI system doesn't recognise her at all. So that means she's not here on the Moon".

Danks was disappointed that there wasn't anything on her. "Then who had sent those signals to the Perigee Hotel?" he thought.

"I wish there was more I could have done" sympathised Lieutenant Price.

"I guess we needn't take up any more of your time" replied Sergeant Francis.

Lieutenant Price stood up and guided them back to the security door. "Maybe we could meet for a drink before you leave?" he suggested.

"That would be great Steve" replied Sergeant Francis as they left.

The security door swung shut behind them and Danks saw Lieutenant Price return to his office.

"Sorry sir" the sergeant said apologetically.

Danks wasn't quite sure. His gut feeling was kicking in again. "I have a funny feeling about this. Didn't you get a distinct feeling he was not quite telling the truth?".

Alicia felt she needed to add something, "My human facial expression analysis indicates he was lying about Dr Taylor".

"So you think she's here? But why would Lieutenant Price lie?". The sergeant seemed shocked at the new revelations as he thought he knew Lieutenant Price well.

Leaving the LPHQ building they turned onto the main street. There was a small café not far away. Danks wanted a pick-me-up so he suggested they try it out while they planned the next move.

Danks's and the sergeant's coffees arrived in cups with the usual valved lid on top.

"What should we do now?". The sergeant just couldn't get his head around the idea that

Lieutenant Price had lied to them.

"Maybe we should make Lieutenant Price think we're getting close to finding Dr Taylor. That might force him to reveal his hand and he might lead us to where she's hiding if she is here" responded Danks.

"How do we do that?" said the sergeant. He just couldn't see a way forward.

"Maybe we should follow him. Find out who his informants are and we could put the squeeze on them to reveal some juicy gossip on Lieutenant Price" suggested Danks.

Alicia responded with the comment, "I could apply the pressure required if you want me to".

Danks thought that was maybe going a bit too far. But for the time being they would stay here in the café and see if anything developed.

Chapter 57

Staking out the LPHQ, both Alicia and Danks watched for Lieutenant Price leaving the building.

The sergeant was too easily recognised by the lieutenant so he waited inside the café for a call from them.

Alicia detected Lieutenant Price leaving on foot heading in their direction. They stepped into the café to avoid him seeing them. When he had passed they followed him at a safe distance. Far enough away for him not to suspect he was being followed but close enough to not lose sight of him.

Lieutenant Price turned down Charles Duke Street and stopped to look into a window. Danks surmised that he was checking he wasn't being followed. Fortunately, he hadn't noticed them and he then slipped into a doorway.

Danks crossed the road so he could see into the passage that the lieutenant had entered. He was talking to another man but he was holding him by the throat and had pinned him up against the wall.

Lieutenant Price dropped the man to his feet and he brushed the man's collar. He turned to leave and Danks had to back up into a shop doorway so he wasn't lit by the street lamps. The lieutenant stepped out into the street and carried on in his original direction.

Alicia met Danks at the doorway and they went inside. Danks could see the same man sitting at a table in a room just off the corridor. Lots of fine detail tools were neatly hanging on the wall. They were strategically placed so the man could pick them easily. "This man is obviously a jewellery maker" thought Danks.

They entered the room and the man looked up. "Can I help you?" the man looked a little shaken from his previous encounter.

Danks closed the door behind him. "The man who was just in here, what did he want?" said Danks.

"What man?" replied the jeweller.

"The man who had you pinned against the wall" Danks said with a stronger voice. He reckoned it might loosen the guy's tongue.

The jeweller picked up what looked like a scalpel and pointed it at Alicia. "I'll slash her wrist if you don't leave" he threatened.

Alicia grabbed the wrist of his hand that was holding the scalpel. Danks saw the look of surprise on his face then anguish as the pain started to register. As soon as he dropped the scalpel Alicia let him go. He slumped back into his seat rubbing his wrist where she had gripped him.

"Look, I've already paid my protection money to him" he said in exasperation.

"He didn't seem happy you'd paid him". Danks felt they were making progress.

"The Syndicate he works for has increased the protection money so what I'd paid him wasn't enough. He's coming back tomorrow to pick up the rest. I barely make a living and paying this protection money is leaving me penniless. If I don't pay it he says he'll break my wrists". The guy was looking really scared.

"Thank you for your help. I think you've answered my questions for now". Danks signalled to Alicia that they were leaving.

Outside Alicia asked Danks, "Why are some of you humans so unbelievably repugnant and yet others are a delight to know?".

"Human nature I suppose. I think some people are born with parents that are poor role models or maybe they're just born nasty people".

They returned to the hotel. It was late so they decided to call it a day. Tomorrow they would confront Lieutenant Price.

Chapter 58

Inspector Danks and Sergeant Francis were sitting in the little café just down from the LPHQ having breakfast. The food was served on metal plates that stuck to magnets that were in the table top. This stopped the plates sliding around in the low gravity. Alicia was sat with them waiting.

"So Lieutenant Price is on the payroll of the Syndicate?" said Sergeant Francis. He couldn't help but show some disappointment in his voice.

"Yes. This Syndicate seems to have its tentacles everywhere" replied Danks.

Alicia added, "Alice has been able to trace communications that originate from the Earth that shows links to the Syndicate. She has compiled a list of suspects on Mars".

"That will be really useful when I return" replied the sergeant. He was looking forward to getting back and investigating how much hold the Syndicate had there. Alice the AI system in Gemma's flat will prove a useful ally for the CMPC he thought.

They finished their breakfast.

"Well, I think it's time we dropped in on

Lieutenant Price and ruffled his feathers a bit" said Danks.

"Ruffled his feathers? I wasn't aware that he was a member of the avian family". Alicia wasn't familiar with that expression.

"It's just an expression meaning we'll pose some questions that will make him do something rash hopefully. You know Alicia, you are full of surprises". Danks found Alicia's comment amusing.

Heading over to the LPHQ, they stepped into the building. Sergeant Francis asked the AI system if he could see Lieutenant Price and soon after his face appeared on the screen.

"Back so soon Stuart. What can I do for you this time?".

"We've come across some information that maybe you could help us with?". Sergeant Francis was trying to sound as polite as possible.

"Okay, I'll buzz you through as usual".

They knew which room he was in and headed straight down the corridor to it. They walked inside and sat down facing him.

"So what's this new news you've discovered?" quizzed Lieutenant Price.

Danks thought he should do the talking, "We've discovered that there is a criminal organisation called the Syndicate operating here on the Moon".

Lieutenant Price seemed to shift uncomfortably

in his chair. "And how does that affect your case?". He tried to deflect the questioning.

"It seems that this Dr Taylor may be part of this Syndicate and there appears to be some corrupt police officers that are protecting her". This seemed to hit the spot as Danks noticed beads of sweat began to form on Lieutenant Price's forehead.

"Interesting, do you have any names yet?". He was obviously hoping his name wasn't on the list.

"We have a few. One of them has given us some details about Dr Taylor. It seems we are closing in on her". He was lying of course but Danks was hoping this would trigger Lieutenant Price into action.

"Well, leave it with me and I'll do some digging around and see if I can uncover any police officers that could be involved with this 'Syndicate' as you call it". He stood up from his desk, took them to the security door and shook their hands as they left.

Danks was sure the smile on Lieutenant Price's face disappeared as he turned back towards his office.

"What do we do now?" Sergeant Francis asked.

"We just wait. We'll go outside and keep a watch on the LPHQ exits". Danks was convinced something significant would happen.

Danks sent the sergeant to watch the front

entrance while he and Alicia went to the café where he ordered a drink. The café was strategically positioned to observe the back exit of the building. Danks's drink arrived and he paid straight away as he knew that he'd have to react quickly when things started to happen.

They waited several minutes before Alicia spoke. "Inspector, Lieutenant Price has just left the back of the building. I can see him walking at some speed towards that street opposite". Alicia's sharp eyes had spotted him and she pointed at the moving figure some distance away.

Danks left the remainder of his drink and he and Alicia started walking briskly to catch up with the figure. He signalled to the sergeant and he dashed over to joined them. They needed to keep sufficient distance so as not to be detected.

Alicia saw the man disappear down Buzz Aldrin Street. They stopped at the corner and checked he was still heading away from the LPHQ. Once they felt he was sufficiently far ahead, they continued following keeping close to the buildings.

He turned left into the Neil Armstrong Street and crossed over about twenty doors down. He stopped at a large arched doorway, pressed his palm on the door and entered the building. The three of them moved down the street and crossed over to the door.

"How can we get in?" the sergeant was

convinced this was as far as they could go.

Alicia stepped forwards, "I believe I can gain access". She pressed her palm onto the pad. There was a period of uncertainty. It seemed to Inspector Danks that nothing was happening. Then suddenly they heard the door lock retract and it swung open.

"Brilliant!" said Danks and the sergeant in unison.

They quickly stepped inside and closed the door quietly behind them. It was dark in the corridor. There was a small amount of light streaming down from the upstairs. They could hear voices, so they crept towards the stairs. Danks led the way. He was halfway up the stairs and could see shadows moving. An argument was raging between two people. It was obvious that the other person was annoyed that Price had come to the house.

"Why did you come here, you could have sent a message telling me that that meddling inspector was in town. I'll have to explain all this to the Syndicate and they won't be pleased".

"I wasn't sure if they were monitoring my communications so I thought I'd come and tell you in person. Anyway, you told me you wanted to know if anyone came snooping around?" came the reply.

The sergeant was following behind Danks. He didn't notice that there were potted plants on a shelf on the stairs. He'd never seen house plants on

Mars as they were a luxury. He knocked one and it toppled off the shelf. For a brief second there was silence until the pot clattered on the solid stone step of the stairs. Suddenly everything changed. Danks looked around to see what had happened and before he could react Price appeared at the top of the stairs pointing a pistol in their direction.

"Well, well, well. Tricky buggers aren't you" said Price with some malice in his voice. "And I thought we were going to have a drink sergeant. Of course, that won't happen now". He gestured for them to all come up to the top of the stairs.

Several desks were arranged in the room with consoles on all of them. There were cables running from the back of a black box up to the ceiling.

"That must be going to an antenna on the lunar surface" thought Danks.

Once they were at the top of the stairs Price signalled for the three of them to move over towards the tables.

"So, Eleanor, is this where you've been hiding yourself?" asked Danks probing for a response.

Price looked confused as he didn't know who this Eleanor was.

"You really are quite a good investigator. How did you find out my real name?" said Dr Taylor.

"We picked up a woman who was caught shoplifting. When we did a DNA test on her it showed she was closely related to you. The tests said maybe an Aunt. It was only when I questioned her that I discovered the real truth and that she was your mother".

"So, you know about Freya?" she said in alarm.

"Yes. How could you bring yourself to leave her?" said Danks in an annoyed tone.

"I had to. Prior commitments meant I had to leave".

Sergeant Francis look confused as he didn't know anything about this new person Freya.

Danks saw the look on his face. "It's a long story I'll have to tell you later".

Price stepped forward, "There won't be a 'later' as you put it. It ends here right now". Price raised the gun and pointed it at Danks. He started to squeeze the trigger. Alicia reacted. She leapt forwards before the gun fired. As she went for him the bullet left the barrel and caught her right arm. She struck Price's hand with her left fist and the gun fell to the floor.

Danks instinctively jumped forward and punched Price in the face with all the force he could muster. Price flew backwards and crashed through the window that was directly behind him.

Danks dashed over to the window to see Price hit the footpath below. Shards of glass were crashing down on top of him.

Sergeant Francis ran down the stairs to check if Price was conscious after the fall. But when the sergeant arrived he could see that a single large piece of glass had severed the lieutenant's carotid artery and he had bled to death. There was nothing he could do to save him.

Danks turned to see Alicia's arm was hanging loose. "Do you need help with your arm Alicia?". Danks was concerned and went over to assist. There was a green fluid leaking onto the floor. Dr Taylor stood aghast with the sight of the fluid dripping from Alicia's arm. Alicia applied a tourniquet to her arm with some cable that was handy.

Danks turned towards Dr Taylor. He grabbed each of her arms, twisted her around and put her hands into a set of handcuffs behind her back. "I think it ends here Eleanor" he said with a heavy heart. He couldn't help but feel for the mother of his child.

"But you don't have the authority to arrest me here" she said defiantly.

Sergeant Francis appeared at the top of the stairs at that moment. Danks nodded in the direction of the sergeant, "No, but the sergeant does".

Alicia said she needed to return to their accommodation to effect some repairs. They all descended the stairs and left the building. Alicia headed for the hotel, Danks and Dr Taylor set off for the LPHQ.

The sergeant had alerted the Lunar police to the

incident and so he remained behind waiting for their arrival.

Chapter 59

On their way to the LPHQ, Danks questioned Dr Taylor some more. "Is this where you've been living since leaving Freya?".

"I didn't want to leave. The Syndicate forced me to come here. They wanted all the politicians and commissioners at that meeting on the Perigee Hotel dead".

"Did you send Lynch to kill me there?".

"I didn't know you were on board. He told me it was someone that needed eliminating, so I simply tried to remove any evidence of him being there using my computer systems here".

Danks slowed his pace as he wanted to dig a little deeper. "How did the Syndicate pressurize you?".

Eleanor hesitated as she didn't want to let Danks know her feelings.

He tried a different angle to see if that would help. "Okay, so would I be correct in saying, does it have anything to do with Freya?". His new tack worked.

"Yes. They threatened to kidnap Freya, so I agreed to helping them".

They were getting near the LPHQ when Danks's watch rang. It was Sergeant Turner.

"Hello Helen what can I do for you?". Danks knew that talking to someone back on Earth was awkward as there was roughly a six second delay before getting a reply.

"Hi inspector, I've just received some disturbing information. It appears that Mrs Halliwell has been shot in her flat and is critically ill in hospital. Also there was no sign of Freya. Video footage shows a man leaving with her. Unfortunately, no identification of him could be made as he was wearing a mask. We have no idea as to where she is at the moment". There was silence for several seconds. "Sir, can you hear me?".

Eleanor looked shocked at the news.

Danks replied, "We'll catch the next shuttle back to Earth. I'll let you know when we've landed. Be ready to pick us up". There was the usual delay before Sergeant Turner replied, "Affirmative sir" and the call terminated.

Danks called Sergeant Francis and told him he was heading back to Earth with Eleanor. "Tell Alicia to head down to Earth when she's able to. You won't be able to come as you've not been conditioned to withstand Earth's gravity".

The sergeant wished them good luck and said he'd forward Danks's belongings on the next available shuttle.

Danks turned to Eleanor and said, "Well, if you are to accompany me back to Earth you can't wear those beautiful looking bracelets". He removed the handcuffs and Eleanor rubbed her wrists where they had left marks on her skin. Maybe he'd put them on a bit tight, but Danks hadn't wanted her to escape a second time.

They caught the next monorail to the moon-port, but it was going to be several hours before the return trip. At least he'd be able to catch up on what happened to Eleanor after she'd arrived back on Earth.

Chapter 60

After a day's journey from the Moon, they were on their descent into the Earth's atmosphere. They had slept some of the way, but they were awoken as the ship entered the upper atmosphere. It was quite a rough ride as they were being jolted around in their seats.

On their way down, Danks wanted to ask Eleanor a question that had been playing on his mind since they had left the Moon. "Why didn't you tell me about Freya?" he said.

Eleanor looked at him with, what he thought was some affection. Maybe she wasn't all bad. "How could I. You would've found out where I was and the whole point was to keep a low profile".

A few more jolts shook the shuttle.

"The Syndicate found where you were though. I could have protected you. Taken you both to a safe location".

"I was in a safe location and yet they still found me or should I say us. I've done this for Freya. It was to keep her safe but that's now gone pear shaped. The web of the Syndicate is everywhere".

Danks could see the bright red and orange streaks of plasma flickering on the other side of the window. It shouldn't take long before they were safely parked up at the spaceport.

After several minutes there was a final bump, he knew they were back on Terra Firma in Australia. The shuttle threaded its way around the spaceport landing strips heading towards a free parking bay. It came to a halt in front of a disembarkation tunnel.

They both got up to leave, but Eleanor grabbed Danks's arm. "Will you promise me you'll do everything possible to find Freya and keep her safe?".

"Of course I will. She is my child as well".

He couldn't quite believe his ears. Was she actually concerned about someone other than herself? Maybe having Freya had changed her. Had she turned over a new leaf? He certainly hoped so. He would do everything possible to soften the sentence, but she had to stand trial for her previous crimes.

After getting priority passage through the border checks, they hurried out of the spaceport. Sergeant Turner was waiting in a police car.

Eleanor was finding it difficult to keep up. A year living on the Moon had reduced her muscle and bone structure. She'd been doing the recommended level of exercise to offset such problems but it didn't prepare her for this sudden change. Breathing heavily she said to Danks, "This feels like the last time I came back to Earth. It's really hard work".

Danks jumped into the front seat and Eleanor climbed in the back.

Sergeant Turner turned to Danks. "Isn't that-" as she nodded in the direction of Eleanor.

He interrupted her. "Yes it is".

"Shouldn't we-".

"No, we shouldn't".

The sergeant turned to face forwards and shrugged her shoulders. She then eased her foot down on the accelerator. "Well, if you know what you're doing". The sergeant sounded a bit sceptical.

She pressed harder down on the accelerator heading towards HQ. Nothing was said for the remainder of the trip.

Chapter 61

At the police HQ the three of them were sitting in a conference room. There was a large screen at one end of the room and a rectangular table with chairs positioned at regular intervals around it. They were all sitting near the screen.

Danks decided to speak first. "Where are we in locating Freya and how is Mrs Halliwell?".

"I'm afraid Mrs Halliwell didn't make it" said Sergeant Turner.

Danks saw Eleanor put her head in her hands and he heard her crying for the first time. He went over and comforted her.

The sergeant continued, "As for Freya, there has been a sighting east of Sydney in a place called Watsons Bay. It's half an hour's helicopter ride away".

"Have any police officers located her?" asked Danks.

"They're observing from a distance. They believe a man is holding a woman and child hostage in a house there" stated the sergeant.

"Any identification on the man?" but Danks had a gut feeling again.

The sergeant pulled a picture up on the screen. Danks and Eleanor recognised him straight away. It was the 'friendly' Mr Lynch.

"What a bastard!" shouted Eleanor.

"Did you tell Lynch about Freya?" Danks asked Eleanor.

"Of course not. He's a mad man. I do know he was monitoring communications at the hotel so maybe he tuned in on your conversation with mum and put two and two together. Either that or the Syndicate told him" replied Eleanor with concern.

Danks had to repeat a part of what Sergeant Turner just said. "Hang on, you think there's a woman hostage too. But who?".

"We don't have an identification on her yet" came the reply.

Danks remembered Gemma saying she was heading towards Sydney. He called Alicia on the Moon to confirm it. "Alicia, do you know Gemma's whereabouts?".

There was the usual delay before she answered. Alicia confirmed that after visiting Canada she was heading to Sydney in Australia. She also confirmed that as soon as the repairs to her arm were complete she would catch the next shuttle down to Sydney. They finished the call.

"Now we know who the other hostage is. He must have seen me talking to Gemma in the hotel. Lynch must have been tracking her when she arrived on Earth" said Danks. He was now really concerned for Gemma's and Freya's safety.

Eleanor added, "There is a mansion that the Syndicate uses in Watsons Bay. I've never been there but it's supposed to be near the cliffs".

Danks had a map of the area displayed on his watch so he swept his finger across his watch toward the screen and a map of the Sydney area appeared. "Can you show me?".

Eleanor expanded the map until there were only four or five buildings displayed.

"I think this is the manor house". She pointed to one of the buildings with a finger.

Sergeant Turner looked closely, "That's the building our officers are staking out".

Danks decided it was time to head over there. So he picked up a gun and holster from the armoury and slung it around his chest. After fitting the magazine into the gun he dropped it into the holster. "Let's get a helicopter and head straight out there".

All three of them made their way up some winding stairs and stepped out into the bright sunshine of the day.

Across the other side of the roof there were four police helicopters. One of the helicopters was just in the process of spinning up its rotor blades.

"You should stay here Eleanor as it's too dangerous for you". Danks was trying to protect her.

"I'm not staying behind when my daughter's in danger".

Sergeant Turner looked at Danks and shrugged her shoulders effectively saying "you can't argue with that".

"Okay, but stay behind me when we get there".

They dashed over keeping their heads down. Running beneath the blades, they pushed through the strong downward wind blasting from above.

They jumped into the helicopter one after the other. They were relieved to be out of the strong wind from the rotors. Danks slid the door shut and it became a lot quieter. They all fitted their safety belts and he shouted to the AI pilot to take off. The engine increased in pitch and the ground beneath them began to drop away. Swooping down from the roof of the building they accelerated off in the direction of Watsons Bay.

They were making good progress and Danks was hoping the backup crew wasn't far behind them.

At the mansion Lynch was getting nervous. He wanted that Inspector Danks here so he could humiliate him. Then he'd put a bullet through his chest. He wanted revenge and then he had an escape route. The Syndicate had promised him he'd be picked up by a team on the beach and taken to a ship just off the coast where he'd get another new identity. He'd return to Mars to start a new life. However, he'd not experienced anything like a sea before so he didn't know what to expect.

"Why are you doing this?" Gemma said with a scared voice. She had been enjoying this holiday when this weirdo had slapped a cloth over her face that was laced with some form of chemical. All she remembers is struggling but then passing out. When she awoke she was tied up inside this room.

"I'm holding you two as bait. Once I have that cretin Danks here I'll humiliate him. Then I'll kill you and the child in front of him before I finish him off. The Syndicate wants him eliminated as he's thwarted too many of their plans".

Gemma could see the sneer on his face.

Lynch dashed over to a window as he could hear the sound of helicopter blades. He picked up the crying child, untied Gemma and then pointed his gun at her. He gestured for her to get to her feet. She stood up, but her legs were shaking with fear. He pushed the gun in her back and shoved her forward towards the door.

"Open it" he commanded.

———

The helicopter came down in a controlled manner and landed smoothly. It was on an open green expanse between the cliffs and the manor house.

Sliding the door back all three jumped out onto the grass.

Danks saw a door open on the house that Eleanor had previously pointed to on the map and Gemma came out first with her hands in the air.

Lynch came out clutching onto Freya. She was crying. He kept prodding Gemma in the back with a gun to persuade her to move in their direction.

Danks signalled for Sergeant Turner and Eleanor to stay where they were as he advanced towards Lynch.

"Drop your weapon or I'll kill the child" Lynch said menacingly.

Danks removed the weapon from his holster with his left hand using only his thumb and index finger. His fingers holding only the end of the grip. He held it out at arms length on his left hand side and he let it drop to the ground.

"And the sergeant" growled Lynch.

Sergeant Turner did the same.

"Now kick the guns away" commanded Lynch.

Danks and the sergeant complied.

"You know we have a couple of officers nearby" said Danks hopefully.

"Oh yeah, I took care of them once I realised they were watching the mansion" and Lynch smiled when he said it.

Danks took a step towards him.

"That's close enough unless you want the child

to die".

Danks had a hunch he wasn't going to shoot the kid as he would lose the child as a shield. But he couldn't take the chance. He suddenly became aware that Eleanor had moved up and was next to him.

Lynch hadn't realised that she was there as the sun was glinting off the helicopter. "Nikola, what are you doing here?". His voice had changed to concern.

Danks realised that Eleanor hadn't divulged her real name to him.

"Let go of the child Alex and I'll come with you. We'll escape back to Mars". Eleanor was trying to defuse the situation.

Lynch seemed to momentarily consider the option as it appealed to him. After all, he always wanted to live on Mars with her at his side. Suddenly he realised that that wasn't going to happen and snapped out of the dream of living with her. "But that won't happen while that bastard's alive".

Lynch raised the gun and his finger started to squeeze the trigger. Eleanor stepped in front of Danks in an attempt to stop Lynch from shooting him. It was too late and a puff of smoke emerged from the barrel.

Danks expected to feel the pain of the bullet but Eleanor was in the path of the projectile. It hit her in the chest and she staggered back and collapsed to the ground.

Lynch saw what he had done and dropped the child. At that moment Gemma saw her opportunity and shoulder charged him knocking him off balance.

This was the chance Danks was hoping for. He leapt forward and grabbed the hand holding the gun. He twisted it and he heard the trigger finger of Lynch break.

The gun fired off a harmless shot as Lynch screamed in pain. But he still managed to punch Danks in the face with a fist from his free hand which stunned Danks momentarily. The gun fell from Lynch's hand as he could no longer hold onto it with the pain.

Lynch realised that his opportunity to kill Danks had evaporated. He decided his best option was to escape on the boat. So, he turned and started running towards the cliff clutching his damaged hand. He knew he'd get another chance to finish off Danks, but that would have to wait for another day.

There was a path down the cliff face to the beach below so he headed for it. As he ran he could see a motorboat out to sea coming towards the beach. The Syndicate had stuck to their promise.

Danks quickly recovered from the punch and set

off after Lynch. He could see his prey just ahead of him. Why hadn't he been to the gym more often? His chest was bursting from the strain, but he wasn't going to let this guy get away. He stretched out an arm and caught Lynch's shoulder. They both tumbled to the ground with sand and soil billowing up in their wake.

Danks was the first to his feet. He took a swing at Lynch but missed his face by a fraction. Lynch threw a wild swing with his left fist as he stood upright. It caught Danks on the arm that he'd lifted to protect himself against the punch.

Before Lynch could throw another punch, Danks drove a right handed tiger fist punch straight into Lynch's throat. He stumbled back clutching his neck. His heel caught on a stone close to the edge of the cliff and before Danks could react, Lynch fell backwards over the crumbling edge.

Everything went into slow motion as Lynch flailed his arms and legs in a desperate attempt to halt his descent. It was all to no avail as Lynch disappeared from Danks's view.

Approaching the edge of the cliff carefully, Danks peered over. Lynch's body was sprawled on the rocks below.

Danks looked up and saw the motorboat turning around and heading back at top speed towards the ship out at sea. They must have seen him fall and decided extracting him was pointless.

Chapter 62

As Danks stood on the cliff edge he could hear voices shouting to him. It was the sergeant and Gemma calling him. He suddenly remembered that Eleanor had taken the bullet meant for him.

Danks ran as fast as he could and dropped down next to Eleanor. Sergeant Turner was applying pressure to the wound in an attempt to stem the blood loss. He took over from the sergeant with his hand pressing on the wound. She stood up with her hands covered in blood.

"I've called for a medical team they should be here soon" the sergeant informed him.

"Did we save Freya?" Eleanor asked with a weak voice.

"Yes you saved her. She's here" replied Danks. He gestured for Freya to come over to him so Eleanor could see her. Gemma helped Freya over to where she lay bleeding.

"Maybe if things had been different we could have been good together" said Eleanor.

"We still will be" he said with tears in his eyes. Danks was trying to reassure her.

"Do you think I've redeemed myself?" Eleanor

asked.

"Of course you have".

But just then she went limp, her arm slid off her chest and her hand fell to the blood covered earth. He couldn't believe that she had gone.

The air ambulance crew came dashing over and pushed him aside so they could treat her. They worked on her for several minutes but it was no use. They were unable to save her.

The ambulance team covered her body, put her on a stretcher and carried her back to the helicopter. A few minutes later he saw it take off and disappear into the clouds returning to police HQ.

Gemma put her arm around Danks to comfort him. It had been the worst day ever.

Other police officers arrived running over to where Danks was kneeling. He told them about the body at the cliff base and the ship that the coastguard had to stop urgently.

Once Danks and the sergeant felt that the police teams were fully in control, they boarded their helicopter. It lifted off, swooped out over the cliffs with the HQ as their destination. He could see a group of officers on the ground cordoning the area off while another group were making their way down the cliff path towards the body of Lynch.

The helicopter climbed up into the clouds and he lost sight of them.

Chapter 63

A year later Inspector Danks was sitting looking out to sea on a striped deckchair. The sand was warm under his feet. He looked up and watched white fluffy clouds drifting across a beautiful bright blue sky.

Danks could hear the gentle crashing of waves onto the light orange beach and seagulls calling in the distance. That fresh sea air, the smell of seaweed and children's voices shouting excitedly in the distance.

There was a picnic basket full of delicious food and drink waiting to be opened right next to him.

He closed his eyes and thought back to that first day on the Perigee Hotel when he believed that it was a perfect holiday. Well he was completely wrong. This is the perfect holiday. Sitting on a Cornish beach soaking up the sun.

A hand touched his and he squeezed it.

"Why don't you go and help Freya build that sandcastle? Aunt Alicia seems to be struggling with making it absolutely perfect". Gemma was sitting in the deckchair next to him. She was under a parasol slowly building up her Cornish suntan.

He thought how beautiful she looked and what a lucky man he was.

A voice floated across to him from not far away. "Daddy, come and help. Aunt Alicia is making the castle too big". Freya looked at Tristan excitedly.

"This" thought Tristan Danks, "is the perfect day".

The End

ABOUT THE AUTHOR

Much of his career has been spent designing integrated circuits. He has always been interested in science fiction and recently wanted to explore the possibility of writing his own books.

Printed in Great Britain
by Amazon